THIS CAN'T BE LOVE

Also by Joanne Pence

Ancient Secrets Series

ANCIENT ECHOES - ANCIENT SHADOWS -
ANCIENT ILLUSIONS

The Cabin of Mystery Trilogy

IF I LOVED YOU - THIS CAN'T BE LOVE -
SENTIMENTAL JOURNEY

The Rebecca Mayfield Mysteries

ONE O'CLOCK HUSTLE - TWO O'CLOCK HEIST
THREE O'CLOCK SÉANCE - FOUR O'CLOCK SIZZLE
FIVE O'CLOCK TWIST - SIX O'CLOCK SILENCE
SEVEN O'CLOCK TARGET - THE 13th SANTA

The Angie & Friends Food & Spirits Mysteries

COOKING SPIRITS - COOK'S BIG DAY -
ADD A PINCH OF MURDER -
COOK'S CURIOUS CHRISTMAS (A Fantasy EXTRA)

Others

DANCE WITH A GUNFIGHTER - THE DRAGON'S LADY -
SEEMS LIKE OLD TIMES - THE GHOST OF SQUIRE HOUSE -
DANGEROUS JOURNEY

THIS CAN'T BE LOVE
THE CABIN OF MYSTERY: BOOK 2

JOANNE PENCE

QUAIL HILL PUBLISHING

Copyright © 2021 by Joanne Pence

All rights reserved.

No part of this book may be reproduced in any form or by any electronic or mechanical means, including information storage and retrieval systems, without written permission from the author, except for the use of brief quotations in a book review.

This is a work of fiction. Any reference to historical events, real people, or real locales are used fictitiously. Other names, characters, places and incidents are the product of the author's imagination, and any resemblance to actual events, locales or persons, living or dead, is entirely coincidental.

Quail Hill Publishing

PO Box 64

Eagle, ID 83616

Visit our website at www.quailhillpublishing.net

First Quail Hill Publishing E-book: January 2021

First Quail Hill Publishing Print Book: January 2021

ISBN: 979-8589869316

THIS CAN'T BE LOVE

CHAPTER 1

Mallory Conway logged out of the Piaget Realty network and checked the clock on her laptop: 6:12 PM. She was at home in a postage-stamp size apartment in midtown Manhattan, a place she could afford only because she was subletting it from one of her boss's clients.

She had forty-five minutes to get ready for tonight's date, but first she had a deadline to meet for her other job.

Her secret job.

By day she was a listing assistant for residential properties at an exclusive Manhattan realty office, but by night she turned into Dear Nellie, columnist for the lovelorn.

The column had begun as a lark.

Seven months earlier, the editor of the *Greenwich Village Gazette*, Brian Abernathy, a tall, pudgy, middle-aged man, happened to be a Piaget client looking for a condominium to purchase. One day, he showed up at the realty office and said he would need to put aside finding a new condo for a while. His current "advice" columnist had been arrested for embezzlement, and the column was the paper's most popular feature. Without it, fewer people would look past page one, which meant fewer advertisers, and that meant less revenue for the paper and less income for him. So he had to find a replacement quickly.

"What kind of advice column is it?" Tom Campilongo, Piaget's top broker, had asked.

"Relationships, what else?" Abernathy had replied. "The 'should I stay with my spouse even though he drinks and beats me?' kind. And the 'does my boyfriend love me when he still goes out with his former fiancée but swears they're just good friends?' questions." The two men laughed.

Hardy har har, Mallory had thought. She sat quietly hidden away in her cubicle behind a massive monitor. She ducked down even further to be sure they didn't see her. The topic they were laughing over was one she had strong feelings about. She guessed they'd never had their black hearts broken. Jerks.

"You won't believe this," her boss, Tom, said. "But I may know the perfect replacement for you. My assistant, Mallory. The girl's been engaged three times that I know of, and she still hasn't gotten married. She could not only give advice to your readers, but sympathy as well. The 'been there, done that,' kind."

"Oh, ho!" Brian said as both men chuckled.

That did it! She no longer could sit quietly by listening to them spew such garbage and laugh about her past. Fuming, she stood up. "Sympathy? You think I'd give them sympathy? Anyone who gets married these days is asking for trouble. It's a one-way ticket to misery and divorce."

"Speak of the devil," Tom said with a big grin, and not an ounce of embarrassment over his words about her. "Brian, meet Mallory Conway. Mallory, this is Brian Abernathy, editor of the *Village Gazette*."

"The only devil around here is you, Tom Campilongo. Hello, Mr. Abernathy." She stuck out her hand to Abernathy. "Nice to meet you. And please ignore my boss's comments. He doesn't have a clue about people. Only real estate."

Abernathy gaped at her as they shook hands, then croaked, "Nice to meet you, too. And call me Brian, please."

Tom chuckled. "She is the most opinionated, and the best, assistant I've ever had. Seems like advice columnist material to me."

"Can you write?" Brian asked.

She was astonished that he would take her boss's comments seriously. "I have a degree in English, and I write puff-piece listings for homes all day long. So, yes, I can write. Especially fiction."

At those words, Brian's head had swiveled between her and Tom, as if he couldn't believe his good fortune. His face glowed. "With her background, it could be a completely different type of column. A 'misery loves company' column where people send in letters and emails, and Mallory could tell them that they don't know what *real* problems are, that she's been close three times but still hasn't gotten married!" Then, the man had the audacity to look at her and chuckle.

"Very funny." With a roll of her eyes at both men at this point, she plopped back down in her chair to go back to work. "You guys are such comedians."

"In fact, I like that name: 'Misery Loves Company,'" Brian added. "It's funny, sassy, and shows it would be an advice column with an edge."

Tom nodded. "Sounds good to me, too. And Mallory does write good listing copy, if that matters."

"For one thing," she added as she scooted her chair away from the desk so that she could see them from the cubicle—and so that they could both see her scowl, "no one would want advice from a three-time loser. So right there, the column would be a dud."

"That's where you're wrong." Brian had moved toward her as he clasped his plump hands together. "They'd want to know your unique take on their situation for one thing, and the second reason is simply because 'misery loves company.' You'd make them realize that their problems aren't the end of the world."

Her mouth wrinkled. How could these two be so clueless? "People don't want to know that. They don't care about other's problems, just their own." She stopped talking as Brian stepped into the cubicle, tore a piece of paper from the notebook on her desk, wrote a number on it, and then folded it in half.

"I would need three columns per week," he said, handing her the paper and then stepping back from her. "Each would consist of one, sometimes two, readers' questions and your answers. Each column is short but pithy and thought-provoking. If you look at our 'Guidance from Gilda' column, you'll see it isn't very many words. I'll give you a couple of test questions, and if everything works out, *that* is your weekly pay."

She stood once more, all the while glowering at her boss. Tom had a grin on his face that told her he was finding all this beyond amusing. She opened the paper.

When she saw the number that Brian had written, her mouth dropped. "This is the amount I'd make each week just for writing three short columns filled with nothing but my opinions?" she asked.

He had nodded vigorously, which caused his jowls to quiver like pudding. "If the readers like what you have to say, and it is reflected in our advertising, it could go even higher."

Her breath had caught; her eyebrows high. Then she had relaxed her face and serenely smiled at both men. Dropping Brian's paper into her handbag, she asked, "When do I start?"

That was seven months ago.

Since then, "Misery Loves Company" had become so popular, it spread from the *Greenwich Village Gazette* to small advertising papers all over the tri-state area. With the now syndicated thrice-weekly, easy-to-write column, Mallory earned almost as much as she made working full time at Piaget.

With the two jobs, she was able to catch up on her credit card payments and might even be able to afford a somewhat decent apartment when the time came to give up her sublease.

Of course, no one except Brian, Tom, and a few other people with a "need to know" had any idea that Mallory Conway was the person behind the answers. All anyone else knew was that Dear Nellie dished out advice that was never sugar-coated and was often hard-to-take. But, ironically, most of the time, people wrote in to say it was spot on.

A few of her friends joked that "Nellie" was just like Mallory in that they'd both had multiple fiancés. She told them it only proved her situation wasn't as unique as they had tried to make it out to be.

Now, since Mallory had time before her date arrived, she opened up the "Dear Nellie" files on her computer. A letter caught her eye.

Dear Nellie,

I'm getting married in two months. Everyone tells me this is supposed to be the happiest time of my life, that I should enjoy all the things I need to do to plan for the wedding and the reception. Instead, I feel overwhelmed and frightened. My parents hired a wedding planner to help me, but now I feel as if it isn't my wedding, but hers. My fiancé says I'm just being silly, and that I really do want a big, beautiful wedding. But, in my heart, I don't. What's wrong with me? [Signed] Miserable to the Max

The letter hit close to home. Mallory didn't have to think twice about how to answer this one. She wrote:

Dear Miserable,

Who is your marriage for? Is it for your parents, who seem to want to give you a big wedding whether you want one or not? For the wedding planner, who seems to be doing her 'thang' and not yours? Or for this schmuck of a fiancé who doesn't listen to what you say when you say you aren't happy. If I were in your position—and guess what, I have been, THREE TIMES—I'd tell them all 'sayonara' and take off for the Himalayas. When you're happily planning YOUR wedding, the way YOU want it—even if it means the only attendees are you, your fiancé, a Justice of the Peace, and a witness—that's when you should say "I do." And not before. [Signed] Free-At-Last Nellie

Mallory reread her answer. Yep, that was exactly how she felt about it. Of course, it was a bit caustic, particularly about the fiancé. And maybe the parents. And maybe she should say something nice about the bride-to-be's predicament. How important was the actual wedding, compared to the years of married life to follow?

The apartment buzzer sounded. She glanced at the clock. She still had ten more minutes before seven. Why was her date here already? She tried to hurry with her answer, but realized she needed time to think of a few niceties to add to her reply.

The buzzer rang again—a harsh, grating sound that she hated. "All right!"

She hit Save and rushed to the intercom. "Who is it?"

"It's me. I'm early, but I want to talk to you."

She recognized Slade Atchison's voice–distinguished, worldly, mature. "Okay." She buzzed him in, then rushed to her computer to log out of the Nellie site. The last thing she wanted was for Slade to know she was writing an advice column. He was the type who wouldn't approve. She didn't know exactly why he wouldn't, but her gut instinct—and it was usually right when she listened to it—told her he would consider it "trashy," to use a word he often employed.

To her horror, she saw that when she left the computer, thinking she had simply saved her response to "Miserable to the Max," she had actually transmitted it to the *Village Gazette*. Well, she'd call Brian in the morning and tell him it was just a draft.

She quickly logged out and was stuffing her Nellie notes into a desk drawer when there was a knock on the door.

She opened it and, as always when she regarded the man before her, she was struck with the thought of how lucky she was to have such an impressive person interested in dating her. His four-thousand (minimum) dollar suit was immaculate, as was his thousand (minimum) dollar silk tie, and equally expensive white shirt. He also spent a fortune having his gray hair styled, his eyebrows shaped, and his nails buffed.

She couldn't begin to imagine what his diamond and sapphire cuff links cost.

He gave her a quick peck on the lips as she invited him in.

"I didn't realize we were dressing up tonight," she said. "Please give me just a minute while I change. I was working late."

His gaze slid over her and he smiled with obvious pleasure at what he saw. "I should object to the way Tom works you. But if it weren't for Piaget Realty, we'd never have met, so I try not to be hard on him."

As she headed off to change, she smiled at his reference to their meeting. It had happened while she was assisting Tom at an open house for a ten million dollar apartment in SoHo. Slade came in only because he was friends with the owner and was asked to check on the open house. As he later explained it, he took one look at Mallory and forgot all about the apartment. He preferred to check her out.

They'd dated ever since—twice a week on Friday and Sunday nights. Soon after they met, he told her he was an "international entrepreneur." Exactly what he did was unclear, but whatever it was, he earned a lot of money doing it, and he had apartments all over the world.

That explained why he reserved Saturday evenings for friendly dinners with business associates. Mallory had heard rumors of him having a mistress, but she couldn't help but suspect the rumor-mongers who came to her with their tall tales were simply jealous of her happiness.

"Some of the magnificent white wine you brought over the other day is still in the fridge," Mallory called from her bedroom. "Help yourself to a glass while you wait."

"I'll pass, dear. And don't fuss too much. You always look lovely. But I'd do have something special planned for tonight."

Something about the way he sounded jarred her. She'd heard that particular combination of excitement and anxiety before. She hoped she was wrong—after all, they'd only gone out for three months. But she drew in her breath, and said only, "Great."

Slade took Mallory to LeCoucou, his favorite intimate French restaurant in SoHo, with dark wood tables, soft lights, and paintings of Paris. She wore a shimmering blue dress, the color of her eyes, that was short, sleeveless, and with a deep V-neck-line. She'd never heard of the designer, but the consignment shop price told her it had to have been expensive. With it, she put on black Manolo Blahnik heels that had cost nearly a week's pay. She'd twisted her naturally wavy jet-black hair into an upswept knot with a few wavy tendrils around her face.

As usual, Slade ordered for them both in French. Mallory had no idea what she was getting, but she had learned after their first date to tell him she was a vegetarian. He had apparently hoped to impress her and ordered some expensive dishes that featured sea creatures and animal parts that left her squeamish.

Slade told her that her vegetarianism was "charming." For that she was glad because as the meal progressed, her food consisted of a vegetable cassoulet and a side of crepes with a wild mushroom sauce, while Slade's was sea urchins and rabbit. No, thank you.

"Now for dessert," Slade said with a cryptic smile. "I have a special treat in store."

"Oh, no need for that," Mallory told him. "Believe me, I'm much too full to even think about dessert."

"Not for this dessert." With that, he nodded to the waiter who approached carrying a silver tray with a half-dome hood over it. Mallory tensed. She hoped he'd place it in the center of the table, but instead he put it in front of her.

She swallowed hard, dreading what it might all mean. "What's this?" she asked, her voice tiny as she faced Slade.

He was beaming. "Open it, my dear."

She did. Seated on white satin was a diamond and platinum engagement ring. The diamond was gigantic. Her heart sank.

Finally, she tore her eyes from the ring, her brow furrowed as she looked at Slade. "This can't be...?"

He chuckled. "Of course, it can. And it is!" He took the ring and held it before her. "I would like you to be my wife."

Her mind reeled as she tried to think of something positive to say. "It's ... it's so beautiful," she said, studying the setting. "And so huge. It can't be real."

He laughed out loud this time. "Of course, it's real! It's a special ring for the most beautiful woman I know, if she'll do me the honor of saying yes. But before you reply, I know your history. I understand all about your dislike of engagements and weddings."

A modicum of hope struck even as she took another shuddering breath. Maybe, since he understood—

"So I've arranged for us to be married by my good friend, Judge Kawamoto, at noon, tomorrow in his office. He'll waive the waiting period so there is absolutely no need for you to get nervous or upset as you have in the past."

Mallory couldn't breathe at all now. Slade knew about her three prior engagements and how they had ended. She had told him about them early in their relationship, opening with, "You don't want to grow serious about me because…"

But he had laughed it off. "It simply means you haven't found the right man yet," he'd told her. She guessed he assumed she now had.

"So, Mallory Conway," he continued, "will you marry me?"

Her mind went absolutely blank. She didn't know what to do. "You … you seem to have thought of everything," she murmured.

"I try to."

"Isn't this too soon?" she asked. "I mean, it's been only—"

"Nonsense! Not for me. I've known it since our first date," he answered. "You're perfect for me."

Perfect. She could think of nothing less than perfection about Slade either. And he was exactly the type of man she'd been looking for. Wasn't he?

The waiter rolled out a cart with a bottle of champagne in an ice bucket, with two glasses and a bouquet of white roses. He stopped the cart right next to her, and then stood by, his eyes on her as he waited to open the champagne.

Mallory's palms felt as cold as the champagne as her gaze jumped from Slade to the waiter. Both stared at her expectantly. And then she noticed people from nearby tables were also watching. All of them. And Slade, the smile on his face slowly vanishing.

It was simply too embarrassing to do anything but to say, in a small but lilting voice, "Yes."

CHAPTER 2

Mallory couldn't sleep that night. Slade had dropped her off at her apartment with a number of carefully planned instructions. After their wedding ceremony, they would immediately leave for a honeymoon in Bermuda, so she needed to pack for a two-week stay. He said he'd take care of informing Tom Campilongo that she'd be out of the office for that period, and most likely permanently. Slade didn't think his wife should be an assistant to anyone. Mrs. Slade Atchison was far too important.

Mallory actually enjoyed her job and the people she worked with. Although, she expected they would treat her differently once she was Slade's wife. His wealth made that inevitable.

Her entire life, she realized, was about to change.

And that was precisely what she had always wanted. Her mother, Roxanne Donnelly, had always told her, "Mallory, it's as easy to fall in love with a rich man as a poor one. So find yourself a rich man." And Roxanne definitely wanted her to marry a very rich man.

With Slade, she would. Finally. Her mother would have been

extremely proud, had she lived to see it. Unfortunately, last year, Roxanne had passed away from a heart attack.

Thoughts of Slade, Roxanne, and life changes swirled round and round in Mallory's head all night long. She had already ended three engagements.

This time, unexpected although it was, she should have realized that Slade was a take-charge guy. It went along with his success in everything he did. He saw what he wanted and went after it. Why wait? He wanted her; she wanted him. Of course, she did. He was everything she ever wanted in a husband.

And even if it seemed a bit sudden, it would work out. Besides, she couldn't bear the humiliation of ending a fourth engagement, could she? Three was bad enough. Four, she could never live down.

And how embarrassing would it be for Slade if she walked out on him after having said "Yes"? For sure, she would lose her job. Slade was too important to Piaget Realty for Tom to risk keeping her as his listing assistant if she were to turn down Slade's proposal.

And since the man whose apartment she was subletting was not only Tom's client but also traveled in Slade's orbit, she'd probably lose her apartment, too.

The only sane thing to do was to marry Slade. Anything else verged on madness. She needed to put such thoughts out of her head. Besides, she'd already said, "Yes!"

She couldn't talk to her friends. She wasn't that close to any of them, and they all worked with her, which meant they wouldn't want to find themselves between her and their boss. Or Slade and his money.

And then there were her two older half-sisters...

Carly, five years older than her, was the logical, practical one. Yet, she had just married a man she'd known only a month! So much for going to "practical" Carly for advice.

Julia, ten years older, had never been in love and never

wanted to be. Mallory and Julia weren't at all close. Julia hadn't even attempted to be present at Mallory's one big wedding day celebration. The one where Mallory left the groom standing at the altar in front of everyone. The one that earned her the ugly title of a "runaway bride." How she hated that name!

No, Julia wasn't one to go to with her problems.

She rubbed her temples. She'd have to work this out on her own. The most promising part of this dilemma was that this marriage would have made her mother proud of her, and she had worked all her life to make Roxanne proud.

Roxanne had married four times ... four that Mallory knew of, at least. She always suspected another marriage or two might have happened because late in her life, Roxanne had cut off contact with all three of her daughters.

That Roxanne's three daughters each had a different father, and that after each divorce Roxanne had given the father sole custody of his daughter, said everything anyone ever needed to know about Roxanne's "motherly" qualities.

Mallory had been six years old when her parents divorced and her mother left the house, leaving Mallory alone with her father. That had been devastating enough, but as time passed, her father didn't want her either. While Julia and Carly's fathers kept their daughters, when Mallory was eleven, her father brought her to Roxanne's apartment. She still remembered her father's words. "This girl is way too much trouble. I've got things to do, places to go, and people to see, and I can't do it with a brat always sticking her nose into my business."

Even worse was her mother's response. "And what am I supposed to do with her?"

But her father had already gone, so she never heard what his answer might have been. She never saw him again.

At least Slade wants me.

And she wanted him. She needed to marry him.

But doubts filled her. It was strange that even now, "officially engaged," he'd done no more than give her a light kiss on the lips. But then, he was older, and perhaps that made him want to take everything slowly and properly. It meant no more than that. She doubted Slade would want a platonic marriage. Not when she saw how he ogled some women when he thought she wasn't looking.

And, frankly, the light kiss was more than enough for her.

Not that it mattered. She'd soon be his wife. All would be well. And she wouldn't feel so alone anymore. So she had done as he said and had dutifully packed her clothes and makeup.

But even after having confirmed her decision to marry him, she still couldn't sleep.

At the appointed time the next day, Slade picked up Mallory in his Bentley for their trip to Judge Kawamoto's chambers. Slade always used a driver to get around the city and said it was the only civilized way to travel. His driver came up to Mallory's apartment with him to help carry down her luggage.

Slade was "charmed"—his word—to discover she had only packed one mid-sized suitcase and an overnight carry-on. "Most women I know would have at least three bags for a weekend trip, let alone a two-week honeymoon."

She just shrugged. She didn't see herself wearing tee-shirts and cutoffs or leggings around Slade, and since they made up most of her wardrobe, she didn't have much left to pack.

He looked fresh and excited, while she felt exhausted and dazed. Lack of sleep, she told herself. That's all it was.

"Are you sure getting married this way is what you want?" Mallory asked him as they sat in the Bentley's back seat.

"Your concern is sweet," he said, lifting Mallory's hand to his lips and then taking a moment to admire the ring he'd given her. "I've already had two big weddings, and I don't want another."

"What about your children? Wouldn't they want to be here?" Mallory asked.

Slade grimaced. "Not when one of them is older than his step-mother-to-be. Don't worry. We'll do this our way. Besides, given your history, I should think this is exactly the way you'd want us to marry."

She nodded. Of course it was.

Since the courthouse was closed to the public on Saturdays, the driver parked near a side entrance as directed by Slade's friend, the judge.

Slade held Mallory's hand and led her through the labyrinth of halls to the office designated as their wedding place.

Her heart beat so hard she was afraid even Slade could hear it thump. She hated this—but it was better than what she had put up with during other engagements. Having to choose a wedding dress, select a wedding party without losing friends in the process, plus the cake, the caterers, finding venues both for the service and the reception afterward, not to mention invitations, party favors, music selections, and even the honeymoon, were all nightmares. She hated all of it and never wanted anything to do with it again. Not ever.

And since Slade didn't either, he was even more perfect for her than she'd previously imagined. Truly, this had to be a marriage made in heaven.

Before Slade opened the door to the Judge's chambers, he stopped and faced her. He was a nice looking man, she told herself. Not too tall, not too portly, and not too leather-skinned despite the many days he spent golfing in Florida. His gray hair was still fairly thick, and his brown eyes not too small. Those eyes stared at her now. "You didn't really love those guys who came before me, did you, Mallory?" he asked.

The question surprised her. Never before had he mentioned anything about love—not his for her, or hers for anyone. Had she loved them? If she were to answer honestly, she would have said that she had no idea. She thought she loved her parents, and that they loved her, but neither one wanted her with them.

She thought she'd loved other men … but something always seemed to go wrong with that love. What was love, anyway? Did she even know?

But this wasn't the time for subjects like that. So she simply shook her head. "They were nice guys, that's all. But love? Probably not."

He took both her hands in his.

"I understand if you don't fully love me, yet," he said. "But eventually, you will. I promise. You'll learn what love feels like. I plan to make your life wonderful. You'll never have to do anything you don't want to. You won't even have to lift your little finger if you don't feel like it. I'll give you everything. Just looking at you makes me happy, and at my age, with my money, that's worth plenty, believe me. Happiness is so fleeting that when you find it, you should do whatever you can to keep it. I hope that's enough for you right now."

Her heart was now not only beating hard, but was beating so fast she felt lightheaded. But Slade's little speech was why she cared so much about him. He was sensitive to her wants and needs. He'd lived a lot and understood a lot. He understood her. "It's enough," she whispered.

"I can only guess what you've been through. I've heard jokes about you as a crazed 'runaway bride.' But that's not you. I know that you were simply looking for the right man and you hadn't found him yet. Your peculiar past isn't a problem for me."

My peculiar past?

"Are you ready?" he asked.

She drew in her breath, her hands tightening on his, then nodded.

"Good." He kissed her cheek.

She had expected some show of passion. She may have even needed it at a time like this. Thoughts of him having a mistress came back to her. But if he had one, she didn't care. She wasn't marrying him for his body. She was no innocent. She knew what it was like to feel lust, to want a man for his looks and his charm. But she also believed those things had nothing to do with the heart of a relationship. Slade wouldn't disappoint her in the "lust" area because she had no expectations with him.

"You're going to be such a beautiful wife for me," he said. "I can hardly wait to show you off to my friends, to introduce you as my gorgeous bride."

Her mother always used to say that she'd make some older, wealthy man a great "trophy wife." *Well, guess what, Mom...*

Her breaths came deeper and longer. Was this the marriage she wanted, the life she wanted? Or was it what she'd been told she should want?

Finally, Slade opened the door to the private area where the judge's administrative assistant sat. As soon as she saw Slade and Mallory, she stood. She clearly was aware of Slade Atchison's reputation and that he was not a man to be kept waiting.

No, he didn't like to wait ... not even when it came to his marriage ...

"Hello, Mr. Atchison," she said. "Everything is ready for you. I'll inform Judge Kawamoto that you're here. I'll be serving as one of the witnesses. The other is Jennifer." With that, she gestured to a woman who was seated in the corner. Mallory hadn't even noticed her until that point.

Slade nodded at both of them. The assistant knocked on the judge's office door, and at the sound of his voice she opened it and said, "The couple is ready for you."

Black and white spots began to dance before Mallory's eyes.

Slade took a step forward. Mallory couldn't move. He barely glanced at her as he gripped her arm tight and again started toward the judge's chamber.

A roaring sound filled Mallory's ears, and the room swirled around her. Slade's hand tightened as he tugged at her arm. Finally, his hand went to her back, as if he were about to physically force her into the judge's office.

"No," she said and yanked her arm free. The roaring in her ears grew louder as she backed away from him.

"Mallory!" His face was a harsh scowl. "It's all right. You can do this."

Her hand went to her throat. The air turned stale, thick, and would close her throat if she couldn't get out of the building, away from these people, these strangers staring at her, calling her name.

Without a word, she yanked off her engagement ring, put it in Slade's hand, then turned and ran from the room.

Slade followed for a couple of steps, but then stopped. The last words she heard from him were, "Stop acting like a child, Mallory! Come back here! You are *not* a runaway bride!"

Slade's Bentley waited for them in a no-parking zone. As she reached it, she saw a taxi approach. She ran into the street to stop it.

"Watch out, lady!" The cabbie leaned out the window and shouted at her after slamming on his brakes. "All you gotta do is wave your arm, not kill yourself!"

She pulled open the door. "I need a moment to get my bags. They're in the Bentley."

At this point, Slade's driver was standing behind her. "What is wrong?" he asked.

She faced him. "Open the trunk, please. I need to get my luggage."

"No, I ... I don't ..."

"Open the trunk!" she insisted.

He opened it. "But Mr. Atchison, he say we go to hotel next."

She pulled out her overnight bag.

"No, no, lady!" Slade's driver grabbed the bag's strap and held on tight. "You cannot take it!"

"It's mine! Let go!" She kept hold of it, and both tugged so hard she was sure the strap would break.

"Hey, what's going on here?" The taxi driver was now out of his cab and standing next to his fare.

"Would you get my larger suitcase, please?" Mallory said to the cabbie.

The cabbie squared his shoulders and puffed out his chest. "Do these things belong to the lady here?" he asked the driver.

"Yes, but—"

The cabbie didn't bother to wait for an explanation, took the suitcase, and put it in his trunk. Slade's driver let go of the overnight bag, and Mallory and the bag got into the back seat.

"Where to, miss?" the cabbie asked.

Without missing a beat, Mallory suddenly knew exactly where she needed to go. "Newark airport, please."

CHAPTER 3

Mallory was stunned at how few flights there were from Newark, New Jersey, to Boise, Idaho, and finally opted for one where she could sleep at the Chicago airport for most of the night, and then get an early morning flight for the last leg. Except that the early flight was delayed.

She was on her way to the cabin in Idaho that she and her two half-sisters had inherited from their mother. Mallory had wanted to sell it, but her older sisters had refused.

It had been in their mother's family for over a century, they said. And they had spent many summers there. Mallory was shocked to learn her sisters had good memories about the place. Hers were all terrible.

When Mallory was quite young, her parents were still married and Mallory would go to the cabin with her mother, Roxanne Donnelly. Roxanne had always used her maiden name, both because of her career in musical theater, and because of her many marriages. She and Mallory would meet her older half-sisters, Carly and Julia, in a month-long, family get-together.

But eventually, Roxanne and Eric Conway divorced and Roxanne sent Mallory to live with her father, just as she had done with her older daughters.

Mallory remembered being hurt and confused by her mother's rejection, except for one month each summer at the cabin. She would cry her eyes out when the month ended and Roxanne would take all three girls to the airport to send them back to their respective fathers.

When Mallory was nine years old, Roxanne didn't contact her about spending a month at the cabin. Mallory had been devastated. Roxanne, she later learned, had remarried and her new husband apparently didn't like her spending time with "other men's off-spring."

From that time, Mallory had never returned to the cabin.

That was why she would have gladly sold it. But eventually, her sisters persuaded her not only to keep it but also to include her share of the money she'd inherited to fix it up. Julia had taken charge of the renovations, and of the cabin itself, since her apartment in Bend, Oregon, was the closest to it.

Now, Mallory phoned her sister and told her she was on her way to the cabin. Julia could scarcely believe Mallory intended to stay there alone. "Mallory, you're a city girl. You don't know how to live all alone out in the middle of nowhere," she said. "You think Central Park is roughing it. Why don't you wait until I can go with you?"

"I don't need a baby sitter," Mallory said. "You've been there alone, right?"

"Yes, but I'm different."

"Carly's been there alone, right?"

"Not exactly. Although she did intend to be alone."

"I can do it. I'm not afraid."

"I'll get there as soon as I can."

"I don't want you to," Mallory said. "I need time to be alone. Isn't that why you and Carly convinced me to help restore the place? So we can go there when we need to? Well, I need to. Now."

"Why?" Julia asked.

"I'm not ready to talk about it yet," she said. "I'll let you know when I am."

"Sounds like man trouble to me," Julia said. The disapproval in her tone could be heard across the miles, which was exactly why she was the last person Mallory wanted to confide in.

"It's nothing I can't handle," Mallory said. "Just give me the garage door code so I can get into the place and tell me where I can find the extra keys to the front door."

The cabin was past the tiny Old West town of Crouch, along the Middlefork Road that meandered northward to the Boise National Forest. Mallory reminded herself of how her two half-sisters had stayed there alone and did just fine. But, as Julia said, she wasn't a tough country girl like Julia, or independent and single-minded like Carly. She was city soft, through and through.

The cabin had never seemed as isolated as it did now.

At the Boise Airport, she had rented a four-wheel-drive Subaru wagon. She didn't know if she'd need it, but she took it just in case the roads were worse than Julia had said.

In fact, the roads weren't any problem at all, not even the dirt road to the cabin. Of course, it was late summer, not winter. Mallory knew enough about this area to understand that made a huge difference.

Now, pulling her rolling suitcase with her carry-on over her shoulder, she punched in the code to the garage door. The garage was small, with room for a car on one side and boxes, old tools, and two lawnmowers on the other. From it, Mallory opened the door that led to a tiny laundry room, half bath, and then the cabin's foyer.

The cabin was hot and muggy from the heat of the day. Of course, the air conditioner was off since no one was living there, and Julia watched the income and outgo of the place like a top notch CPA.

Mallory scarcely remembered the foyer, but she did remember the rough-hewn wooden staircase that led to the three upstairs bedrooms and a full bathroom. Late at night, she would crawl out of bed and hide on the stairs to listen to her older sisters and their mother talk. Julia was ten years older than her, and Carly five years older, so they could stay up much later than she did.

That was when she first learned about the ghosts that lived in the cabin, and in particular, about Elijah Donnelly. All she remembered was that Elijah had built the home for his wife but then she died, and then he died, and the cabin went to their son. When he grew up he went to war, but then he died, and now the three of them were said to haunt it.

No one seemed to know why they haunted it, however.

She wished she'd asked for some clarification of the story, but if she had, her sisters probably would have laughed at her. She couldn't tell if they believed in the ghosts or not. Most of the time they said they didn't, but Julia told her that she once saw one of the ghosts, the mother, and that the ghost was searching for her baby.

Mallory grew so scared when Julia told her that, she started to shake, but then Julia laughed and told her she was just teasing. At such times, Mallory hated her eldest sister. Carly was always much nicer to her.

Mallory stopped believing in the ghosts as she got older, and eventually she didn't care what the true story was of the three people who all had died so young.

Mallory left her suitcases at the bottom of the stairs and

walked into what was once the parlor and stopped. It was nothing like she remembered.

There had been lots of little rooms. In one, they would sit and play games near the fireplace, in another they ate, and in the very back was a small kitchen.

Now, all that was gone, replaced by a large open space with a seating area near the fireplace, a dining area, and then a large granite-covered island that separated the kitchen with its stainless steel appliances from the rest of the room. It was all much nicer than Mallory had expected.

She strode into the great room, which was larger than her apartment. Her gaze jumped to the portrait hanging over the mantle. Elijah Donnelly. From an adult woman's perspective, she now saw that the cabin's builder had been a rather nice-looking young man with blond hair parted just slightly off-center and slicked down in the style of the 1890s. He wore a gray suit with a vest, and a white carnation on the lapel. She guessed he was still in his twenties when the portrait was painted—and he probably died within years of it being finished.

Next to him, as if seated on his lap while posing for the portrait, was a white, orange, and black cat. Odd, Mallory thought. She didn't remember seeing a cat before. It should have caught her attention as a child, especially since she'd never had a cat and had always wanted one. She guessed it was one of many things she'd simply forgotten over the years.

At the same time, she remembered Elijah Donnelly's face well. There was something off-putting, almost fierce, in his strange lavender-blue eyes. They used to scare her and, she had to admit, still made her shiver.

His eyes seemed to follow her. She suddenly remembered Roxanne telling her if she acted bad, the ghost of Elijah would come down from the portrait and pinch her hard and make her cry. No wonder a chill went down her back whenever she looked at the painting!

If she ever had a child, especially a sensitive little girl, she would banish anyone who tried to scare her—no matter who it was.

She rubbed her arms against goosebumps even now over Elijah's picture. She turned toward the kitchen, but as she did, from the corner of her eye it seemed she saw Elijah's hand move to pet the cat. She froze, then turned back to the portrait.

His hand was where she'd last seen it, but he seemed to be smiling a bit broader.

No way! My sisters tormented me about those darn ghosts when I was a kid. I'm not going to let them scare me now!

She stormed to the kitchen area. Clearly, her mind was playing tricks on her. In the pantry she found a few canned veggies and broth, but nothing else to eat. She had bought a burger at the Boise airport and ate it while waiting for her rental car, so she was fine for the moment.

She heard a noise and jumped, spinning around. Of course, nothing was there. It was probably something outside. She was sure she was quite alone here.

She steeled herself and carried her suitcase upstairs. She already knew which bedroom she wanted—the one her mother had always used, the one with a view of the river.

The room was every bit as pretty as she remembered it. The wallpaper was the same—a traditional yellow and cream striped design, and the furniture was the same—cream colored and early twentieth century with floral carvings on the edges of the pieces and the headboard. But the ceiling and woodwork had been painted white, and everything appeared to have had the grime of time scrubbed away, making it fresh and lovely.

The view from the window was beautiful. As a child, she hadn't appreciated it, although she had heard her mother remark on it a few times. As an adult, she could see why it was special. The cabin had been built high enough over the river that the vista stretched quite a distance north and south, with touches of river water appearing now and again through the trees and shrubs along its bank.

Driving up here, she had learned the river's name—the Middle Fork of the Payette. As a child, it was simply The River.

One look at the bed and the physical exhaustion she'd fought through the night, uncomfortably trying to sleep at the Chicago airport and then on the plane to Boise, finally caught up with her. Also, her mind, that had raced incessantly ever since she ran out of the judge's chambers, was now so tired it had gone completely numb. She lay down on the bed and shut her eyes.

When Mallory opened her eyes, it was dusk. She glanced at her watch. Seven-thirty.

She put on the lamp by the bed. The room was warm and cozy, but she hesitated to go out to the rest of the cabin. Had she even shut the garage door? She didn't think so.

The area immediately around the cabin had no other houses or cabins, nothing but trees and shrubs. Down the hill, one could reach the river. Her mother had constantly warned her about the dangers that lurked outdoors. Wild animals could kill her and maybe eat her, and the river could carry her downstream and she'd never be seen again.

Between the dangerous outdoors, and the ghostly intruders indoors, she had spent most of her childhood at the cabin afraid.

No wonder she now sat in the bedroom too scared to venture out of it!

She wasn't a child anymore, and well she knew that there were no such things as ghosts. Maybe outdoors there were dangerous animals... but here, she was perfectly safe.

And she was still wearing the suit she'd put on to marry Slade. It seemed like a lifetime ago. She wanted it off.

She opened the door to the hallway. All was quiet. She hurried to the bathroom. Much as she didn't like the idea of taking a shower in a place that frightened her, remaining in that suit after her awful past twenty-four hours was even worse.

Finally, she steeled her nerve, locked the bathroom door, took a shower, and washed her hair. She felt much better when that was done.

As she was getting dressed, she noticed that the mirror over the washbasin had steamed up. She took the washcloth and wiped it and as she did, she saw someone standing directly in back of her—a woman, her face very pale, her dark brown hair pulled back tight, and her dark eyes so sad they took Mallory's breath away.

Mallory cried out, dropped the washcloth and spun around to confront the stranger. But when she did, the small bathroom was empty, and the door to it shut tight. And still locked.

Spinning toward the mirror again, she was the only one in it.

The vision had left her quaking, gasping for breath. It had to be nothing more than her imagination as she'd faced the steamy mirror—although how steam could look so much like a small woman in a calico dress was hard to say. And, strangely, an overwhelming sorrow washed over her.

She tried her best to pull herself together, to shake off the sense of sadness as she dried and styled her black hair so it fell in loose waves well past her shoulders from a side part.

Be not afraid, she told herself. After all, she was home—a part owner of the cabin, and here, she didn't have to worry about rents or landlords or cranky neighbors telling her if she didn't do x, y, and z, she'd be kicked out.

And here, she was away from New York City, away from Slade, away from Tom and Piaget Realty, and even away from the few friends she had there. She didn't have to hear their opinion of her latest fiasco with Slade, or hear them trying to psychoanalyze her "fear of marriage," or "fear of commitment," or fear of anything else. She wanted to be far away from all of them.

And she was.

She went downstairs because, more than anything, she hated being alone with her thoughts.

She looked again at the empty kitchen, the empty refrigerator and pantry, and then the cold, watchful eyes of Elijah Donnelly.

Quick as she could, she grabbed her car keys, ran out to her rental car and drove to town.

CHAPTER 4

The Old West town of Crouch was smaller than Mallory remembered it. As a child, to walk from one store to another, especially in the heat of summer, could be tiring. Julia and Carly had bicycles and went all over town with them. Finally, when Mallory was five, she was given her own bicycle, training wheels included. Roxanne put the fear of God into Julia, who was then fifteen, that she was to make sure Mallory was safe riding with her. Julia hated it, but did as Roxanne demanded.

The bikes gave the girls freedom to meet other kids and soon, each of them had a friend or two close to their own age that they liked to visit. Mallory's best friend was named Darlene, who lived half-way between the cabin and Crouch's only ice cream shop.

Now, Mallory's gaze went to a place called the Rusty Nail, where food as well as strong drink were served. At the moment, a relaxing drink seemed to be what the doctor ordered—or would have ordered if the town had a doctor, which she doubted.

She needed something to help calm her nerves.

She parked right in front and entered. The place had the vibe of an old Western saloon, with a long bar and a number of smaller tables and booths. A couple of older men sat at the far end of the bar, and in the nearby corner sat a man with an unhappy looking woman standing and talking to him. Mallory took a stool between the two groups, having learned in Manhattan to overcome any awkwardness at sitting alone at a bar.

"What'll it be?" the bartender asked. He was a skinny, white-haired man with a mustache and a broad, pleasant smile.

"I'll have a cosmo," she said.

He feigned a sad expression and shook his head. "Well, let me tell you. Some years back, when cosmos were real popular I bought a bottle of Cointreau. Some fifteen years later, when I finally used the last of it, I was so happy I never bought another."

She couldn't help but grin at his tale of woe and the way he told it. "How about a dirty martini, then?"

"That," he said, "I can handle. Gin?"

"Right."

He soon put it in front of her. "You here for vacation or just passing through?"

"A vacation, so to speak." As she said that, she noticed the woman who'd been standing, turned and stomped out of the bar.

The bartender ignored the angry customer. "So to speak?" he asked.

"I own a cabin nearby. I haven't been back for some time, though."

He smiled. "Well, then, welcome back."

"Thanks." The word was a whisper, and the bartender left her alone.

The martini went down much too quickly and too smoothly. It didn't do anything for her nerves. She still felt trapped somewhere between misery and tears. One drink was usually her limit, but there was nothing usual about this situation. "I'll have another," she said.

The bartender nodded and soon put a second martini before her. "So, you mentioned you own a place out here?"

"Actually, my mother owned a cabin. When she passed away, my sisters and I inherited it. It's been in the family a long time."

"And that's what brought you back?"

"It is. That, and needing to get away from New York City for a while."

The bartender chuckled. "Well, you've come to a spot that's probably about as different from New York as you'll ever find in this country."

That brought a small smile to her lips. "That's what I want to hear." She raised her martini to him. "Cheers."

"You, too." He said with a nod and lifted his glass of tonic water with a twist of lime toward her. "Hope you have a nice stay here."

"So do I."

The two fellows further down the counter waved their empty glasses at him and he headed their way.

She continued to sip her martini, trying not to think of all the things her mind wanted to think about.

"Excuse me." The fellow sitting in the corner called to her.

She ignored him. The last thing she wanted was to be hit on. She was in an official "no males allowed" mood. She didn't care if Brad Pitt wanted to talk to her. Well, maybe…

"Excuse me, again, please," he said, a little louder.

Persistent, isn't he? She turned and gave him her iciest glare.

"I couldn't help but overhear you and Butch, and I wondered if you were by chance talking about the old Donnelly cabin."

By his side was a tan cowboy hat. She didn't think anyone wore cowboy hats any more—although she now remembered that they were popular around here when she was a kid. He had pale blue eyes and wavy dark blond hair. Not bad at all, she had to admit, but she wasn't interested. "Yes, I was," she said with the curt "drop dead, it's none of your business" tone that she'd perfected in Manhattan.

His blue eyes seemed to widen while his lips slowly curled into a half smile. Something about the way he did that, something about *him*, niggled in the back of her mind.

He cocked his head. "You wouldn't be little Mal, would you?"

Mal. That's what she'd been called by kids around here when she was a child. As an adult, she insisted on being called Mallory.

"I am." She studied him. Blue eyes, blond hair ... her sense that she should know him grew.

His gaze softened. "As soon as I heard you and saw that charcoal-color hair of yours, I started thinking it might be you. I ran into your sister, Carly, a while back, and ever since, you gals and your mama have been on my mind. Your sister hasn't changed much, but you have." He grinned. He had a nice smile. "You were just the scruffy little kid who always tagged along. You've grown up."

"So I have. You do look kind of familiar," she said. "What's your name?"

"Gunnar McDermott."

"Gunnar!" He was one of the kids she used to play with in summer. The memories flooded back, and she smiled. She must have been five, and he was about eight when they first met. She and Darlene always liked playing with Gunnar and his best friend, Nathan. Boys did neat things, like catching frogs, that Mallory wouldn't have dreamed of doing on her own. Gunnar was always pretty nice to her, but Nathan was hell on wheels, and even convinced her not only to climb a tree but to keep going up it, until Mallory was too scared to try to come back down.

They all got into trouble for that stunt.

Mallory looked forward, each summer, to seeing Darlene, Gunnar and Nathan. For three years, until she was eight, she'd had great summers with them. She even remembered how she and Darlene used to play "brides"—when the boys weren't around, of course—and she would pretend she was going to marry Gunnar, and Darlene was going to marry Nathan.

Now, that made her laugh. "Oh, my God," she blurted. "I used to have the biggest crush on you."

"You *what?*" he asked with a laugh.

Seeing how good-looking he was now, she had to admit "little Mal" had a good eye. "I was eight, so don't think it meant anything." She gave him a wry smile and sipped more of her martini.

He raised one very cocky eyebrow. "And I guess I was young enough and dumb enough not to appreciate the attention. Although, I remember I used to look forward to seeing you in summer."

"I'm glad to hear that," she said, surprised at the admission. "I remember that you used to hang out with a kid named Nathan."

"He was my best friend. Still is, matter of fact." Gunnar shook his head. "I'm sorry to say we did surely enjoy teasing you and your friend, Darlene. I guess that's what boys do around girls at that age. But we liked you both. And Carly, too. Your older sister, Jules, though, she was something else. I'll never forget the time she came after us with a broom when we set off some firecrackers near her. I think I can still feel the bruises on my backside where the broom connected a few times. And they were just little firecrackers."

Something about the way he spoke, the way his eyes mischievously twinkled and his tone, caused Mallory to laugh aloud at his story. He joined in her laughter. "Oh, my!" she said finally. "How could I have forgotten that? She was so furious! You're lucky you two could run faster than her or she would have pulverized you."

Gunnar nodded. "We used to play tricks on Carly, too, but she was a good sport about it, and sometimes got back at us. You were too little and too nice, so you were spared."

"I was nice?"

"You sure were!"

"That's good to know," she said with a grin.

She finished her martini and reached for her purse. Time to go.

"Do you have to leave already?" he asked. "Let me get you another for old times' sake."

She should leave, get a sandwich somewhere and go back to the cabin. And then she thought of the emptiness there, the ghosts, the strange air of sadness. "That sounds good."

Gunner signaled to the bartender for another round. She expected Gunnar to move closer to her so they could talk more quietly, but then she noticed the cane propped up against the wall at his side. She moved instead, leaving a single empty barstool between them.

"Thank you," she said to him when the bartender approached with their drinks, a beer from the tap for him, another dirty martini for her.

He acknowledged her thanks with a simple nod. "So, are you staying out at the cabin?"

"Yes. Julia renovated it. It's pretty nice."

"So I've heard. And your sisters are with you?"

"No. I'm alone."

"Really?" His eyebrows rose. "Well, I'm glad to hear you got over your fear of that place. When you were little, your mama and your sister Jules scared you so much about those ghosts, you wouldn't go inside if someone wasn't already in there."

His words surprised her. "You knew that?"

"Of course. Carly used to tell me about it. She felt bad about the way you were treated. Jules was just being Jules, but I thought your mama wasn't very nice scaring you, but what did I know? Still, I never heard the Donnelly ghosts were dangerous or even mean. So I didn't think you had anything to worry about."

She raised her eyebrows. "You make it sound as if they're real!"

He shrugged. "Half the town swears they are. The other half, not so much."

She didn't realize the ghosts were that popular. "You're saying everyone in town knows about them?"

He nodded and faced straight ahead as he took another sip of his beer. "This is a very small town."

Just then, an attractive young woman with long, silky brown hair, entered the bar and stepped between them, her back to Mallory. "Hello, Gunnar," she said in a high voice that set Mallory's teeth on edge. "You busy?"

"As a matter of fact, I was having a conversation here."

"Oh?" She glanced over her shoulder at Mallory and frowned. "I should let you two talk, I guess?"

Gunner nodded.

"Oh, well." She gave a toss of her head and shrugged. "I gotta get home, anyway. See you around, sweetie."

Mallory didn't know women still sashayed, but that one did, and Gunnar seemed to appreciate it as his head swiveled to watch her leave. *Men!*

She concentrated on her martini.

"That was, uh..." Gunnar began, facing her again.

"Nothing. I know," she said with a grin as if she knew exactly what he was about to say. "Tell, me, do you live in Crouch?" she asked.

"I still live out of town at my folks place," he said. "I'm helping my dad with the farm when he lets me. He's up in years, but still ornery. Not that I'm that much help."

"I'm sure you're a big help," she said.

"Not really." His voice dropped with that, but almost immediately he forced a smile. "But I do own the auto shop in town, so that keeps me out of trouble."

"Glad to hear it," she said.

"Did I hear you say you're living in New York now?"

"Yes. Manhattan."

"Nice." His voice was flat.

"It can be. Sometimes."

He sipped his beer. "Other times, you just need a little peace and quiet, right?"

She was curious. "How d'you know?"

"I haven't always lived in Garden Valley."

"I see. Where else were you?"

"Wherever the Army sent me. For a time, at least."

"Ah. Got it." She looked around the bar. "I understood they served food here, but I don't see anyone eating."

"Food service closes about eight-thirty unless there's something special going on," Gunnar said. "Lots of places close up plenty early in this community."

Her watch showed 9:30 p.m. "It's later than I thought," she said and finished the martini. "Well, I need to find something to eat. Thank you for the drink." She slid off the bar stool, and to her surprise, her legs were a bit wobbly.

"You okay?" he asked.

She gripped the edge of the bar until her head stopped spinning. "Guess I shouldn't have had three martinis on an empty stomach. Oh, wait—they had olives. Three, six, nine olives for my dinner."

"Let me help you," Gunnar said. He stood, too, put on his hat, and then picked up the cane he'd had beside him. "With this," he nodded toward the cane, "I'd say I'm steadier on my feet than you are."

"I'm fine," she said, then took a step and listed leftward.

Gunnar grabbed her arm. "Right. I can see you are steady as they come. Let me drive you to the cabin. The Middlefork Road is tricky at night if you don't know it. It's not lit up around your cabin and there are no stripes painted down the middle or along the sides."

"I don't want to put you out," she said.

"The thought of what your sister Jules would do to me if I let anything happen to you is too frightening to contemplate. I'm taking you home, Mal. No argument."

She kind of liked that he remembered Jules as Julia's nickname. The image of Jules being furious popped into her head making her laugh all the way to his truck. Or, she couldn't help but think, those martinis may have hit her a teensy bit harder than she imagined.

He helped her into the truck. "You mentioned you haven't eaten dinner," he said before he put the key in the ignition. "Is that a fact?"

She gave him a puzzled look. "I wouldn't lie about starvation."

"I think you need some food in you. We've got ten minutes before the grocery closes." He put the truck in gear and started the engine. "We can do it."

Gunnar had her wait in the truck while he hurried into the grocery store. She saw that his knee could bend, and she wondered if it was a pain issue more than anything else that caused him to need the cane.

She leaned back against the headrest as memories flowed of what an active, athletic, and fun kid Gunnar had been. He'd always been great in sports. Sometimes she and Carly would ride their bikes to the kids' baseball field to watch him and Nathan play Little League. To see him, now, with a cane, hurt her heart.

He was soon back in the truck. She was feeling sick to her

stomach as the truck bounced and rocked over the curvy, winding road and it was all she could do to hold down those martinis.

Finally, at the cabin, she saw that he'd bought two steaks, butter, mushrooms, and a pre-made salad. The cabin was well stocked with pots, pans, dishes, utensils, and seasonings, so while Mallory sat on the sofa feeling woozy and bleary-eyed, he quickly fried up the steaks, sautéed the mushrooms, and then served them with a side salad.

"Come on." He all but lifted her to her feet and helped her to the dining table.

"I usually can hold my liquor better than this," she said as she dropped into a chair. "I haven't gotten this blitzed since high school. This is crazy. And embarrassing."

"Butch sometimes pours heavy, especially if he's trying to impress someone."

"Oh?" Butch was trying to impress her? Why?

She took a bite of the steak. She hadn't realized how hungry she was. The steak was deliciously cooked and seasoned. "I'm in heaven. Are you an angel, Gunnar McDermott, come here to feed me and save me from the cabin's ghosts?"

"Not that anyone's ever told me," he said. "In fact, most would say I'm more likely the opposite. But if it suits you, I'll take it."

"How did that happen?" she asked, pointing to his cane.

His back stiffened ever so slightly and didn't answer for a moment, then he quickly spat out the words, "Afghanistan. It was nothing."

She had met enough vets to know better than to ask more when a soldier said, "It was nothing." It was always something. And he clearly didn't want to talk about it.

"What brought you back to Crouch?" she asked.

"It's home."

She tried but failed to stifle a yawn. "Tell me about the kids that were around when I was little. You and Nathan are still here. What about Darlene? Is she still around?"

"I do believe her folks moved away quite a few years back. This is not an easy land to make a living on, believe me."

"Oh. Poor Darlene. Do you remember other kids?"

"Sure. But I don't know much about the girls. A lot of them moved to Boise where the jobs are, got married and never came back."

"Not surprising," she said, yawning.

"You seem plenty tired."

"I've had an unbelievable weekend."

"Why don't we move over to more comfortable furniture," he said. "You might want to stretch out on the sofa."

"What if I fall asleep?"

"That's okay." He gave a slight grin. "I'll make sure the ghosts don't bother you."

Her lips tightened. "Well, I will lie down, but I'm not about to go to sleep with you here."

She stretched out on the sofa. As soon as her head met the armrest, her eyes shut, and she was out.

CHAPTER 5

Mallory opened her eyes to find she had a splitting headache and immediately shut them.
When she opened them again, she saw that she'd been covered with a chenille bedspread from an upstairs bed. She sat up. Gunnar wasn't in the room.

She looked at her watch. Six-thirty in the morning. She padded over to the front window. The sun was just peeking over the eastern sky, casting the land in a golden glow as she looked outside.

Gunnar's truck was gone. And she had no car. Her headache suddenly seemed a whole lot worse.

Coffee. She needed lots of coffee. As she crossed the great room, running her fingers against her scalp, and trying to straighten out the mess her hair had become, the prior evening was a blur. She could have believed it hadn't happened at all except for the dirty dishes in the sink, and the frying pan on the stove top.

With a mug of coffee in hand, she returned to the sofa and curled up on it. Elijah Donnelly stared down at her. And the cat was no longer in the portrait.

Wait ... had there really been a cat in it? She'd been so dead on her feet yesterday, and she couldn't remember seeing a cat either before she went into Crouch or when she returned to the cabin with Gunnar.

Gunnar ... whatever must he think of her drinking so much? Well, she'd probably never see him again, so what did it matter? Still, what was she thinking? But then, considering she'd just run from yet another fiancé and had caught a plane to Idaho on the spur of the moment, she probably wasn't thinking at all.

Elijah Donnelly was frowning at her. "You don't approve of me either, I see," she said to him. "Well, join the club."

Now, alone in the cabin, no longer dealing with the rush she'd had when she first arrived, a mixture of astonishment that she'd actually traveled here, disappointment over Slade, and fear of being alone in this isolated spot struck. The totality of her action at coming out here, the strangeness of the place, and the mess she'd made of her life intertwined with the worst hangover she'd ever had.

She rubbed her temples. She didn't belong here. She scarcely remembered this place. It was funny, but talking to Gunnar last night, she realized he knew her sisters better than she did. Once the summers in Garden Valley ended—she was only nine at the time—she scarcely saw her sisters at all. They communicated almost completely by email, and very infrequently at that.

Their mother's funeral had brought them together briefly. Since Mallory was the one who had most recently communicated with Roxanne, Julia and Carly left it up to her to arrange everything. At least she had the names of some of Roxanne's close friends, but in Los Angeles, even close friends seemed far away.

Few people showed up for the small service at the funeral home, and not one of Roxanne's former spouses attended. Julia had frowned with bitterness throughout, and Carly had kept checking her watch, as if she couldn't wait to get back to San

Francisco and her catering business. Mallory was the only one who even shed a tear, but it was more for the memory of what her mother should have been to her, but never was. Roxanne had taken a great interest in Mallory's love life and, as Mallory grew older and more attractive, seemed thrilled as the men in Mallory's life had become wealthier and more important. Roxanne's last conversation with her was to warn her that good looks were fleeting, and that she really needed to find someone rich before she got much older. Mallory had been twenty-two at the time.

Mallory always went along with whatever Roxanne had to say. She believed pleasing Roxanne would be the surest way to win her mother's love. But try as she might, she hadn't been able to do it.

How ironic that she might have finally pleased Roxanne by marrying Slade. Roxanne would have adored Slade, and his money. Actually, he was closer to Roxanne's age than he was to Mallory's. She could hear Roxanne praising him as a great catch.

If she had listened to her mother, she wouldn't be sitting in a lonely old cabin in a forest—a creepy, dangerous forest. She wondered if Slade could forgive her for running out on him.

His words rang in her ears. "You are not a runaway bride."

But she was. Not only a runaway bride, but a complete screw-up. Roxanne would be ashamed of her. Again. Tears came to her eyes.

All she ever wanted was a little peace and security. Nothing more.

Slade would have given that to her if she hadn't mucked up that relationship just as she had all her earlier ones. But this was her worst screw-up ever.

She heard a car engine. It sounded nearby. And then it stopped.

Wiping her eyes angrily for being such a softy and for feeling so ridiculously sorry for herself, she hurried to the front window.

Her rental car was on the driveway, a truck behind it. Gunnar got out of her car, and she saw another man getting out of the truck. On the truck's door she read McDermott Auto Repair.

She hurried out to meet them. "Thank you so much!"

Gunnar approached, looking carefully at her eyes. His brow knitted as if she might not have done as good a job wiping away her tears as she'd hoped. "I didn't want to wake you if you were still asleep," he said, and held up her car keys. "I had to take it upon myself to borrow these, but since I have an automotive shop, it's not the first time I've driven someone else's rental around here. And given the circumstances, I didn't think you'd mind."

"No. Of course not." She took the keys. "Thank you."

He lightly touched her arm, still studying her face. "Are you okay?" he asked softly.

She pursed her lips, then nodded. "Yes," she whispered.

The other fellow approached—tall and broad-shouldered, with curly brown hair and dark brown eyes. "Oh, my! Nathan!" she said, and gave him a quick hug.

"You remembered!" he said with a big smile. "Good to see you, Mal."

Her heart warmed at his greeting. "Come in, you two," she said. "I don't have much, but I have coffee."

"We've got to get to work," Gunnar said. "But I'll check on you later, if you don't mind."

"I don't mind at all. You're always welcome here. Both of you."

She watched them drive off, and couldn't help but think how lucky it was that she met Gunnar last night. If not, how would she have faced being in the cabin all alone last night?

She went back inside. After the brief encounter with Gunnar

and Nathan, the cabin seemed lonelier than ever.

She locked the front door, and as she entered the great room, she saw the small rocking chair in the corner moving back and forth, back and forth. She backed into the foyer, and stood there staring at the rocker, watching it move for no reason she could fathom.

Julia had left a few antiques in the cabin, and word was that the chair had been owned by Elijah Donnelly's young bride. It was too small and delicate to be used, but too pretty to be stored away or sold, so it was merely decorative.

Mallory told herself there must have been a draft or a wind gust through the room caused by the front door being open. Or maybe her walking on old floor boards had started it moving. "There's a logical explanation for everything," she whispered as she stepped into the room. As she got closer to it, it stopped moving.

The hair on her arms stood on end.

It was almost as if someone, like the chair's owner, was sitting and rocking in it.

She sat down on the sofa where she'd slept and stared at the little chair. Strangely, as she did that, the fear she felt drained away. She had no idea why it left her, why she wasn't afraid anymore when every bit of logic told her she darn well should be!

But it had been Elijah's wife's chair—a loving young wife and mother—who died way too young and too sadly. People said she was one of the ghosts that haunted the cabin, and somehow, the thought of her possibly being here, relaxing in her chair and watching over the place, was oddly—in a weird kind of way—comforting.

"Oh, my God!" Mallory said aloud as she ran her fingers through her hair. "I must be losing it completely!" She then headed upstairs to shower and change the clothes she slept in last night.

Halfway up the stairs, the thought came to her that she'd been wrong about the cabin. She wasn't alone here after all; she had ghosts with her.

And with that thought, a cold chill rippled down her back.

Mallory found the house key in her purse and then cradled the bag of groceries with one arm as she walked to the cabin's front door.

A rugged "welcome mat" lay on the stoop in front of it. And a cat lay on the mat.

As she neared, the cat sat up. It was tri-colored: white, orange, and black. Her breath caught. It looked exactly like the cat she saw in the portrait with Elijah Donnelly. The cat that was no longer there.

It wasn't the same cat, of course. That would be impossible. Crazy, even.

Okay. She'd figured it out. She must have seen this cat at a window or something. He was looking in at her and she was so tired, she remembered it as having been in the portrait with Elijah. Her mind had played tricks on her. Nothing more.

"Where did you come from?" Mallory asked, relieved that everything made sense now.

The cat stepped away as she unlocked the door, but as she turned to shut it again, the cat darted inside the cabin.

"Oh, you know this place, do you?" Mallory asked. "I'll bet Julia spoiled you when she was here, right? And that's why you're now lurking around scaring me. You think this is your home. Well, you're wrong. But that doesn't mean I can't give you some water. And I'll bet you wouldn't mind a little of the canned tuna I just bought."

Sure enough, the cat followed her into the kitchen area. She took two small bowls from the cupboard, put water in one and some tuna in the other. The cat closely eyed them both, then walked away.

"Okay, so the water isn't Perrier and canned tuna isn't the same as wild salmon, but in this house you get what you're offered, or you're on your own," Mallory said, hands on hips as the cat strolled around the great room.

"Cat, you are the perfect colors for Halloween." Its face was white while the top of its head had splotches of orange and black. Its underside and front legs were white, and the rest of its coat was a mixture of the three colors. It was a pretty, but odd looking cat. "I'll call Julia and ask if she knows who you belong to, and if you have a name."

When the cat reached the seating area near the fireplace, it jumped on an overstuffed chair and curled into a ball. By the time Mallory finished putting away the groceries and making herself some coffee, the cat was asleep.

"That," Mallory said, "looks like a very smart move. But I have work to do. I suspect I only have one job now, so I need to give it my undivided attention."

She retrieved her laptop from the bedroom and opened up her Dear Nellie files. She'd been so engrossed with Slade's proposal and then her mad dash to Idaho, she'd forgotten to amend the answer she'd given to the poor bride that called herself "Miserable to the Max." The quick answer she'd dashed off had been printed.

She wasn't surprised to see a number of unhappy letters about her last column. As she suspected, people said Nellie had been much too nice to the ungrateful bride-to-be who had objected to her parents generously paying for a large wedding, and to her fiancé for siding with them. Most of the respondents called the bride a spoiled, selfish brat—or worse—and believed Nellie had completely missed the mark.

You can please some of the people some of the time ...

She was glad when she noticed a letter from someone who

didn't start out immediately complaining about her response. With a sigh of relief, she began to read.

Dear Nellie,

On my wedding day, as I walked down the aisle with my father, my fiancé suddenly turned away from the altar and ran out of the chapel. I couldn't believe it. By the time my father and I reached the minister, the groom was gone and the best man and the groomsmen were running after him trying to find out what was wrong. The church was filled with family and friends who witnessed this with both horror and, I'm sorry to say, amusement. It was the worst, most embarrassing day of my life.

You said you pulled this same kind of terrible stunt on three different men. You're an awful person! How could you be so cruel? I feel so sorry for your fiancés and hope they never forgive you. You don't deserve forgiveness. [Signed] Hiding in the Closet

Mallory gasped. She was all but shaking with rage as she read the last paragraph. What kind of idiot—who didn't know her or anything about her life—would write something like that? And today, in particular, was not the time for anyone to send her such a letter. She had a quick reply:

Dear Hiding,

Get out of that closet. It's very possible that his running off isn't your fault. It might be all his, and you have nothing to be embarrassed about except that you picked the wrong guy to want to marry. It's his loss.

On the other hand, could it be that he realized you're the loser? Could it be that he took off rather than to be stuck with you, a "person" (I won't use the term I'd like to use—hint: it starts with a "b") who writes a letter accusing me of being awful when you know nothing about the circumstances? I wouldn't blame your fiancé if he ran so far from you he ended up in another continent!

And, as for me being cruel to the men I walked away from, they should be thankful. It saved them the time and expense of having to divorce me—and to pay me beaucoup alimony to boot!

Now, brush yourself off and stop whining and pointing fingers at others. [Signed] Lessons Learned Nellie

Mallory had to admit that she may have gone a bit too far. But she said nothing that wasn't true. And "Hiding" had attacked her first. Mallory Conway, who everyone said was nice and sweet and a pushover, might meekly take such abuse, but Dear Nellie never would. Nellie hit back. Hard.

She sent her response off to Brian for the next edition of the *Gazette* and then turned to see if the cat was still asleep on the chair. As she turned, from the corner of her eye, she saw what appeared to be a woman with dark brown hair pulled back in a bun and a high-necked calico dress, bending over the cat and petting it. The cat was purring.

Mallory jumped to her feet. "Who are—?" But the woman seemed to have disappeared into thin air.

Mallory dropped back into the chair, her heart pounding. The woman had looked far too much like the vision she'd seen in the mirror. Who ... or what ... was she?

The cat still seemed to be sleeping soundly. So maybe, hopefully, it wasn't a woman at all. No, as she thought about it, she realized that it was nothing but a play of light. Not a person. And definitely not a ghost.

"Okay, kitty," she said, her mouth dry and her heart still beating way too fast, "it's time for you to go outside. There's something about you that is making me uneasy. Besides, I don't have a kitty litter box in this house, and I don't intend to get one."

She opened the French doors and, as if it understood, the cat bolted from the chair and scampered into the backyard.

CHAPTER 6

As dusk fell, Mallory made herself soup and a sandwich. She was alone in the cabin and dreading being there at night. As much as she tried to deny it, whatever she'd seen certainly had looked like a woman petting the cat. And the cat certainly had appeared exactly like the one that had been in Elijah Donnelly's portrait. But thinking such a thing was illogical. It had to be the result of a mixture of stress over the situation with Slade and having heard too many stories about the cabin's ghosts as a child.

Tomorrow she was going back home. How completely insane of her to have left New York and everything she knew and loved for this wild emptiness! This place was horrible. And scary, ghosts or not. Okay, she would have to spend one more night alone in the cabin. Or would she? She could drive to a motel near the Boise airport and wait there until she got a flight heading east.

But then she heard a car.

She hoped it was Gunnar. He said he'd come by and check on her. She had hoped he might be there by now although, for all she knew, he could be quite busy and might even have a wife and children living on the farm with his parents.

But since he hadn't bothered to phone anyone last night after he brought her home, she was probably wrong about that. And when she thought about the young, attractive women at the Rusty Nail—one who seemed angry with him, and the other who acted more than a little interested—he had better not be married!

Anyway, he and his women were none of her business.

She went to the window and peeked out.

To her amazement, her sister, Julia Perrin, was getting out of a Jeep. She was small, thin, with long light blond hair pulled into a single braid, and wore rugged, baggy outdoorsman clothing. Julia swore they were the only style of clothes that she found comfortable, and that no one cared how she dressed anyway.

With a ten-year difference in age and since they were raised apart, Mallory had never grown close to Julia. But she was elated to have her company now. She pulled open the door. "Jules! It's great to see you! But I told you, you didn't have to come here."

"It's okay. I thought you might like a little company." Julia pulled a duffel bag from the back of the Jeep and slung it over her shoulder, then went to the passenger side and pulled out two big bags of groceries. "This place can feel awfully lonely until you get used to it."

You don't know the half of it, Mallory thought. "Let me help you," she said, hurrying to the Jeep, and took a bag from Julia.

"Thanks. I figured you could use some basic groceries to stock the pantry. You probably ran to the store whenever you needed something in your little city apartment. But in an area like this, people tend to shop for several days at a time. And since I've found that this cabin has a habit of drawing people to it, I brought plenty extra. Anyway, it's good to see you, kid," Julia said.

"You, too," Mallory remembered that Julia wasn't a hugger which was good since their arms were full. "But I doubt anyone but you and I will end up here. I didn't tell anyone I was coming."

"We'll see." They carried everything into the cabin.

Julia, at age 35, had never been engaged, let alone married. She had watched, with horror, the way her mother had lived, always looking for "true love" and convincing herself that the *next* man she met and fell for would be "the one." Julia saw love wreck her mother's life and had decided years ago that it would never wreck hers.

They quickly put the groceries away as Mallory told Julia how much she liked the renovations to the cabin. Once they finished, Julia took out two bottles of beer, and handed one to Mallory.

"You'll find beer's good in this dry climate," she said. "And it's tastier than water. Water's fine, but as a great man once said, fish make love in it."

Mallory chuckled as they took their beers out to the back porch, now bathed in the evening shade. A bench and chairs with fluffy pillows covered the seats and back making them a comfortable spot to relax. A couple of steps went from the porch down to the fenced acre of land that Roxanne called "the orchard" because she'd planted apple and pear trees in it. They were bearing fruit now.

"So, tell me about your latest victim," Julia said, taking a chair.

Frowning, Mallory sat on the bench. "What are you talking about?"

"Come on. You're here. You're upset. I know a man caused you to suddenly flee the city you always said you adore and would never leave. So, what's the story?"

Mallory took a deep breath. "Nothing you haven't heard before. This time, we'd only dated three months before he proposed. Slade is older, and very, very rich. Plus, divorced twice. He was kind, considerate, generous, and not a lech. I'd have had a wonderful life with everything I ever wanted at my beck and call—or so he promised. He's everything I should want in a husband."

"A prince among men," Julia said with a smirk.

"So it seemed."

"Love?"

"He told me he was aware that I wasn't in love with him yet, but I would come to love him in time. And the strange part is, he could have been right. If a person is that good and giving, you do eventually come to love them, don't you?"

Julia eyed her sister and was not happy with what she was seeing. "That's the way a lot of arranged marriages work, from what I've heard. But in the US, we don't do arranged marriages. People here supposedly marry for love."

"And look at the divorce rate that's gotten us."

"Good point. That's why I've never wanted to try it. But it doesn't mean you go to the other extreme and marry solely for finances." Julia drank down some beer. "I know Roxanne thought you should, but she was hardly a paragon of motherhood—or wifeliness."

Mallory found it jarring the way Julia never referred to their mother as anything but "Roxanne." She wondered if the word "mom" had ever passed Julia's lips. "It wasn't just our mother," Mallory said pointedly. "There's a lot of truth in what she advised."

"Really?" Julia grimaced. "You sound as if you're having regrets about not marrying this Slade fellow."

"I just don't know. I've been down this road before, and nothing good comes of it. He really is a good man and deserved better from me. Because of my past, he said he didn't want a long engagement. So, he asked me to marry him and the very next day we went to the office of a judge, a friend of his. But then—as always—I got cold feet. I wondered what I was doing. Should I really marry someone I wasn't in love with? I didn't think so. So I bolted. I left Slade alone with the judge and, I suspect, completely mortified. I'm sure he'll never want to see me again."

"Good guess, I'd say."

"And Slade is one of my boss's biggest clients. He knows lots of real estate developers and sends Piaget business. I'm sure my boss won't want me there after this. Better get rid of me than risk losing Slade."

"I'm sorry about that."

Mallory took a sip of beer and looked out at the orchard before she added, "And on top of all that, the apartment I'm subletting is through my boss, which means when the job goes, the apartment probably won't be far behind."

Julia, too, drank a little more beer. "Sounds like a clean sweep, little sis. Is that why you're here? Looking for a place to live?"

"Oh, God no!" Mallory rubbed her forehead. "I could never live in a small town like this. I'll return to New York, but I need a moment to catch my breath and figure out what to do next. I'll have to find a job and an apartment. It's not fun looking for one of those, let alone both at the same time."

"Well, you can stay here as long as you like. It's not as if people are clamoring to rent it. Besides Carly's new husband, we've only had one couple renting the house, and they were only here for two nights."

"Do you want renters?" Mallory asked.

"Of course! I could use some extra income, couldn't you?"

Mallory hesitated, but finally couldn't help but ask. "Has there been any talk about ghosts connected with the place?"

Julia pursed her lips. "Of course not!"

"No ghost sightings?"

"What are you talking about?"

Mallory didn't want to say anything about the young woman she'd seen, or the weird cat, or the way Elijah Donnelly's portrait kept changing on her. It was surely her overwrought imagination and upset about her miserable love life that was causing her to imagine things. But still... "I did a lot of marketing when I was with Piaget Realty, and sometimes all it takes is a little something extra—like the possibility of a ghost—to make a house rise above the rest and become popular with renters. And Carly did meet her true love at the cabin. Doesn't that go along with the story about the ghosts? That they help people meet their true love?"

Julia sneered. "I think the last thing Carly or Alex would want is for people to think they met and married because of some ghostly matchmaking."

"Think about it a minute." The more Mallory thought about it, the more she warmed to the idea. She raised her arms high as if she were spreading an overhead banner. "I can see it now in travel magazine ads and mailings: *If you haven't met your true love yet, come to the Cabin of Love and Magic in Idaho. Here, true love waits.*"

"Love and magic?" Julia scoffed. *"Puh-lezz!"*

"Seriously. It would work," Mallory said.

"Who has money for all that? And besides, what happens when they don't meet their true love and sue us?"

"They'd be laughed out of court." Mallory couldn't stop a smile at the thought. In fact, the more she thought about it, the more she liked it. "But we would also need to tell them about the second half of the ghost's tale. That if you reject the person the ghosts bring you, you're doomed to live alone, forever. So, if no one finds true love, we just say our lodgers were too fussy and turned down the ghosts' choice. Or, if a lodger didn't stay for a minimum of a week, how could they expect the ghosts to find them a true love? What were they looking for, a miracle?"

"Yes," Julia said. "Obviously."

"Even miracles take a while."

"Forget it, Mallory." Julia scowled. "The last thing I want is a bunch of lovesick yahoos coming to the cabin looking for love. Spare me! But, since you brought up our ethereal ancestors, did Carly tell you she found a letter written by Lucas Donnelly?"

"Lucas Donnelly? You mean Elijah's son? No, I've heard nothing. In fact, I haven't spoken to Carly since congratulating her about eloping with that sexy thriller writer."

"Well, let me show you." Julia went to the pantry and got a step stool so she could reach the top shelf. Pulling down a tin container, she placed it on the kitchen counter. "I figured no lodgers would go looking through the pantry for anything of value. But here's the letter."

Mallory took it and read Lucas's letter to his cousin Theodore. In it, he not only willed the cabin to Theodore, but strongly suggested that his parents lived there as ghosts and that he hoped to join them.

"Oh, my," Mallory said. "This letter is actually very sad. I knew Lucas died at a young age, but to read his letter makes him and the story of the ghosts so much more real. Do you know what happened to him?"

"A little. Roxanne used to tell us about the family. You were probably too young to remember. Anyway, she said that after his parents' deaths, Lucas was raised by an aunt. He joined the Army and was sent to Europe to fight during World War I. After that, he returned to the cabin, suffering from shell shock and something else—no one knew what, maybe tuberculosis—and he soon died after willing the cabin to Theodore, who also lived a lonely life."

"But then, one day, a woman showed up at the cabin for help when her horse went lame. She'd been guided there by smoke from the cabin's chimney, but Theodore swore he had no fire burning that day. Anyway, the two fell in love and married. He was our great grandfather, the one Roxanne referred to as her

Grandpa Teddy. That started the rumor of the ghosts as matchmakers. Other members of the family had similar experiences, and several—including Carly—ended up marrying someone they met because of the cabin."

"Oh, my, that's an incredible story," Mallory said.

"I've heard more details about other family members. But, actually, the most interesting to me are those who say the reason Roxanne married so many times is that she never met her true love. And *that*, they say, is because when she was young, the cabin found a man for her and she rejected him." With that, Julia gave a sharp, knowing nod.

Mallory was astounded. "Who was the man she rejected?"

"I have no idea. I don't know if anyone else does either. It might just be a rumor. A ghostly cabin rumor."

"That's incredible. I'd love to find out more about it."

"Unless you can go back in history, I doubt you ever will," Julia said.

"All of those stories only convince me more than ever," Mallory said, "that this would be a popular vacation rental if people heard the story of the ghosts who help people find true love."

"Forget it!" Julia scoffed.

"It's true! In fact, I should get Slade out here to see what happens. Maybe the ghosts would help me fall in love with him, and then all my problems would be solved!"

Julia rolled her eyes. "Oh, yes, that's a great reason to believe in ghosts." The sarcasm dripped from her lips.

"It's a better reason than most," Mallory stated.

"Or, go with your gut and forget about him," Julia said in her usual, no-nonsense, forceful way. "Rest up here, and when you go back to New York, you might find someone who appeals to *you* instead of someone Roxanne would have loved you to marry."

Those words were like a stab to the gut. Mallory was

outraged. "I do *not* choose men I think Roxanne would approve of."

"Oh?" Julia raised an eyebrow. "Could have fooled me."

"Our mother always wanted what was best for me!" Mallory cried.

"Yeah, I'm sure she did." Julia sounded tired of arguing and picked up her duffel bag. "I'll move my things up to a bedroom. I'll only be here a couple of days. After that, I'm afraid you're on your own."

"Fine!" Mallory snapped. "I'll probably only be here a couple of days myself."

"Oh? Don't get ahead of your skis, here. Give yourself time."

Mallory folded her arms. "You're not my babysitter anymore, you know!"

With a harumph, Julia went upstairs.

Mallory heard a knock on the front door and went to open it. She sat in the great room with a slice of the pizza Julia had ordered, while Julia sat out on the back porch eating. She knew the pizza was a peace offering, but she was still irritated at the way Julia had spoken to her. Although, it wasn't completely Julia's fault.

She pulled open the door. "Gunnar, nice to see you. Come in."

He stayed on the front stoop. "Do you have company? I don't want to interrupt."

"No. The other car belongs to my sister Julia. She's out back."

"Julia?" His smile vanished and his already large blue eyes widened further as he entered. Mallory couldn't help but laugh as she remembered all he'd said about her sister the night before.

"I wanted to give you this." He handed her a round

container. "It's the best cherry pie in the state, locally picked cherries, and baked by my mom."

"Thank you so much. This is so nice of her."

"My mom says welcome back."

"Well, tell her thank you."

"I will, and now, I'd best be going."

"No way." She linked her arm with his. "You're coming outside with me to meet Julia."

His lips tightened. "I don't—"

"No arguing."

She led him out to the porch. "Jules, you remember Gunnar, don't you?"

"I sure do." Julia grimaced and remained seated. Her gaze went to his cane, then lifted to his eyes. "You could get on my last nerve faster than anybody else, Mr. Gunnar McDermott. I hope you've managed to change your ways."

He raised his chin. "I hope you have, too, Miss Julia Perrin. My ears still ache from the way you used to twist them with those strong, bony fingers of yours."

With that, Julia laughed out loud. "Good! Glad I did something right."

Gunnar also chuckled, and it seemed to Mallory that his tension about Julia seeped out of him.

"Gunnar's mother made this pie for us," Mallory said putting the pie on a little outside table, and then ran back into the kitchen to grab plates, forks, a knife to cut the pie, and beer for Gunnar. The three were soon eating, drinking, and talking about childhood memories as the sun dipped below the western range.

"Carly told me she found tapes of Roxanne singing old show tunes," Mallory said. "Maybe we should look for them."

"If you're going to do that, I'm going to say goodnight." Julia stood. "It was a long drive from Bend, Oregon, and I'm feeling tired. It was good seeing you again, Gunnar. And thank your mother for that delicious pie."

"Will do, Miss Julia," Gunnar said. "You take care, now."

He and Mallory soon went into the house.

"Are you interested in looking for those old tapes?" Mallory asked.

"It's already nearly eleven. I had no idea it'd gotten that late. I'd best be going. I'm glad to see you've got company here tonight."

She smiled. "Were you worried about me?"

"Until I determine what those ghosts' intentions are, I'd planned to keep an eye on you. But with Julia here, they're probably more scared of her than they'll ever be of me. I think you gals will be just fine."

Mallory laughed. "I suspect you're right."

CHAPTER 7

Mallory's morning began with an email from Tom Campilongo at Piaget Realty saying her work was no longer required due to a "restructuring" of the staff. She was being let go immediately, with two-weeks severance pay.

It was actually a relief not to go back there. If she thought her "friends" at work were merciless about her being a runaway bride in the past, they were going to be brutal when they learned she'd left Slade Atchison at the courthouse ... unless they already knew. She suspected the Slade debacle had much more to do with her firing than any sudden desire to restructure the staff.

Tom then sent an email asking where he should send her final paycheck.

She knew he was trying to find out where she was, probably at his buddy Slade's request. She said to send it to her home address, and then she promptly put in a change of address with the post office to her sister Julia's address. She expected to hear any day from the man whose apartment she was subletting, saying he'd need it back. She wasn't sure where she'd go next.

Life had suddenly become very complicated.

A little later that morning, she received a call from Brian Abernathy, the *Greenwich Village Gazette* editor. She was so surprised when his name flashed on her cell phone, she answered, and immediately regretted it. The connection was beyond terrible. She ran through the house and outdoors hoping she could hear what he was saying past the loud static, but nothing worked. Finally, she hung up. She thought about using the cabin's landline to phone him back, but the Idaho area code showing up on his caller ID would give him information about her location. Instead, she drove into Crouch, and phoned him back on her cell phone.

"Sorry about that. I'm out of town, and cell service is bad here," she said.

"Where are you?"

"Just … west. A tiny bit west. I don't know these areas all that well."

"Hmph. I was hoping you could come into the office to talk."

"Talk? We can talk now, can't we? I mean, what's going on?"

"We've got a problem," he said.

Her mind was racing. Slade couldn't have gotten her fired from her newspaper job, could he? She'd tried to keep it a secret from him, and it was her only source of income now. "What do you mean?" she asked.

"There's a backlash going on. It started small, but it's growing. And now a few people are saying our advertisers should quit us if we keep going this way."

"A backlash? What are you talking about?"

"It started with your response to Miserable to the Max who was unhappy about her big wedding. But it really is getting out of hand with your response to Hiding in the Closet—the woman who chastised you for ditching three fiancés."

"Wait—that column wasn't supposed to run until tomorrow."

"I loved your response, so it ran in this morning's paper. I expected it would get people riled up, and that's what I wanted."

"Hold on, Brian. This doesn't make sense. Are you happy about the column or angry about it?"

"It's getting attention. Lots of attention for the *Village Gazette*. And that makes me happy. But, if things get out of hand and too many people complain to our advertisers, you'll have to back off. Got it?"

"How out of hand might things get?" she asked.

"I might have to fire you."

"*What?*"

"Don't worry. I won't want to do it, believe me. But sometimes these things happen. Besides, no one knows you're Nellie. If she gets fired, you can become someone else. Maybe Dear Lucretia. Who knows? You're talented, so it's not a problem."

She couldn't believe what she was hearing. "What do you mean, not a problem?" she screeched. "I love 'Misery Loves Company.' From the start I used a 'tough love' approach. Yes, sometimes very tough, but I used myself as an example in my answers. I mean, how many people are more miserable than me? I showed I was able to talk about my experiences and not be a complete basket case. Or, almost not. That's what we wanted, and I believe that's what the public wants despite this current batch of complainers. I mean, who in the world has such a boring life that they have time to write letters of complaint about an advice column?"

"I know, I know. But the public is fickle," Brian said. "For now, just keep up what you're doing and we'll play it by ear."

"Thanks loads."

"You aren't fired yet," he said, his voice higher and whinier than usual.

"Are you expecting a thank you?"

"Listen," he continued. "You're the writer. You can fix this. I've taken all the letters and put them in a file and I'll send it as an attachment. You can see why people are getting increasingly angry. I want another column for tomorrow's paper."

"Tomorrow?"

"Yes."

They soon hung up.

She stayed sitting in her car as she read through the emails she'd received from outraged fans.

One was completely nasty:

Dear Nellie,

You should be the LAST person giving advice to anyone. My heart broke for Hiding in the Closet. Your advice to that girl was first to call her fiancé a loser. And then, even worse, you attacked her. The victim. Why not have the girl find out what the problem was? If she loves him, and I think she must or she wouldn't have said 'yes,' she should want to know why he got cold feet at the last minute. Was the problem fixable?

I don't believe that you, Nellie, should be giving advice about relationships to anyone until you find a good, loving relationship for yourself.

I could do your job better than you. I've been married for fifteen happy years. What are your qualifications? It seems your "badge of honor" is actually one of dishonor. You've been a three-time loser at the wedding game, and I think your column sucks! [Signed] Happily Married

Mallory saw red. The knives were out now. Brian said to keep doing what she was doing. Well, Dear Nellie was never one to shy away from a fight, and wasn't about to start now.

Dear Happily,

Bully for you. It's easy to 'go along to get along' and marry the first jerk who asks, and then stick with him because it's too hard, too expensive, and simply too much work to get a divorce. But when you want to break out from what everyone else expects of you, that's when you need to apply Nellie's tough love. It might be difficult, but it's called being true to yourself. It's great. You should try it. [Signed] Tough Nellie

She put down her phone. She could go back to the cabin, but no one was there. Julia had left a couple of hours earlier to go to Boise. She texted Julia to say she was going to the Rusty Nail and if Julia returned soon, to join her there.

Gunnar sat in a booth at the Rusty Nail with one of his employees named Sam. Sam was having trouble getting to work on time, and when he got there, he looked hung-over. Sam had been in Iraq years before and had battled through major PTSD as a result of what he experienced there. Sam had been doing better over the past few years, but every so often he had a slip.

Gunnar believed the best way to help with men like Sam was to give them a job and lots of understanding, but not leeway. He had rules he expected to be followed, but he could be forgiving when his employee felt overwhelmed.

He saw Mallory come in. She waved to him and he nodded, but apparently she recognized by the expressions on the two men's faces, that theirs wasn't a social lunch. She took a seat at a table and was handed a lunch menu.

Turning his attention away from her wasn't easy, but he did his best to focus his attention back on Sam, who was telling him about his latest fight with his wife, Sherry. It was the same issue as in the past and had started long before two months ago when Gunnar hired Sam to work at his auto repair shop. Sherry wanted kids. Sam didn't. He didn't want to bring any kids into a world that was so screwed up.

The situation wasn't one that Gunnar could directly deal

with—and it wasn't his place to try to give advice. The only thing he could do was to be a sounding board and to, hopefully, get Sam to realize the importance of keeping the job.

Despite that, his gaze kept wandering over to Mallory. She certainly had changed from the quiet little girl he once knew. She was now beautiful. Her long hair shimmered as she walked, reminding him of the glint of moonlight on the ocean at night. Her eyes, though, kept the same sweet innocence he saw when she was a little girl, when those large, clear blue eyes would look up at him as if he were the cleverest, bravest boy she'd ever met. How he'd loved that. And, despite her being three years younger than him and Nathan, she never gave up trying to stick with them. He suspected, now, she had that same gumption.

He was mesmerized by her, but for the life of him, he couldn't understand what she was doing back in Garden Valley. He had the impression she'd left New York abruptly, but whenever their conversation veered in that direction, she changed the subject.

Women made no sense to him.

And Mallory Conway made less sense than most.

Just then, Emma Hughes, local realtor and accountant, came into the Rusty Nail. He nodded dismissively and turned back to Sam, but that didn't stop her from coming over to him and gently rubbing his shoulder.

"Gunnar, how nice to see you here," she said, then faced Sam. "Hello. I'm Emma."

"Sam," he muttered.

She faced Gunnar again with the hopeful smile he hated. He'd made the mistake of dating her twice. How was he to know that in her mind a second date equated to some kind of everlasting commitment? He had been trying, nicely, to make it clear to her ever since that he wasn't interested.

"I just came in to have a quick bite for lunch," she said. "I know I'm going to have a busy afternoon, probably working until evening, and won't have time for anything later in the day…"

She was clearly fishing for an invitation to join them.

"We're talking about some work-related matters," Gunnar said.

"At lunchtime? Gunnar McDermott, I never took you for a workaholic. Let the poor man enjoy his lunch."

"Sorry, Emma," Gunnar said.

Finally, she understood she needed to leave. "Well, you can make it up to me at dinner sometime this week. Give me a call, okay?"

He nodded, and she walked off to sit at a table by herself.

Gunnar noticed that Mallory had watched Emma's exchange with him and that her gaze followed Emma to a table. When Mallory then looked back at him and saw his eyes on her, she quickly turned away.

Julia didn't arrive back in Garden Valley until nearly dinner time. There was nothing of interest to eat at the cabin, so Mallory went back to the Rusty Nail with her for dinner. Of course, Gunnar was long gone by that time.

When they returned to the cabin, the three-colored cat was lying on the welcome mat. "Do you know that cat?" Mallory asked.

"Never saw her before," Julia said as Mallory opened the door and the cat ran inside. "She certainly seems familiar with the house, doesn't she?"

"How do you know it's a she?" Mallory asked.

"It's a calico. They're almost all female. The three colors are caused by some strange genetics going on with the two X chromosomes all females have. Since it's extremely rare for a male cat to have two X chromosomes along with the Y that makes them male, there are almost no male calicos."

Mallory gawked at Julia as if she couldn't believe her sister knew that. "I had no idea."

As they entered the cabin, Julia continued her explanation. Julia loved it when she knew more about a subject than anyone else around her and always explained exhaustively. "Most cats are only two colors with lots of shadings of those two colors. Calico's are rare and many cultures consider them good luck. Several cultures, spread throughout the world, believe they have special powers. What's also interesting is that they aren't any particular breed, and can't be bred. Male calicos are sterile because of their extra X chromosome. Which means that such cats are created only by chance, or as some people say, by an act of God."

"How did you become such an expert on calico cats?" Mallory asked.

"A calico stray moved in with me some years back. She was a very neat little cat. I cried buckets when she passed away."

Mallory couldn't help but gape as Julia confessed that. Julia was the toughest person she knew and the image of her ballsy sister crying over her cat was more than a little hard to believe. Julia had once told her she hadn't shed a tear when she learned that Roxanne had passed away. Mallory initially had found that hard to believe, but that was because she didn't know Julia well. Now, she found it easier to believe with every Julia encounter.

Julia grabbed the second—and last—can of tuna in the cupboard for the cat and opened the can, dishing out for her. But just as when Mallory tried to feed her, the cat sniffed the food and walked away. "Fussy, isn't she?" Julia remarked.

"Since calicos are said to be good luck," Mallory said, eying the cat, "and right now, I need all the luck I can get, I'll run down to the market and get some cat food and a litter box for her. She looks like she'll be happy to stay here tonight."

"She does." Julia smiled as she watched the cat licking its front legs. "The only problem, if she gets used to staying here, will be what to do when the house is empty."

"She looks well cared for, so she might have a home. Maybe she's treating this as we are—a nice place for a vacation."

Julia smirked. "That could be. And if not, I'll just have to take her back and forth to Oregon with me. We'll work it out."

"I'm sure you will." Mallory had no doubt. Julia always worked things out. She wished she had half so much self-confidence.

When Mallory returned from the store, she found Julia asleep on a chair by the fireplace, and the cat curled up on her lap.

CHAPTER 8

When Mallory got out of bed the next morning and all but stumbled, half-awake, into the bathroom, she discovered that Julia had placed the cat's litter box in it. She'd never lived with a cat before so she didn't like it being there. But as she considered the alternatives, it was definitely better than having the box in a bedroom. Or any other room in the house for that matter.

As she passed by Julia's bedroom, the door was open. Her sister was asleep, and the cat was also on the bed, awake. It looked up at Mallory with a jaundiced eye. Something about the cat wasn't quite right.

Downstairs she made herself some coffee and then headed up to the extra bedroom which she had set up as an office. There was essentially zero Internet service inside the cabin, so Mallory would take her cell phone outdoors, waving it around until she found a spot where it would connect. There, she'd transmit and receive emails.

In her latest group of emails, she found one from Slade.

My dearest Mallory,

I forgive you.

I should have realized I was pushing you too fast. I've asked your neighbors and the people you work with where you've gone, but no one knows. Please tell me where you are, and that you're all right. I'm worried sick about you. I want to work this out so we can enjoy the wonderful life we always talked about.

Yours forever,
Slade

He forgives me? she thought. That's big of him!

But then she reread the letter and a bit of guilt began to seep through her. He was apologizing, sort of. And he did say he was worried about her. On the other hand, she didn't remember them ever talking about their "wonderful life together." Maybe he thought it, but never said it.

She was so confused. If he'd simply accept they were over, O-V-E-R, things would be much easier to deal with. Now, she guessed she was supposed to feel sorry for him, for worrying him, for making him regret he'd acted too fast simply because he loved her.

Frankly, she didn't know what to feel.

Maybe she was being too hard on Slade. In all fairness, she had agreed to his proposal.

All he wanted to do was to make her life easier. Why didn't she appreciate him more? Roxanne would have married him in an instant!

With that in mind, she wrote an answer:

Slade,

I'm so sorry I put you through this embarrassment, I really am. I don't know why I do these things. But, if you still care about me at all, know that I never wanted to hurt you. I'm in Idaho, at the cabin I own with my sisters, so please don't worry. It's a quiet place for me to try to unwind, and to try to understand what devils are in my head that cause me to upset the people I care about. And, I must say, myself.

Sincerely,

Mallory

She no sooner hit "Send" than she searched for an unsend button. There wasn't one.

Doubts about her response assailed her. Maybe she should have told him she'd go back to New York and try to work things out. Or, maybe she needed to say she didn't think she'd ever be ready to marry him because, deep down, that thought was also there.

She was pondering what to do when she heard Julia walking about and went downstairs to see what her sister was up to.

Julia's duffel bag was by the front door, but she was sitting at the kitchen island with a cup of coffee.

"That's a really sweet little cat," Julia said as soon as she saw Mallory. The cat now lay in a beam of sunlight streaming through the window. "Cats hate change, so I won't take her to Bend with me unless I have to. But in the meantime, we should put a cat door in the garage so she'll be able to go into it at night when we aren't in the cabin. Night is when foxes and coyotes and such are out there hunting. I hired a gardener to come by here every other week to keep the land cut down and free of weeds, and I'll ask him to also put out lots of food and water in the garage for her when he's here. Is that okay with you?"

"It's fine," Mallory said, joining her at the island. "And she can stay inside with me while I'm here. But why are you leaving already?"

"I can see you're handling things here just fine," Julia said. "Any idea how long you'll stay?"

Mallory got up to make herself some tea. "Not yet. I'm not quite as ready to turn around and head back to Manhattan as I was yesterday, but I doubt I'll be here long."

"Play it by ear. This place might be what you need. By the way, I don't suppose you've seen your neighbor around, have you? He's around my age, brown hair, gray eyes. Tall, and would be good looking except he's kind of gaunt, as if he'd been ill for a while."

As Mallory placed a teabag in the hot water, she couldn't get over the question. What neighbor? Something about the way Julia asked—a tightening of her voice, a slight blush to her cheeks—made her wonder if her tough sister had, at some time, actually met a man out here that intrigued her. But if so, she knew Julia would never admit it. "I didn't even know we had any neighbors," she admitted. She hoped they did because the thought of being so isolated and alone once Julia left made her nervous.

But she was being silly. Nothing in the least bit scary or dangerous ever happened in this area. Truth be told, she was probably ten times safer all alone in the cabin than she was surrounded by people on the streets of Manhattan.

"Anyway, let me know how everything goes," Julia said with a shrug, "and I'll come back if you need me."

Mallory nodded. "I'm glad you came, and for our talks. Thank you."

Julia gave what was, for Julia, a smile. "I'm glad, as well. Long overdue, in fact."

Mallory smiled at that, then placed her hand on Julia's arm even though her sister wasn't one for touching. "Quite a pair, aren't we?" Mallory said giving Julia's arm an affectionate squeeze. "Thank God, Carly turned out normal."

"Oh?" Julia gave her a slight grin. "I don't think I'd go that far."

They both laughed.

Julia strode to the front door, slung her duffel bag over her shoulder, and went out to her Jeep. Mallory followed, standing on the driveway and waving goodbye until the Jeep disappeared.

When she turned to go back into the cabin, the cat was near the front door. It gave a loud meow and then ran under some bitterbrush shrubs that grew along the edge of the property.

Alex Townson was looking through some tourist brochures with his wife, Carly, in their suite overlooking the Spanish Steps in Rome when his cell phone began to buzz.

He didn't recognize the number calling, but the area code was New York City. Although they were on an extended honeymoon, he thought the call might be about his latest Rip Tarrington thriller, so he answered. "This is Alex."

"Mr. Townson, my name is Slade Atchison, and I'd like to speak to your wife if she's available. It concerns her sister, Mallory."

Alex glanced at Carly with worry. "Is she all right?"

"I don't know. That's why I'm calling."

Alex was perplexed. "Who are you again?"

"I was Mallory's fiancé."

There was a momentary silence, and then Alex said, "Hold on a minute." He put the phone on mute and handed the phone to his wife. "Mallory's ex-fiancé."

"Which one?" she asked.

He shrugged.

She then put the phone on speaker so that Alex could hear as well. "This is Carly. I understand you're calling about my sister, Mallory. What's going on?"

"My name is Slade Atchison. I was engaged to her."

Carly grimaced at Alex and lifted an unhappy eyebrow. "You *were* engaged to her, you say? Recently?"

"Last Saturday, we were going to get married—"

"But didn't," Carly finished the sentence for him.

"Right."

She rolled her eyes. "How did you get this phone number, Mr. Atchison?"

"Call me Slade, please, since we were nearly in-laws. Mallory told me about your recent marriage—congratulations, by the way. Anyway, I'm a good friend of"—he stopped himself—"of someone at your husband's publishing house. I told my friend it was extremely important that I get hold of you since I have some vital information concerning your sister, so my friend gave me the phone number needed."

Alex was shocked to hear that.

Carly nodded. "And what is this vital information?" she asked, not sounding happy.

"Look. I know about your sister's history with weddings. I had hoped she could get past that with me, but she couldn't. I also know she loves me. She sent me a message saying so, and also that she's at an Idaho cabin that the three of you own. But I have no idea where in Idaho it is. I need to see her and talk to her."

Carly sighed. "Every man she left at the altar believed what you do now."

"I understand. Mallory explained about the others to me and swore it wouldn't happen again. I believe she truly wants to be my wife. I need to see her, to talk to her face-to-face and help her through whatever is causing her to walk away from love. From life, if you want the truth. We shared so many dreams of what we hoped our life together would be, I simply cannot believe she means to throw it all away. Please, Carly, she told me that she and her two sisters aren't close, that you all had different fathers and never lived together except for one month each summer at the cabin. But despite all that, if you care about her at all, please tell me how to find her."

"As you said, we aren't close, so she hasn't contacted me. I just don't know if I should tell you where the cabin is located."

"I'm begging you."

Carly waited a moment. "Let me call the cabin. If Mallory's there, I'll ask her."

"You know, as I do, that she'll say no. And then we're right back where we started. I need to see her, face-to-face."

"All right. Tell me the name of the person who gave you Alex's phone number. He'll phone that person—and others—and if you check out as a decent fellow, I'll give you the address."

"Not a problem," Slade said. "And thank you. You'll find I have an impeccable reputation and credentials."

CHAPTER 9

The house was beyond quiet with Julia gone. Even the little cat seemed to have disappeared. Mallory had no idea if either one would return while she was here. The cat seemed fonder of Julia than of her.

But she had promised Julia she'd have a cat door installed in the garage.

She went down to the hardware store. It was ancient, and the hardware might have been there for close to a century. An elderly man sat behind a high wooden counter with a glass top and glass front so that she could see the variety of knives he was selling.

"What can I do you for?" he asked with a slight drawl that matched his backward wording.

"I'm hoping you can suggest someone to help me put a cat door in my garage," she said.

"Well, that shouldn't be too tough. Say, aren't you one of the gals that owns the old Donnelly cabin?"

"I am." Mallory was surprised he knew who she was, but then realized that she shouldn't be. The whole town probably was aware the Donnelly cabin had been renovated.

"I remember you three as little kids running around here. And I remember your mother. Real pretty, she was. I'm Fred Wilkins."

Mallory smiled. "I thought you looked familiar."

"That's kind of you to say. You didn't need to stop in here much, but if Sandie hadn't retired from the ice cream store across the road, you'd surely remember her. You kids went there nearly every day. Her daughter's running the shop now."

"You're right. I remember that!" Mallory smiled at the memory of the enormous single scoop cones Miss Sandie used to give them.

"In fact, I believe I heard you and Gunnar had a nice long conversation at the Rusty Nail the other evening," Fred said, rubbing his chin.

Her eyebrows rose. She'd always heard small towns knew everything going on in them, but she never imagined talking to Gunnar McDermott would land her on the town's hot line.

"No need for you to look further. Gunnar's the best man for the job," Fred said. "Putting in a cat door is a small thing, and most carpenters are real busy doing big jobs. Have to get ready for winter, you know."

"That makes sense," Mallory said. "But I don't know how to contact him."

"His auto shop is on the Middlefork Road as you head toward the highway. It's on the right. You can't miss it. I'm sure he'd be more than glad to help out."

"Thanks." Mallory bought a hammer. Not that she needed it —or, hoped she didn't—but it seemed she should buy something. She then headed out to her car and drove as directed.

For some reason, the thought of seeing Gunnar again brought a smile to her face. Of course, it was only because they'd been such good friends as children.

She saw a big garage with two bays and twice as many cars parked in front of it.

She parked and headed for the office. She hadn't gotten very far when a car, going backward, careened out of one of the garages right toward her. "Watch it!" she yelled as she flung herself out of the way.

Nathan was in the driver's seat and stomped on the brakes, then gawked at her as if he'd seen a ghost. "Oh, no!" he cried as he jumped out of the car. "I am so sorry! I didn't hit you, did I?"

"No," she said, but she was shaken by the near miss, and her voice quivered.

Nathan waved his arms, as if he didn't know if he should help her to the office, or have her sit somewhere—but where?—or exactly what he should do. "I've never seen anyone walking out here. I know I should have looked. I'm really, really sorry!"

"It's okay," she said. What had she recently thought about safety in Garden Valley versus Manhattan?

"What happened here?" Gunnar hurried toward them from the shop, looking more than a little worried. He had a streak of grease on his cheek, his cane in his hand.

"I didn't see her," Nathan wailed. "I didn't mean it."

"It's okay," Mallory said, this time to Gunnar. "I'm fine, really. I didn't realize I was in a 'no walking' zone. I just stopped by to see if you could help me with something."

"It's all right, Nathan," Gunnar tore his gaze from Mallory to pat his friend's back. "She said she's fine. You finish parking the car and then go on inside and relax. I'll take care of this."

Nathan nodded, got back into the car, and then, as slowly as a very senior citizen, backed the car into a parking space along the road.

Gunnar turned back to Mallory, again studying her as if to make sure she was all right. But at the same time clearly wondering how or why she was standing outside his auto shop. "Let's go into the office," Gunnar said, taking her arm and directing her away from the street and the stares of the men working in the garage.

She stepped into an office crammed to the rafters with stacks of paper, books, binders, sets of auto repair manuals, a desk, computer, and a counter for receiving customers.

"So what brings you out here?" Gunnar asked. He put the cane down and leaned against the high counter, remaining with her on the customer side.

"I'm really sorry to bother you," she began. "I guess I didn't realize how busy you are."

"You're no bother. Besides, I'm fortunate to have good help." His words, his expression, were serious.

Through the indoor window to the auto shop she could see he had two men working on each car. "That's good. Well, I was at the hardware store talking to Fred Wilkins about a little project I have at the cabin, and he suggested I contact you."

"Oh?" Gunnar's eyebrows rose in surprise.

"Yes. It's small. He said all the carpenters in the area are busy and probably wouldn't want to take on something like this."

Gunnar's brows crossed. "Fred said that?" Again, that wasn't the reaction she was expecting from him. "So, what is this little project that caused Fred's thoughts to turn my way?"

"A cat door." It did sound like a really tiny project when she said it.

His head bowed closer to hers. "Excuse me?"

Her mouth went dry. Her request suddenly seemed silly. "A little cat has been hanging out at the cabin for the past few days. I'd like a door put into a wall in the garage so that the cat can get into the garage at night when no one is at the cabin to help her."

He slowly took that in. "So … this isn't actually your cat?"

"We don't know whose cat she is. But Julia's fond of her. She's a pretty little thing, and I'd hate to abandon her when I leave Garden Valley. This way, she could at least stay warm and dry in the garage."

Gunnar studied her a moment, then said simply, "Well, there is that."

She turned so she, too, was leaning back against the counter, side-by-side with him. She thought a moment, then said, "I can understand cat doors aren't your thing. And if you're too busy, it's okay. I'll ask Fred for another name, and maybe one of those carpenters isn't exactly as booked up as he seemed to think."

"No, no. It's all right." He straightened, looked her in the eye and nodded. "If Fred says this is the job for me, I'll take his word on that. Why don't I come out tonight and take a look at what you want, and then I'll figure out what's needed. Of course, it'll mean a trip down to Boise to one of the big hardware stores. I suspect they have cat doors all set up, and I'd just need to cut a hole in the garage siding to fit it."

"That doesn't sound too hard," she said.

"Shouldn't be."

"Great. Whenever you have time to come over, I'll be there. It's not like I have to be anyplace else."

"Okay. How about after dinner, say around seven? It'll still be light enough to see what I need to."

"Sounds good. But before I go." She stepped closer and reached up, resting her fingers on his jaw and with her thumb she tried to wipe away the grease on his face. His eyes brightened at her touch. "You have a smudge."

"A smudge?" he repeated.

She met his eyes and realized how close they now stood. Her heart skittered and suddenly her fingertips burned where they touched his skin. She dropped her hand and stepped back.

"Better now," she proclaimed, and hurried from the shop.

Mallory scarcely remembered the drive from Gunnar's shop to the cabin. All she could think about was her reaction when she touched him. She'd touched him without thought when they were kids—pushing and shoving over toys and games, holding his hand or arm when they went climbing around the hillsides. She'd even share her ice cream cone with him when he didn't have money to buy one for himself. But she never felt anything like she did that moment in his shop as she lightly grazed his face.

Once back at the cabin, she decided to look for the calico cat. "Hey, kitty, kitty," she called. The cat really did need a name. She'd love to call her Callie, but that was way too close to her middle sister's name. She suspected Carly might not find the name amusing.

Mallory had the strongest desire to phone Carly, which was something she almost never did, and talk to her about the cabin, Slade, and maybe even Gunnar. Carly had a softer personality than Julia. Carly could be logical and practical to a fault, but she was never bossy. When they were kids, Mallory would often play with Carly, while Julia always took on the role of babysitter cop.

Where is that darn cat? Mallory was going to feel quite foolish asking Gunnar to install a door for the cat if it never came back. But Mallory was also used to doing whatever Julia demanded— "or else!" as her big sister used to say.

At five minutes before seven, Gunnar arrived.

She showed him into the great room.

"I still can't get over how much nicer this cabin looks than in the old days," Gunnar said. "It was old and spooky. Not anymore."

"Thank goodness. Would you like some beer, wine, or iced tea?" she asked.

"Let me take a look at the job first," he said. "Is the cat in the house somewhere?"

"No. I haven't seen her for a while. But she's very independent. For all I know, she has an owner and just comes here to visit. A second home, so to speak. But Julia wants a cat door."

Gunner smirked. "And whatever Julia wants, Julia gets. Didn't your mom used to sing a song like that?"

"You're right. It's from *Damn Yankees* and in the musical, the woman's name was Lola and she was a devil or demon or something," Mallory said with a chuckle.

"Well, then, that Lola sounds more like Julia every minute."

Mallory grinned and shook her head as she led Gunnar out to the back porch. Gunnar, like everyone else who'd been in town back when her mother would visit, knew Roxanne was a fine singer. She had performed in musicals off-Broadway in her younger years and often went on tours. By the time Mallory was born, however, she no longer toured. Still, Roxanne loved to sing, and when in Crouch, if she was in a restaurant or pub with musicians who would ask her to join them in a song, she'd do it. They were often in town for the Fourth of July celebration, and Roxanne would sing the national anthem along with a song or two from old musicals. She would always get a big cheer singing "I'm in Love With a Wonderful Guy" because of it mentioned the flag on the Fourth of July," at which point she would turn to the flag and salute. Mallory used to believe her mother was singing about her father as the "wonderful guy." But then one day, *poof*, Roxanne announced that the two were getting a divorce.

Gunnar stood at the porch railing and gazed out at the orchard. "I remember playing out there. It was fun except for the time Nathan convinced you that mud pies were delicious. Your mom was furious. She said we could have poisoned you, and then we'd go to the gas chamber. She scared us half to death!"

"I don't remember that."

"You were really little then—but so were me and Nathan."

"We had quite a few years out here, didn't we?" she murmured.

"We did." He hesitated, and she could see the struggle in his eyes before he said, "But then it all stopped."

She nodded. "Our mother simply changed her mind about coming here." She had no better explanation.

"None of us knew what happened to all of you," he said after a while. "The cabin stood empty and neglected for years. But then, last winter, we saw workers out here and heard the family still owned it and that you guys were fixing it up. We figured it was being done to sell it."

Mallory sat on the bench and invited Gunnar to join her. "After Mom passed away, I definitely thought we should sell it, but Julia didn't want to, and Carly always went along with whatever Julia wanted. I was the odd-man-out. They said I didn't appreciate it because I didn't remember it well enough. They believed it was worth fixing it up, so I went along. I didn't realize it was in such bad shape it would take my entire inheritance, but here we are."

He turned to face her, looping his arm along the back of the bench. "So what brought you here?"

Her mind went blank. She couldn't tell him the truth, but she couldn't think of what to say instead. "If I own it, I should see it, right?"

"Absolutely!" His gaze went out over the land, and when he faced her again, his voice was softer. "If I owned this cabin, right near the river but on ground high enough you shouldn't ever have to worry about flooding, I wouldn't sell it. In fact, I'd do just what you are—come out here and enjoy it."

She smiled. "It is nice, but not at all what I'm used to."

"It must be like a completely different world from Manhattan."

"It is," she admitted. "But in a good way."

"Not boring?"

"I suspect it can be," she murmured.

He leaned forward, looking out at the land and mountains

beyond. "When you were a little kid, you really loved it here. I always knew when it was near time for your family to leave, because you'd cry for a couple of days that you'd have to leave."

"You remember that?" she asked. "I thought I hated it."

"Maybe, but that wasn't how I saw it." Large blue eyes, soft with kindness, faced her. "I used to feel real sorry for you. I even asked my dad about it—how you and your sisters had different fathers, and all, and how you three were all split up once you left the cabin. I tell you, I really didn't understand anything of what was going on there. My dad told me to mind my own business and hush my mouth, so I never said anything. But I could see that you and your sisters had strange lives. Not like me and my friends in Garden Valley, that's for sure."

"I had no idea," she said. "Of course, since that was my life, I didn't think it was odd, but I did wish my mom and dad were still together and that my sisters could live with us. I liked the idea of having sisters and still feel bad that I never got to really know them. In fact, the first real conversation I ever had with my sister Julia—other than talking about fixing up the cabin after we learned we'd inherited it—was right here during this visit. It was a good talk—for Julia."

He smiled at the proviso. "Glad to hear it. Speaking of Julia, let's take a look at the garage to see where to put the cat door. I'd hate to have her come back and get mad at me for not doing it. She can be one scary little lady."

Mallory laughed. "Ha! That she can."

A door near the cabin's small laundry room and half-bath led to the garage. They entered the garage, and Gunnar began his search for a spot. But he no sooner got started when the door to the back yard blew open.

"I thought that door was locked," Mallory said going to it to check the lock. It had a dead bolt. "I guess I was wrong."

Gunnar went out back and looked around. He wanted to put the cat door high enough that little animals like toads and lizards and voles and such wouldn't find it and wander inside. At the same time, it should be small enough that raccoons couldn't make use of it.

He slowly walked along the garage perimeter. "What in the world?" He walked to a spot where the cabin met the garage—the garage was a "young" fifty years old, having been added on decades after the original cabin was finished.

He saw a small horse carved out of wood. The carving was quite rough. "What's this?" he asked Mallory, picking up the small horse and standing it on the palm of his hand.

"I have no idea. It looks like it might have been a child's toy, but I've no idea why it's here."

"A little boy's toy, most likely. It doesn't look very weathered, though, so it can't have been out here long," Gunnar added.

As Mallory looked at it, she could feel the gooseflesh rising on her arms. It looked like the sort of toy a child might have had over a century ago, not at all like the plastic, painted toys of today. "Who knows what goes on here when the cabin is empty. Let's find a place for the cat door."

"Actually," Gunnar eyed the spot where the wooden horse was found. "This might be it. There's an overhang from the roof, and the ground slopes away from the garage, so snow will run off as it melts. I can put the cat door right here."

Mallory told herself she was being paranoid, but for the strange toy to happen to be in exactly the right place ... She steadied her nerves and said, "I doubt you'll find much better."

"I agree. Now, we just need to find the cat. Is it big or small? I checked out cat doors on the internet and found that most doors come in sizes for cats under twelve pounds and those over."

"I have no idea. Should we just get the big one?"

"We could, but the bigger the opening, the bigger unwanted animals can get inside—like foxes and raccoons. If we must get a big one, so be it. But we should be sure."

"Such animals coming into the garage sound dangerous. Maybe we don't want a cat door."

"It's more likely your cat will encounter one of those outside than inside the garage, but it's up to you."

"That's true. Okay. The cat will probably show up later tonight. If you'd like to wait awhile, I've got wine, chips and guacamole. If not, I'll do my best to measure and weigh her, and then I'll call you."

"I don't mind waiting with you," he said. "Let me get a couple measurements inside."

Mallory tried not to let him see how relieved his words made her feel. She still was a bit nervous about being alone in the cabin. "Great. But first, let's leave that old toy out here. Some kid might come looking for it."

He put the horse back where he found it. "I doubt it, but okay, sure."

Back in the garage he knelt down and measured between the studs. "This will work. And the wall is plywood and siding, so it won't be hard to cut through."

She was at the door to enter the house when she noticed that he was slow to stand and was using the cane for support as if it hurt too much not to use it. Once again, she wondered what had happened to him and how bad the injury was, but hesitated to ask.

But soon, Gunnar caught up to her. He said nothing, and neither did she.

CHAPTER 10

Mallory opened the refrigerator door. "I have some Sam Adams if you'd prefer it over Chablis."

Gunnar grinned. "Actually, I would."

"Thought so," she said and took out two bottles. "I think I would as well." She poured a bunch of tortilla chips into a bowl, grabbed the container of guacamole Julia had bought, and placed them on the coffee table in front of the fireplace.

She couldn't help but look up at Elijah Donnelly's portrait. Of course, the cat wasn't in it. What, she wondered for the umpteenth time, had ever possessed her to think she saw a cat there? Too weird.

Gunnar immediately loaded a chip with guacamole and took a bite. "Delicious!"

"Good," she liked seeing him enjoy it and took a taste herself. "By the way, I don't have a name for the cat yet. I think I ought to name her."

"What color is she?"

"She's a calico cat."

He smiled. "I hear they're good luck. It's nice one has adopted you."

"Adopted me?" she said with a laugh. "Yes, I guess that's what happened, isn't it?"

"With a stray cat, always. It says good things about a person when a stray cat shows up at your house and then doesn't want to leave."

"That's nice to hear, although I think it was more to stay with my sister Julia than me."

"I doubt that," Gunnar said with a grimace, even as he continued to plow through the chips and avocado mixture.

Mallory grinned, but also shook her head at his persistent aversion to Julia.

"So tell me," Gunnar said, turning away from the food to face her as they sat on the sofa, "what brought you here? And why all alone?"

"I just wanted to get away from everything for a while. To think."

"Is this a vacation? Do you work?"

It felt strange to say she wasn't working. "I recently lost my job. I was a listing assistant at one of the top real estate firms in Manhattan."

She saw a mixture of surprise and concern cross his face. "I'm sorry to hear you're no longer working." His always velvety voice was soft now.

"Well, I have a lot of experience, so I'm not too worried about finding another job in that area."

"That's good. So ... you left New York to think about stuff?"

"One of the reasons." She guessed it sounded silly. And since she figured he'd hear about it one way or another, she added, "I left because I broke off my engagement."

Shock filled his face. "Oh? Sorry to hear that," he said. "That must have been hard for you."

"It was. But, it's complicated."

He nodded. "I can well imagine. Matters of the heart usually are. This is probably a good place to be alone and try to get over it."

"That's what Julia said." She paused a moment and then tried to sound more upbeat. "Enough about me. What are you up to? You mentioned helping your dad run the farm."

"My dad's still in charge, but he's slowing down a bit, and more and more farming information is online. He hates computers, but I'm pretty good with them."

"Nice." Then, as casually as she could, said, "I take it you aren't married."

"No."

She hesitated, but was now too curious not to ask the obvious question. "Seeing anyone special?"

"Not at the moment," he replied.

She suddenly sat a little straighter. "Why not?" And she couldn't help but tease. "I've certainly seen more than enough women interested in you!"

"Is that so?" His face slowly formed into that brash half-smile she remembered so well, and she knew a zinger was coming. "Well, then, why pick one tree when there's a whole forest?"

"Ooooh, give me a break!" She groaned.

They both laughed.

He shook his head, apparently uncomfortable with the whole topic. "I do keep looking. How's that? Satisfied now?"

"What about the girls we used to play with? Some were very nice. And cute."

"Do you remember Emma Hughes?" he asked.

She wondered what made him mention Emma Hughes. "I don't think so."

"She has the only insurance office in town, and she also handles rentals for the area. You might want to talk to her about caretaking the cabin for you when you and your sisters aren't here. But other than Emma, I'd say just about all the girls you used to play with got married and moved away. Or, they moved away and then got married. Whichever, they've left town. Seems to be the way in rural areas like this."

Mallory nodded. "I've heard that about quite a few small towns. It's got to be hard to deal with," she said. "But thanks for the tip about Emma Hughes. I'll look for her. And maybe some day you can come visit me in New York. I have a few girlfriends who say they'd love to get out of the city and move into the country. One of them might be 'the one.'"

He scoffed. "Somehow, I doubt that. Country life seems idyllic until you try to live it, and discover you might get snowed in during winter, have to tend the land all year-round, and you might have to travel many miles to buy those things city people have at their fingertips. Look at how you left and didn't come back for years—and you sound ready to leave again."

She took in his words. "Maybe."

He lifted an eyebrow, clearly not believing her "maybe." "I noticed you have a landline. Give me the number so I can reach you if necessary and also make sure you've got my number near it in case of emergency. Things happen, and you being alone out here might not be the smartest thing."

She picked up on his worries, which only added to her own. "I understand. Luckily, Julia mentioned that we have a neighbor."

He scoffed. "What, a mile away?"

She had no idea. "She didn't say. In fact, this is the first night I'll be spending here alone."

He grew increasingly worried. "I don't mind sleeping on the couch tonight."

She could have kissed ... or at least hugged ... him for his offer. But quickly realized that might be misconstrued. "That's very kind of you, but I've got to learn to do things on my own. Being here should be perfectly safe."

He nodded. "I think it is, but the location is fairly isolated."

"Fairly?" she asked with a smile.

He shrugged. "Some parts of Idaho, like the roadless areas deep inside the national forests, make the Middlefork Road look like your city's Fifth Avenue."

"I wish!" she said with a grin. "But really, I'm fine. Besides, you have work tomorrow! You need a good night's sleep."

He checked his watch. "It's already ten. Looks like that little cat of yours isn't going to show tonight. If you can weigh or measure him, give me what you find out and I'll see about getting the right size door for you."

"It's a she. And I'll do what I can. Thank you!"

She walked him to the front door. He opened it, but suddenly stopped and faced her.

"I really can stay." His voice was low and soft.

Something about the sound of his voice, the way he looked at her, his sudden nearness made her mind go to places it shouldn't. Not when she was confused about how she felt about Slade. And Gunnar was a childhood *friend*. The thought of having him spend the night with her shouldn't feel so enticing. She stiffened. "No need, I can do this."

He nodded then headed out to his Ford pickup.

The house was emptier than ever after Gunnar left. No sister. No cat. No old friend.

And then her phone went missing. She searched for nearly an hour before she found it in the refrigerator. That made no sense. She must have been distracted looking for the cat.

Mallory took the phone outdoors into the dark of midnight, moving it all around until she found a spot with two bars.

With that, a text message from Slade popped up, written some three hours earlier.

Would a visit help? With my private plane—and your directions—I suspect I can be with you in a matter of hours.

She wrote back: *Right now, I need to be alone. But thank you for the offer.*

Turning to her newly downloaded emails, she found lots of reactions, mostly negative, to her response to "Happily Married." She chose the most interesting yet typical reaction for her next column.

Dear Nellie,

You don't get it. You're so ready to fail at love and marriage, you don't give yourself or your readers a chance to overcome whatever their problems are and find a way to be happy. Before you tell others how to develop a loving and lasting relationship, why don't you try having one yourself? [Signed] Happily Married

After all she'd been through the last few days, her response was immediate:

Dear Happily,

As the old song says, "A Good Man is Hard to Find." And there's always the old adage that "you doth protest too much." Could it be that things are not as blissful in your marriage as you pretend? [Signed] Not looking Nellie

She no sooner sent it than she couldn't help but wonder if she wasn't the one overly protesting. After all, Happily Married had more than a little truth to what she said.

Mallory shut her eyes a moment. No one would trust Dear Nellie ever again if she were to turn soft! With that, she locked up the house, checked and double-checked the doors and windows, grabbed a poker from the fireplace to use as a weapon in case anyone broke in, and started up the stairs to her bedroom when she heard the cat crying.

She followed the sound to the French doors and opened them but the cat wasn't anywhere that she could see. She stepped onto the porch. "Hey, kitty, kitty," she called. But there was no sign of the cat, and it was no longer crying.

She gave up and went indoors to find the cat sitting on a chair by the dining table.

"What? How did you…?" She decided she didn't want to know. The cat had obviously been hiding somewhere in the house, and Mallory had missed finding her. "We've really got to give you a name so you'll understand when I call you," she said. Then, she put out some water and grain-free dry cat food, checked the door locks once more, and retired for the night.

CHAPTER 11

In the morning when she woke, she found the cat asleep on the bed. "You're already a spoiled little creature, aren't you?" she said as she sat up. The cat opened her eyes and gave a long stretch. "I wonder if I should take you in to a vet, Cat. I don't know if you have fleas, worms, or anything else, and if you're going to sleep on my bed, that'd be good to know. Especially since I suspect you do."

The cat gave her a sour look, jumped off the bed and strutted out the door.

After some toast, coffee, and searching the house for anything to use to measure the cat, Mallory phoned Gunnar.

"I've got the cat shut up in the house, but I can't find a scale or a measuring tape in the cabin. If you could bring one by some time today…"

"I can come by right now, if that works," he said.

"You don't have to drop everything for this," she said.

"I don't mind. I'm doing the books, and the numbers are already jumping all over the screen. It's quiet today, so my guys can handle things here."

"In that case, see you soon."

Gunnar arrived twenty minutes later. She ran to the door when she heard his truck on the driveway. The sun glinted off his blonde hair as he got out of the truck, peeled off his sunglasses and left them on the dash. As he approached with a small scale in one hand, his cane in the other, his snug-fitting, light gray tee-shirt showed every movement of his muscular chest and shoulders. It was all she could do to ignore the way her pulse quickened.

"Greetings," she called, rushing out to meet him. "Thank you for coming to help."

"Helping damsels in distress is my most favorite thing in the world," he said with a half smile.

"Well, I'm not exactly in distress," she began, taking the scale from him.

"Oh? Should I leave?"

She took his arm. "No way!" She liked holding his arm, and definitely like the way he smiled at her when she took it.

They went into the kitchen and she put the scale on the kitchen island. The cat had been curled up on a chair cushion in the sun, but as soon as she saw Gunnar, it was as if she knew something was up because she ran up the stairs. Mallory and Gunnar went after her—Mallory continued up the stairs, while Gunnar waited at the foot of them. Mallory chased the cat from one bedroom to the next.

"Get her to run to me," Gunnar called.

Mallory tried hard to catch her, but the cat proved much more slippery than she imagined, although she couldn't remember ever having tried to catch a cat before. She especially hated it when the cat ran under a bed and she'd have to lay on her stomach to try to reach it. She soon realized she needed to shut all the doors except for the room the cat was in. Then, when she chased the cat from that room, the cat had no choice but to take the stairs. Gunnar managed a soccer goalie block and grabbed her as she attempted to leap past him.

"Success!" he shouted. The cat was furious, but he held it against his chest and petted it, and it soon stopped yowling.

"Thank goodness," Mallory said, breathing heavy. "I don't think I could have handled chasing that little monster another minute. That cat can move!"

"They all can."

The cat wriggled more and more as Gunnar neared the scale, but then he put her down. "No need to weigh her. She's no twelve pounds. I've had chickens that weigh more than her. She's like a feather."

"That's because she doesn't eat anything," Mallory said. "She won't touch any of the food I put out for her."

"She's probably getting her fill of birds and field mice. Some say that's actually healthier than processed food, anyway."

"Please! Now, I really don't want her sleeping on my bed!"

He grinned at that. "Now that I know the size, I'll drive down to Boise and pick up a door."

"You don't have to do that. I'll go," Mallory said.

"It's okay. I've got a shopping list of supplies I need from a hardware store a lot bigger than Fred Wilkins'. I've got to get some lumber to rebuild the hen house, among other things. I've been putting off going, but now I need to just get it over with."

"Oh." Disappointment struck until she added, "Want company?"

Mallory had forgotten how pretty the trip was from Garden Valley down to Boise, especially viewed from the height of a pickup truck's seat. Most of the trip followed the Payette River. She had driven from the airport up to the cabin, but now, sitting beside Gunnar in his big pickup, she realized how upset she must have been making that drive, because the beauty of the tall mountains dropping steeply down to the fast moving blue river had barely registered. The river was a bit low now, and she could see large rocks in it, making it a challenge for rafters. But despite that, there were a number of rafts out on the water.

"Have you ever gone rafting?" she asked Gunnar.

He gave her a quick sidelong glance, then went back to watching the road. "Used to."

"Did you like it?"

"Loved it." He smiled as if pleasantly remembering being out on the water. "Just have to make sure you've got a good guide and an even better life jacket."

"I can imagine."

"If you want to try it sometime, just let me know."

"I would. Thanks."

He glanced at her as if to make sure she wasn't joking. She wasn't. "By the way," he said, "I made some inquiries about some of the kids you might have known during your summers at the cabin."

"Interesting! What did you find out?"

As he talked, she was surprised at how many of the kids she actually remembered. He had a great way of telling stories about growing up with them, especially their high school days and the crazy stunts they pulled. At times she laughed so hard tears came to her eyes, and before she knew it, they'd arrived in Boise. Gunnar drove to one of the big box stores that carried all the tools, lumber, and hardware on his list.

As they pulled into the parking lot, about three-quarters of the vehicles were trucks. "This looks like pickup truck heaven!" she said.

"You saying it doesn't look like Manhattan?" he asked with a grin. She noticed he didn't bother to put on his cowboy hat. They apparently weren't used in Boise anymore. But quite a few men wore baseball caps, mostly with logos of Boise teams, Idaho locations, or beer brands. Again, not typical Manhattan headwear.

Gunnar got a flat pushcart and he and Mallory first went to the area with cat doors. Once they reached the correct aisle, it took less than thirty seconds to find the one they needed, but then off Gunnar went to the lumber department, and Mallory entered a whole new world. She had no idea there were so many sizes and grades of wood that could be used to built a chicken coop—and the wire that would enclose it seemed to engross Gunnar even more. She was ready to beg him to simply buy both size chicken wire he was debating over just so they could get out of there.

When the bill was rung up, she handed the clerk her credit card. "I know you won't let me pay you for installing the door, so the least I can do is buy the supplies for your chicken coop."

"Hen house. But you really don't need to—"

"I know. But I want to."

Before heading north again, they stopped for lunch at a small restaurant in Eagle with outdoor seating. This time, Gunnar insisted on paying.

Once more, he was able to tell Mallory stories about crazy things that happened to him or friends, like the time they snuck into a high school rival's team clubhouse and spray painted the basketballs pink with orange polka dots. When their own school principal found out, the boys were made to wash and hand detail all the rival school's coaches' cars. Gunnar had dishpan hands for a week.

Hearing his stories, Mallory remembered that even as a kid, whenever Gunnar showed up, there was always laughter and fun. As an adult, he had story telling down to a science. She didn't know any of the people Gunnar told her about, but it didn't matter. She'd already come to recognize that whenever he began with, "I should tell you about the time that my friend ..." it was going to be a story she didn't want to miss.

What was nice, was that he seemed to enjoy the way she

laughed at his tales. He carefully watched her expressions, and when she would laugh he'd join in.

"You two seem to be having a really nice time out here," the waitress said at one point when she came by to check on how their lunches were.

"Delicious, ma'am," Gunnar said. "I'll take the check now. We'll be leaving soon."

The waitress pulled out her pad. "You seem like a nice young couple. Ex-military, right?" she asked Gunnar.

"Army, ma'am," Gunnar said, then flashed a glance at Mallory and added, "But we're just friends."

Since Gunnar was looking at her, she felt compelled to add, "That's right. Friends."

"Oh, I can see that," the waitress said with a smirk before she turned to Gunnar again. "What did you do in the service?"

"I flew helicopters."

She drew in her breath. "My son's in Afghanistan now."

Gunnar nodded. "Thanks to you both for his service."

The waitress smiled. "Hopefully, he'll be coming home soon. Well, you two just keep enjoying each other's company like you are—friends and all. Me and my old man have been together thirty years. Being able to laugh at the things life throws at you is the key." She put the bill on the table.

"Thanks, ma'am," Gunnar said, once he got his voice back.

Mallory's smile was more stiff, but she murmured a thank you before the waitress walked away.

"Sorry about that," Gunnar said to Mallory.

"No problem." Mallory said with a chuckle. "Helicopters, huh?"

"Mostly Apaches," he murmured, then turned away. She could see that it wasn't a topic he was comfortable with, and made her suspect his injuries might have something to do with it. She couldn't help but wonder if Gunnar had loved flying, loved being a pilot. Considering what a dare-devil he was a child, she could picture him thrilled to be out there with his Apache helicopter. And she could also picture herself scared to death at the thought of the danger he'd been in.

When he flipped over the bill, she noticed the waitress didn't charge them for her wine or his beer, leaving a smily face on the bill instead. Gunnar left her a generous tip.

CHAPTER 12

It was early evening when they arrived back at the cabin, the sky brilliant streaks of orange, red, and white as the sun sank low on the horizon. The day remained warm and the air still. With no air conditioning in the garage, Mallory made some iced tea to bring out to Gunnar as he worked.

She thought about giving him the tea and then leaving him alone while he worked on the cat door, but soon realized she'd rather be out there than sitting in the cabin alone. She only hesitated because some of her friends had said she accepted so many marriage proposals because she was "needy" and afraid of being abandoned since her own parents hadn't wanted her. She hated such two-bit psychoanalysis and didn't see herself as needy at all. And so what that her parents hadn't wanted her? Who needed them, anyway?

She marched into the garage in a strong, determined fashion.

Gunnar was sitting on the floor and sawing through the wall. She had guessed that would be the area requiring the most concentration so as not to make the hole too big or lopsided, and that the rest would be a more methodical step-by-step process.

"How is it coming?" she asked.

"I think I can handle it," he mused.

"I should hope so." She put her hands on her hips. "If you can't do this, heaven only knows what you'll end up with trying to build a chicken coop."

"That's just mean, Mal," he said with a grimace.

"Guess so." She grinned to let him know she wasn't serious.

"So, since you're already feeling mean, why don't you tell me about your ex-fiancé?" he said, not looking at her. "I'm surprised to hear he's an ex. In my experience, once you women get the guy to put a ring on your finger, you go nuts planning the wedding."

"Some do," she admitted.

He waited, and when she said nothing more, he asked, "Have you known him long?"

"Three months."

"That's not long."

"My sister, Carly, after being single nearly to age 30, married a man after knowing him only a month. And two weeks of that month, they were in different states."

He faced her, his eyebrows high at this bit of news. "Did she marry that writer fellow I met?"

"She did."

"I suspected there might be something going on there." He gave a knowing nod. "I figured they either loved or hated each other the way they were acting—but I guessed it was the former. Short engagements work for some people. And Carly was always so level-headed and practical, I'm sure she knew exactly what she was doing. So the timing of it means nothing. But then, there are some couples who can be engaged for years and still don't end up happy."

At his last comment, she looked away, her reaction powerful. "And some are unhappy no matter what they do."

He must have heard something in her tone because suddenly his hands stilled and he slightly cocked his head as he studied her. His voice turned soft. "And others, it seems, never find the right person at all. No matter how hard they search."

"Unless they come to the cabin," she said, forcing a lilt to her voice and a smile to her lips.

He went back to work. "Ah, yes! I've heard all the ghost stories about the cabin, how Elijah Donnelly, his wife, and their son haunt the place."

"There's much more to the story." She stepped closer, her words forceful. "Carly found a letter when she was here, and it confirmed what our mother used to tell us."

"Oh? Can you tell me or is it a family secret?"

"Not a secret." She went on to relay the stories Julia had told her about how the son, Lucas, had willed it to a cousin who found true love because of the cabin, and that there were other family members who went to the cabin alone and ended up married. Mallory stopped speaking a moment as the stories struck her. "This seems to mean the Donnelly clan isn't very good at finding people to love us on our own. But you should know that there are also stories about Donnellys coming to the cabin and ignoring the person the cabin sends to them. Those Donnellys end up alone and miserable."

"Oh?" He studied her a moment. "And which kind of Donnelly are you?"

The question took her aback. "I don't know yet. Although, judging from my history so far, I'd say I'm doomed to be alone and miserable."

His eyebrows rose. "I'm surely sorry to hear that."

"Me, too. A part of me thinks I should get Slade here and see if the ghosts like him and want me to stay with him." She realized, with horror, how that sounded. "I mean, if there really were such things as ghosts, of course."

"Of course." His mouth wrinkled into a wry grin.

"You stop that, Gunnar McDermott!" she said hotly. "I think the ghost story is very touching."

"Touched in the head, you mean," he said. "I can hear you now: 'Oh, Slade, honey, would you come to Idaho so some ghosts can check you out for me?'"

She threw an old rag at him. "It's not funny!"

"Oh, but it is." He laughed.

She couldn't help but join him. "Stop that! What if the ghosts hear you and get mad? This isn't smart, Gunnar."

"You aren't the first one who's called me not smart, Mal Conway. Anyway, I just finished putting the inside screws in this door, now I have to go outside and attach the outer plate to the wall. Maybe they won't hear me if I laugh at them out there."

"I don't know. How good do ghosts hear, anyway?" she asked, trying to look serious.

"I don't—Ow!" He tried to get up, but then the knee of his bad leg seemed to buckle and he went back down. She could tell if she wasn't there, he'd be swearing a blue streak, as his face went white with pain.

He tried using the cane, but it was too tall and insecure for him to get enough support from it.

"Let me help you," she said, standing next to him.

"Just give me a minute." He spoke through gritted teeth and seemed both angry and embarrassed at what was happening to him.

She waited without a word.

"Okay, it's better," he said, although his jaw was still clenched.

"I'm going to help you, Gunnar. Don't go getting bossy with me." She stood beside him. "Tell me what to do."

He took a moment to get past stubborn independence, but

then he nodded. "I've got the wall on one side, but bend down and let me hold your shoulder on the other side."

She bent low, and he looped his arm around her neck, his hand on her far shoulder. She put her arms around his back and chest.

"When I count to three, start to lift," he said, still not looking at her.

"Okay," she murmured.

"One, two, ... thr*eeee*." He was heavier than she imagined and she struggled to stand up as he used her to brace himself to get off the floor. Finally, he was high enough that he was able to shift most of his weight onto his good leg and made it upright.

"We did it!" she said, smiling up at him. And just as suddenly she realized her arms were still around him, her body pressed hard against his. She could feel the contours of the muscles of his arms and back, smell the earthiness of a man who'd been working, hear the harshness of his breathing from the strain of working through his pain. And most of all, she liked his arm around her—liked it very much.

His blue eyes seemed larger and even more fascinating this close, and she couldn't look away. As she studied them, she could see he was hurting, but she saw something beyond that, something that drew her even closer to him. Her breathing all but stopped. He seemed to feel it too, but his reaction was the complete opposite and he let go of her as if his arm was on fire. He backed away, breaking her hold. "I'm sorry," he said.

It took her a moment to remember how to breathe. She never expected to feel such a reaction standing close to Gunnar of all people. What was she thinking? He was a friend, a childhood buddy. Nothing more. "Sorry? Don't be. I should have known better than to ask you to do something causing you to have to get down like that—"

"No. You couldn't know. Let me finish this job." He grabbed

his tools and without a glance her way, went to the outside of the garage.

She went into the cabin.

About a half hour later, Gunnar came into the great room. "It's done. It works fine. You'll have to teach the cat how to use it. Make sure it doesn't scare her when you're introducing her to it, or you'll never get her to go through the door flap. Prop it open, throw treats through it so she'll go get them and associate walking through the opening with good things."

He sounded much more formal than he had previously, as if he might still be embarrassed or angry over what had happened in the garage. She hated to see him that way. "Okay," she murmured. "Thank you."

"I'll be on my way." He turned to the door.

"Wait!"

He stopped.

"How about some dinner? I can make some spaghetti with a meat sauce. It won't take long to cook them."

He shook his head. "Those hamburgers in the city were belly-busters. I'm not hungry. But thanks."

"Gunnar, stop." She went to the kitchen and grabbed two beers from the fridge. "At least join me for a beer."

"No, I should get back."

"It's too late to work on your hen house. You know it and I know it. Come on. Besides, I need help to come up with a name for the cat. Now that she's got a door, I can't just call her cat, can I?" She stepped closer to him and took his hand. "Please?"

He shook his head, giving up. "Okay." The word was a whisper.

She took their beers out to the back porch, and they sat

together on the bench. The moon was three-quarters full, and the stars were brilliant.

She opened the bottles, and they drank the beer in silence for a long while until she said, "Would you tell me about it?" She didn't need to say what "it" referred to.

His entire demeanor seemed to harden. She had never seen his face so serious. A long while passed before he began to speak. "It happened in Afghanistan. There were six guys on patrol who were attacked. It was my job to get them out of there on my helo. Gunfire. Mortars. A bomb went off near me. Tore up my hip and femur. My medic—Nathan—managed to patch me together enough so I could fly us out of there. To this day neither of us knew how he did it. But only four of them survived. I wasn't fast enough to help the other two guys." He shut his eyes. She couldn't imagine what he must be feeling—the pain of his injury, the chaos around him, and still being able to take off with gunfire around them, all the while regretting the two men who didn't make it.

"I'm so sorry. That must have been horrible for you."

"Yeah. Not a fun time. I touched down back near base and didn't wake up again until I was in Germany. I was in and out of surgery over three days putting the hip and leg back together, getting out most of the shrapnel. The big problem was infection. But I survived."

"And that's why you left the service?"

"Part of flying a helo is being able to help once you land. If I can't even stand up after putting in a cat door, you can see how worthless I am."

His words stabbed at her. "I suspect you're one of the least worthless men I know. But I can see why going to a war zone isn't in the cards for you," she said. "Can you have more surgeries to fix whatever's wrong?"

"Some things can't be fixed," he said. "It's mostly okay. But sometimes, like if I'm in an awkward position such as in the garage on cold cement for a long period, the leg just gets cranky. Then every spot that was ever cut, every nerve that ever had anything done to it, seems to wake up and say, 'hey, remember me?' It's bad. There are times I wish they'd have just cut it off. Maybe I'd even get myself one of those neat prosthetics that look like a long, flat ice skate, and maybe become an Olympic athlete."

"Gunnar, no." She placed her hand on his arm. "Thank God you got out of there with your life and managed to bring four men to safety. The doctors saved you, and your poor leg. That means a lot."

He took a deep breath. "Now you're sounding like my mama, so knock that off."

"She's right, you know."

"I tell myself that. But sometimes, I wonder why anyone bothered. So I can make cat doors and hen houses?"

"And help your parents and your friends and me. So we can smile and laugh with you instead of grieve."

"I know," he whispered. "Don't mind me. It's the pain talking. It takes a while after one of these for things to settle down."

"You need meds?" she asked.

"No. I've learned its better just to wait it out. Those pain pills cause their own set of demons. Most of which are real bad."

"I'm glad you can get by without them."

"Most of the time," he admitted.

She nodded. "Thank you for telling me. I know it wasn't easy."

"Thank you for listening, and for the beer. Both helped."

She smiled.

This time, he was able to get up from his chair, but she could see he was still in pain. It hurt her to think helping her had caused all this.

"Say, we never did name my cat," she said as they walked to the front door.

"Well, you could always give her a common cat name like Bella, Chloe, Zoe, Daisy, and so on."

"How do you know what are common cat names?" she asked.

"Most people in the country have cats. They keep mice out of your house and barn."

"Good point! But common names, no. Not for this one."

"How about something that goes along with having a possibly haunted cabin? Let's see, you could call her Boo, Crystal, Tarot, Ouija, Shadow."

"I don't know. Something more Halloween. That's what she reminds me of."

He thought a moment. "She's got a lot of the color of a pumpkin pie, but—"

"Pumpkin! That's perfect. I love it."

He smirked. "You are joking, right?"

She laughed. "No, really! Thank you. You've named my cat." She kissed him on the cheek.

His arm went around her back and his gaze held hers. His look darkened, strained, as his voice softly murmured, "That was nice. But I'd say we can do better." He drew her close and kissed her. A real kiss, one with passion and promise. She let her arms go around his neck as she realized she'd wanted to be kissed that way for a long time. And she liked it—far too much.

What am I doing? She drew back, her heart pounding over all his kiss made her feel. But she had no business feeling that way. Not now. Not even a week had passed since she'd left Slade. She decided the best thing to do was to make a joke. She smiled. "Yes, that was definitely much better."

He grinned. "I think your little Pumpkin will do a good job watching over this place. Or, at least, keeping the mice out of it."

He opened the door and stepped outside.

"Gunnar," she called, unable to keep a quaver out of her

voice. "Will you come back soon, even if I don't have a job for you to do?"

His blue eyes met hers and she saw a slight frown appear on his face. She wasn't sure why, but then he nodded and gave her a slight smile. "Sure. I'll be back."

The cat walked out of the shadows in the front yard.

"There she is," Mallory said. "Come on, Pumpkin. Come inside."

And to both their amusement, the cat did just that.

CHAPTER 13

After a breakfast of two cups of coffee during which Mallory did her best not to think about Gunnar and how right it felt to kiss him ... which meant she played the scene over and over in her mind, she turned to her email as a distraction. The first thing she learned was that Brian hadn't waited for the usual day to publish the last column she had sent him, but had put it in that morning's paper. A number of emails in reaction to it followed.

Before she opened them, a text came in from Brian. "I tried calling, but the call won't go through. Where the hell are you? I need to talk to you right away!"

She got in her car and drove closer to town until she had decent cell service, then pulled to the side of the road and phoned.

"It's not working," Brian said.

"What, exactly, isn't working?"

"More and more readers are questioning Nellie's responses. It's like some mass hysteria going on. What began as a few letters questioning her credentials for giving relationship advice has hit social media and turned into a torrent to the editors of all the syndications, saying Nellie is a fake and a scam-artist, trying to ruin their lives. They all come back to the same reasoning, if her suggestions are so great, why isn't she married? Instead of answering questions with the voice of experience, her voice has only bitterness."

"But the column is called 'Misery Loves Company' for a reason!" she complained.

"I know, but the letters are now causing the other editors to question you—her—as well. I'm sorry, Mallory," Brian said. "But this situation is out of control. It's gone from more people reading the paper due to the column, to people not reading it because they're angry at the column."

"You're kidding me."

"People pick the *Gazette* up at newsstands for free. If we find lots of papers sitting in the stands when the new edition comes out, we know we have a problem. And now, we have a problem."

"You can't blame that on my column," she reasoned.

"Nothing else has changed. So there's nothing else to blame it on."

"How do I fix it?"

"You have two choices. One is to do a mea culpa and tell everyone you're sorry you spoke so harshly to people who asked for advice. But that isn't especially easy, and might not end the complaints about your qualifications. The other way could take care of the problem, and might get more people wanting to read your column."

"Oh? Tell me!"

"Get married."

She hung up on him. There had to be a better way.

All of a sudden, an idea popped into her head. What if she were to write about the ghosts in the cabin? What if "Misery Loves Company" went from an advice column in which Nellie shared misery with her readers, to one where Nellie shared stories about matchmaking ghosts? Who didn't love a touch of the supernatural these days?

She had already talked to Jules about using the ghosts as a marketing tool. Julia had objected, but she'd come around if it worked. Besides, the advertising would be free—and would be in the New York area markets. It wasn't as if scads of New Yorkers would suddenly travel to Idaho to look for true love. But a few might. Of course, the possibility existed that the column would become so popular newspapers throughout the country might start to run it, papers closer to the Pacific Northwest. And then it might bring many more lodgers—and their money—looking for ghosts.

The cabin had a few quirks, and if she were a person who believed in woo-woo things, she might have been scared at times. But so far, she could always find a rational explanation, sort of.

The bottom line was simple: there were no such things as ghosts. But that shouldn't stop her from pretending they existed and were living in the cabin.

Since Mallory had already driven close to Crouch to find cell service, she decided to continue along the Middlefork Road until she saw a sign that read "Emma Hughes - Insurance - Real Estate." It was a little white house with a front porch and a green roof. The sign was scarcely visible.

She parked right in front of the house. No other cars were nearby. The office was empty when she entered. Not even a receptionist. Instead a bell chimed when the door opened.

A young woman stepped out of the back room. "Good morning. I'm…"

She stopped talking and gawked at Mallory. Mallory stared

back at her. She'd seen her before, in the Rusty Nail, talking in a very friendly manner to Gunnar.

"Emma Hughes?" Mallory asked.

"Yes! I'm Emma. I'm so sorry. Something distracted me. Er, can I help you?" She was trying to pull herself together but not doing a very good job of it. Basically, she was nice looking with shoulder-length light brown hair, brown eyes, and a ready smile. She wore a dress and mid-heeled shoes, but she looked like a person who'd be much happier in blue jeans. She had a healthy, tanned look that Mallory could only describe as country rosy as opposed to Manhattan pallid.

"My name is Mallory Conway and I'm part owner, along with my sisters, of the old Donnelly cabin off the Middlefork Road north of town."

Emma kept nodding as Mallory spoke. "I know the place you're talking about," Emma said. "It looks like an interesting property."

"It is. It's been in my family for generations. We've got it on the YourB&B website as a vacation rental, but a friend of mine, Gunnar McDermott, said you handle local vacation rentals. I was wondering what would be involved for you to handle renting the cabin."

Her eyes widened. "You know Gunnar?"

"Yes," Mallory said.

Emma's lips tightened. "That's a ... a good recommendation." She pushed a lock of hair behind her ear. "Are you talking about vacation, short-term rentals only, or are you seeking a full-time tenant?"

"Vacation only. I think my sisters and I will want to use it part of the year."

Emma pulled out a sheet of paper and handed it to her. "This has my fee schedule. I can provide everything from simply renting the property, to doing advertising, to overseeing its care."

Mallory gave the paper a quick scan. Since she had worked with realtors in New York, she was used to these kinds of service. Emma's write up was professionally done, appeared thorough, and the prices were dirt cheap compared to what Mallory was accustomed to. "This is great. I'll talk to my sisters about it."

"Good." Emma stood up straighter. "In the meantime, if it's all right with you, I'd love to take a look at your cabin. For all I know, someone might phone or walk in here anytime—and they do—wanting to know if anything is available for a week or even a weekend. People tend to come up here without realizing how pretty this area is with our little town and the Middle Fork of the Payette and then decide they really like it here and want to stay for a while. Since we have only one motel in town, cabins for rent are very popular and profitable."

"Sounds great. When would you be available to see it?"

"I'll be closing the office at five tonight. I can be there some fifteen, twenty minutes later. I won't bother you for long. I'd just like a sense of the place. You mentioned it's now on YourB&B?"

"Yes, and I'm sure my sister Julia would want to keep it there as well," Mallory explained.

"Not a problem. Plus, that'll give me a sense of what you think it's worth. Are you getting many renters?"

"Not at all."

Emma nodded as if that answer was what she expected. "Well, we'll see what we can do about that."

CHAPTER 14

As promised, Emma showed up at 5:15 that afternoon. Emma no sooner said "Hello" to Mallory than she meandered through the foyer and into the great room taking in everything as she went. "I've always wondered what the inside of this cabin was like. I heard that several workmen were out here earlier this year. They said the place was pretty and didn't seem to be haunted at all."

Pumpkin had been stretched out across the back of the sofa as Emma entered the great room. Seeing her, the cat stood up, arched its back, and gave a loud hiss before springing from the couch and running upstairs.

Emma stood still, her mouth open, looking afraid to take another step.

"Don't let Pumpkin bother you," Mallory said. "She was a stray, so I guess she's afraid of strangers."

"I see." Emma kept glancing at the stairs as if afraid the tiny cat might come back down and attack her.

"So you've heard the stories about the ghosts?" Mallory asked, hoping to distract Emma from being nervous about Pumpkin.

Emma's lips tightened. "Every longtime resident in town has, I'm sure. People say the cabin is haunted by the man whose portrait hangs in the parlor." With that she walked closer to the fireplace, studying the picture hanging over the mantle. "That's him, right? He's the ghost? Or one of the ghosts? I've heard some people say there's only one, others say there are two or three, although most say the whole thing is hogwash."

"I'm glad most people don't believe in such nonsense," Mallory said. One of the French doors blew open and crashed against the wall. Mallory hurried to it and shut it again. She noticed the wind had come up a little.

Emma had jumped at the noise the door made and now put her hand to her chest. "Some people say the ghost story was started by someone who only came up here infrequently and didn't want to worry about the place being vandalized. What better way to keep people out than to say it's haunted?" Her voice sounded unnaturally high.

"Actually," Mallory said with a frown, "I should think talk of ghosts would bring more people here—particularly kids trying to prove their mettle and show they aren't afraid."

"A little *Ghostbusters* thing going on, you think? 'Who you gonna call?'" Emma had worked her way to the kitchen area, was looking in the pantry and then checking out the new stainless steel kitchen appliances.

"Of course it's all silly." Mallory was feeling increasingly exasperated by the ghost talk. And when she glanced up at Elijah Donnelly's portrait, the look on his face said he was exasperated as well. "Let's go upstairs."

She showed Emma the three bedrooms and bathroom. Pumpkin must have ducked under a bed because Mallory didn't see her anywhere.

"Is there an attic?" Emma asked.

"No attic, no basement. And the garage was an afterthought, but at least we have one."

"You're quite close to the river which is a great point for renting. Let me take a quick look at your land."

Mallory led her downstairs and into the back yard.

"Nice large porch," Emma mused, taking a quick glance at the landscape. Then they returned to the great room. "It's a very nice cabin," Emma said, her back to the fireplace as she faced Mallory. "I think the problem you're having with rentals is that the price on YourB&B is simply wrong for the area. I suspect people accustomed to high priced vacation homes might find it low enough to give them pause. They could think it's a great bargain, or that there's something wrong with the cabin. But most of them probably have never heard of Garden Valley and have little to no interest in coming here. On the other hand, for those in Idaho who know this area, the price is too high. They can get much better deals, bigger and newer cabins, by contacting me. So you need help. And that's where I come in."

The fireplace mantle had some antique pewter pieces, and Mallory could have sworn a small vase moved from one side of the mantle to the other. Her breath caught, even though she told herself she was seeing things since Emma was stressing her out for some reason.

"Makes sense" Mallory murmured, tearing her gaze from the mantle and trying to pay attention to Emma.

"I can easily have this place booked almost constantly, if you wish. Best would be to simply let me know when not to schedule anyone to stay here because the family wants the place, and then I'll make sure there's no conflict. And I would gladly oversee care of the property while you and your sisters aren't here. If my plan for using this as a vacation rental works out the way I hope, the three of you could stay completely out of it if you wished."

Ker-thud!

Mallory and Emma both jumped and spun around. The peripatetic pewter vase had done a swan dive onto the fireplace hearth.

"What in the world?" Emma squeaked, her voice high. "Why did that fall?"

Mallory had been equally startled, but she refused to show it. "That darn cat! She must have jumped up there, and when the vase fell, she got scared and ran." In truth, Mallory had seen no sign of Pumpkin as she picked up the vase and put it back on the mantle.

"But... look..." Emma yelped.

Mallory spun around to see Emma pointing at the coffee table. The candy dish that had been centered on the table, was now at a far edge. Emma's mouth dropped open as her gaze jumped from Mallory to the candy dish.

"How did you do that?" Emma whispered.

Mallory tried to laugh. "I must have bumped the table as I went to pick up the vase. Ha, ha."

Emma was about to call her on that blatant lie but right then, the ice maker in the refrigerator door started spewing ice all over the floor.

Emma spun around at the noise. "Are you kidding me?" Emma screeched, glaring at Mallory. "What's going on here?"

"I'm sure it's nothing," Mallory shouted over the noise of the ice maker grinding out little cubes and then them bouncing all over the hardwood. She could imagine the stories Emma would tell about all this. "The part that holds back the ice must be malfunctioning."

Emma looked as if her hair was standing on end. "That's not the only thing malfunctioning around here!"

"Please," Mallory said, "it's just—"

The CD player suddenly turned itself on and blasted, "Every Breath You Take." Mallory gasped. She had no idea CDs from groups like The Police were even in the cabin. When the song got to the words, "I'll be watching you," Emma picked up her handbag and not saying a word, ran out of the house, pulling the door shut behind her.

Immediately, the CD player went quiet.

The ice maker stopped spitting out ice cubes.

And Mallory stood in the center of the room not knowing what in the world had just happened. It was almost, *almost,* as if the house understood when Emma said she'd take over care of the cabin. And absolutely hated the idea.

Gunnar sat in his favorite corner at the bar of the Rusty Nail when Emma stumbled inside looking white, pale, and shaky. She saw him and made a bee line in his direction.

He normally would have gotten up and left at that point, but she looked desperate to talk to him.

"Emma, what's wrong?" he asked. "Sit down before you pass out."

She dropped onto a barstool and faced him wild-eyed. "Did you tell the woman from the Donnelly cabin about me?"

He was surprised at her question and the way she was acting. "Yes. I thought it might help you both."

Butch the bartender came over.

"Whiskey. Straight," she said.

"That's not like you, Emma," Butch said as he put a glass in front of her and added a shot of whiskey.

"It is when I've encountered a ghost!" It took her three tries, but she finally drank down the shot, and then spent longer trying to get her breath back than she'd needed to finish the drink.

"A ghost?" Butch placed both hands on the bar top. He wasn't about to serve anyone else before he heard Emma's story.

"She's joking," Gunnar said.

Butch tucked in his chin and gave him an amused stare. "Doesn't look that way to me."

"Actually," Emma said, slowly calming down. "Now that I think about it, that ... that Mallory Conway is scamming me! That's what it was. She had all afternoon to rig up the cabin, and I fell for it! I think she wants people to believe the cabin is haunted."

As much as Gunnar didn't like to get involved in anything involving Emma, he couldn't help himself. "I truly cannot imagine her doing anything like that."

"I can. She's a hateful person! Conniving and awful. I don't know what her game is, but I'm not playing!"

"What do you mean by 'game'?" Gunnar asked.

Her eyes cast daggers at him. "Why don't you ask her yourself, since she's your good friend? I still can't believe you wanted me to help her. No way! Butch, how about another?"

Gunnar stood. "I'm sorry you're so upset, Emma, but Mallory isn't a person who'd scam anyone. There's no reason for her to want you to think the cabin is haunted."

"She's good," Emma added derisively. "I'll give her that. She almost had me believing her. All I can say, Gunnar, is watch your back if you're having anything to do with her. She's not as sweet as she plays at being."

He didn't have a clue what was going on, but he was going to find out. "I'm sorry, Emma," he said. "Sorry I mentioned you to her." With that, he said goodbye and fled.

CHAPTER 15

Mallory was surprised to hear a knock at her door some forty minutes later. She wondered if Emma had forgotten something in her mad rush to leave. For a moment, a twinge of uneasiness struck, but she shook it off and marched to the door. As she did, that darned CD player started playing again, this time with her mother's voice softly singing the jaunty "This Can't be Love."

Mallory paused, tempted to go and shut it off, but she was already near the front door. More convinced than ever Emma Hughes had returned—and with her came the strange electrical vibes that had caused the cabin to run amok earlier—she angrily flung the door open.

Gunnar stood before her. The last time she'd seen him, they had kissed. She froze as the memory of that kiss and what it had felt like, swarmed over her. She stared, her mind empty of words. He, too, said nothing.

Finally, she found the ability to say, "Gunnar. How … why …?"

He shifted uneasily. "Just wondering how you did last night being here alone."

She searched his eyes. Something was wrong. "I did fine. Won't you come in?"

He nodded and entered the cabin.

"Would you like some beer? Or maybe coffee? Wine? How about wine?" She hoped she didn't sound as rattled by him as she felt.

"Actually, a cup of coffee sounds good. Black."

"Coming up." She headed to the kitchen but stopped as the song continued about being too happy to be in love. She couldn't take so much joy! She spun around and marched toward the player.

Her heart was beating fast as the words reminded her of how she felt around Gunnar. She shut the player off.

"What was that?" he asked.

She swallowed hard as she rushed back to the kitchen and with shaking hands put a pod in the coffee machine, then sucked in her breath. It was just Gunnar—her pal, her buddy. He was nothing more to her ... despite the way she'd liked his kiss. "My sisters found CDs of my mother singing. I was just listening to one."

"I thought the voice sounded familiar," he said. "It's truly amazing I'd remember her voice after so many years."

"Isn't it though?" She gripped the edge of the counter.

"Have you had any luck getting Pumpkin to try her new cat door?" he asked as he sat on a stool and waited for the coffee to finish brewing.

"None whatsoever. I've never had a cat before, and this one seems to have a mind of her own."

"Typical cat. I brought you some catnip. Cats often love the smell and will follow it. Is she around?"

"She was, but then Emma from the realty office came by, and things got ... well, they got weird. Emma practically ran out the door, and I haven't seen Pumpkin since."

She handed him the coffee and proceeded to make a cup for

herself.

He took a sip. "I should tell you, I ran into Emma at the Rusty Nail. She was upset."

Mallory rolled her eyes. "Upset is mild compared to the way she left here. You'd have thought her hair was on fire."

"Or that she saw a ghost?" Gunnar suggested.

Mallory's jaw clenched. "Which is impossible."

"That's what I said," Gunnar added. Big blue eyes seemed to bore into her very soul before he added, "She thinks you played some kind of trick on her."

"*What?* Me? Is she crazy?"

"Why don't we sit out on the back porch and you can tell me all about it," Gunnar suggested. They took their coffee and sat side-by-side on the bench. "Any idea what had Emma so ... spooked?"

Mallory groaned at his bad joke, but then stared out at the mountains a moment before speaking. "I honestly have no idea. Maybe it had something to do with electricity. Can a short cause an ice maker to run by itself? Or a CD player to come on ... with a song by The Police?"

Gunnar's mouth wrinkled. "You are joking, right?"

"I wish!" she said miserably.

He pondered that a moment. "Some kind of surge, maybe? But it's hard to imagine. Although the wiring is probably old. Maybe an electrician should take a look."

She shook her head. "A big part of the renovation cost was to update the cabin's electric wiring. Julia is a stickler for things like that, so I suspect the electricity isn't as bad as you fear."

He looked stumped. "If not electricity, what's doing it?"

"Whatever it is, Emma surely won't be coming here to help us figure it out."

He snorted a laugh. "I'd say not. You should have seen her when she first showed up at the Rusty Nail. She really did think you've got ghosts out here. It was pretty funny."

"Lordy, that's all I need," she said, trying not to laugh along with Gunnar.

Pumpkin suddenly leapt onto the narrow porch railing.

"Oh, my God!" Mallory said and started to jump up before Gunnar caught her arm and stopped her.

"But she might fall off," Mallory cried.

"She's more likely to fall if you scare her by trying to grab her. Let her be, she'll be fine. And, we can see if she likes catnip." Gunnar let go of Mallory's arm and opened the little box of catnip he had put in his shirt pocket. He sprinkled some on the deck and tapped at it to make her curious.

Pumpkin jumped down and sniffed the catnip for quite a while and then rolled onto her back.

"What's she doing?" Mallory asked.

"I'd say she likes it." He stood back and watched. "I'm surprised she's not eating it. Most cats do."

"She doesn't eat anything that I've seen," Mallory said. "She never touches her food or water."

"So she's got a source outside somewhere. Maybe another home," he said.

"That's what Julia suspected." Mallory wasn't about to say her own growing suspicions about the cat—especially after watching Pumpkin's reaction to Emma Hughes.

As Gunnar added more and more catnip towards the garage, he and Mallory inched closer and closer together as they watched Pumpkin sniff it.

Gunnar propped open the cat door flap, put some catnip inside, and Pumpkin jumped through the opening.

"Success!" Gunnar said. "We'll leave the door propped open so she'll learn there's nothing to be afraid of."

"This is great," Mallory gave his hand a light squeeze of thanks, but simply touching him made a spark go through her and she let him go. Not smart, Mallory! "I want to be sure she's safe when she's here alone."

His eyes captured hers. "Does that mean you'll be heading back to New York soon?"

She wasn't sure how to answer. "After my first weekend here, I was ready to leave right away. But now, I'm starting to get used to the silence around me, and even the isolation of the cabin. Also, I'm subletting my New York apartment and expect it to be gone soon. And my job's already gone."

Gunner shook his head. "No job, no apartment. That's got to be hard, Mal. You might be here longer than you thought."

She shut her eyes. "Don't remind me."

"Come on, now." He grinned. "It's not that bad."

"That's because you didn't see the cabin when Emma was here. Sometimes …" She stopped, thinking better of what she was about to say, but she noticed Gunnar's eyebrows lift. "Anyway, I haven't had any dinner yet since I was waiting for Emma to show up. So, if I ordered a pizza to be delivered, would you help me finish it?"

"Only if I can go out and get some beer to go with it."

"I've got plenty in the fridge," she said, then added, "But you can replenish the supply next time you come by."

"I'll gladly do that." He gave her a half-smile as they both recognized her invitation and his agreement.

She smiled back, inordinately pleased by his response, and then used the cabin's landline to phone in an order. "It'll take about forty-five minutes before they make it out this way," she said. "Would you like to go down by the river for a little while?"

"Let's do it."

It was dusk as they left the house. Without thinking about it, both turned right at the end of the driveway and automatically walked to the footpath to the water's edge that they'd used as kids.

The path was rocky and even a little steep in spots as it led down to the river. Mallory had to slow down because she wore loose sandals while Gunnar went slowly because of his hip injury. "Those shoes," Gunnar said, "are going to cause you to twist your ankle as you step on a slippery rock that makes the shoe go one way and your foot another. You'd better take my arm. This stick I carry is like a third leg, so I'll be plenty steady for you."

She took his arm as they went, and did feel considerably more secure on the loose silty soil, and considerably warmer just touching him.

As the footpath turned, they saw Pumpkin sitting in the center of it as if waiting there for them. "Hello, Pumpkin," Mallory called. "How did you get down here?" But then the cat darted into the underbrush.

"I told you she doesn't like me," Mallory whispered, leaning closer to him.

Gunnar laughed. "Then there's something wrong with her."

A cooling breeze rose off the water as they neared it, the air scented with pine and a hint of sage. They could hear the soft lapping of the water against the rocks. At the river bank, several birds waddled along the water's edge, as if enjoying the evening. Gunnar pointed out a hooded merganser, and some mallards. He suddenly put an arm around her waist and pulled her to the left. "Look over there, where I'm pointing. It's a cormorant. You don't see them often."

The bird stood about three feet tall, with an orange spot on its throat. "It's huge."

"There are probably more nearby. They're usually in a group like the Canadian geese. It's not often you see one so close."

"What a beauty."

"I wouldn't go that far, but it's a neat bird."

She found she was enjoying being by the river with him. Vague memories returned of coming down here when she was young. She was only allowed to go to the river if Julia was with her, to watch her. And Julia made it clear that if Mallory put even one toe in the water, Julia would remove it from her body.

She knew Julia wouldn't really, but at the same time, she didn't dare test her.

Gunnar went over to a felled log and sat looking out at the water, now a dark greenish-blue in the setting sun.

She sat next to him. "It's so pleasant here this time of day," she said, her shoulder brushing his.

"It is," he agreed, then cocked his head as he faced her. "Of course, being with the right company helps."

Why hearing him say something sweet like that should make her heart beat faster, she had no idea, but it did. Why would simple words such as he just spoke make her feel so much happier than when Slade had asked her to marry him? What, she wondered, was wrong with her?

She couldn't help but turn to him, to meet his pale blue eyes. She never before realized how much she loved that particular eye shade ... or maybe it was because he looked back at her with such obvious, sweet desire. He leaned closer. Memories of their one kiss filled her, and she was sorely tempted for one more. She inched the tiniest bit closer, but it was enough for him to wrap her in his arms again and give her the kiss she craved.

Her arms circled his neck, and she held him tight, kissing him back. She loved the feel of him, the scent of him, even the shape of his mouth against hers. Her fingers raked through his wavy dark blond hair, to his ear, his neck, feeling the warmth of his skin, of him, even as his hands traveled over her body, as if seeking to know it, to ...

"Oh my God, the pizza," she said. She drew back and looked at her watch. "We better hurry back to the cabin so we don't miss the delivery."

"Who's hungry?" he whispered, giving her one last, quick kiss. "Okay, I guess you are."

She stood and took his hand, helping him up without saying a word. Instead of simply taking his arm, she put her arm around his waist, and he draped his arm over her shoulders as they trudged uphill on the footpath.

Back at the cabin, Mallory got them each a bottle of beer and they sat down together on the sofa. He no sooner put his arms around her than they heard a knock on the door.

"Food," she said.

"Saved by the bell," he told her with a devilish smirk.

Wearing a huge smile, she rushed to the door, opened it, and froze.

"Hello, my love."

Mallory blinked once, twice, but the image remained. Perfect suit. Impeccable tie. Styled gray hair. "Slade. What are you doing here?"

"I'm here to see you," he said. He didn't smile, but simply looked at her.

She stared, wondering how he'd found her, but then shook her head as if to clear it. "Come in."

He walked in, looking at the walls and ceiling as if he couldn't believe he was in such a place. "This is quaint," he said.

As they walked into the great room, Gunnar slowly stood.

Slade's eyes went from Gunnar to Mallory, then back to Gunnar. He stuck out his hand and approached as he introduced himself. "Slade Atchison," he said. "Mallory's fiancé."

Gunnar's mouth tightened as he shook Slade's hand. "Gunnar McDermott. Mallory's friend of many years."

"Oh?" Slade glanced at her again.

"That's right," she said, standing so that Slade had to turn his back on Gunnar to face her. "Gunnar and I knew each other as kids. We were just waiting for some pizza." Something about Slade tracking her here made her uneasy. "How did you find me?"

Slade lifted an eyebrow as he glanced over his shoulder at Gunnar, who had now sat back down. He again faced Mallory. "I tracked down your sister Carly. I remembered you telling me she'd just married the author, Alex Townson. His book publisher's CEO is a personal friend, so I gave her a call. I explained how important it was, and she gave me his phone number. Carly was easy to convince that I needed to talk to you about our wedding plans."

"But," she felt herself growing increasingly nervous about him, and raised her chin, "there are no plans."

"There will be," he stated. "We'll get over this little setback. It'll be something we'll tell our children about someday and laugh."

Children? He was aware she wanted them, but he'd always said he was too old to start over again with a baby. He must want her back even more than she imagined he did. Her mind was reeling, and she forced herself to focus on the here and now.

"Are you planning on staying here at the cabin?" she asked.

"I didn't know how you'd react to seeing me, so I thought I'd better find a different place to stay. I spoke to a very nice realtor, and she found a beautiful home for me on the other side of the highway. It's at the top of a bluff, and from there you can see the entire valley and the river. Quite charming. She called the home a cabin, but it's larger than most penthouses in New York."

"Yes, they tend to be out here," she said. "Although I suspect you'll be much more comfortable in a nice hotel in Boise. Garden Valley doesn't have the kind of amenities you're used to."

"Garden Valley has one amenity I like. You. You're the reason I'm here. To win you back. And I will."

Something about the way he said it, his level of confidence, made her realize it just might happen. Slade wasn't a man to take "no" for an answer in business. Maybe that went for his personal life as well. As he began to stroll around the room, she turned and glanced over at Gunnar. He was looking at Slade as if he were some kind of swamp creature, and he must have felt her eyes on him because he met her gaze with confusion and—she hated to see it—disappointment.

"I find this cabin terribly isolated," Slade said. "Is your sister staying with you? Or, perhaps, someone else?"

Mallory lifted her chin. "No one is."

Slade's brows furrowed. "You're alone? Are you comfortable staying in a place as remote as this all by yourself? Maybe I should stay here."

"I'm fine. I don't need protection!"

"Of course you do," Slade insisted. "You're young and beautiful and far too naïve. I hate to think of anyone taking advantage—"

"I'm sure I'm safe here," Mallory interrupted. "So there's no need to worry about me."

"But—"

"If the lady states she doesn't need your protection," Gunnar said, his voice low and firm. "I do believe it would be best if you accede to her wishes."

Slade spun toward him, and did a head-to-toe raking of Gunnar's clothes, body, the cane ... "And I suppose you're ready to offer any help that might be needed."

Gunnar eyed him coldly. "I am a neighborly sort."

Just then, there was another knock at the door.

"I'll get it," Gunnar said, slowly standing and making his way to the door. "It must be our pizza."

Slade faced Mallory and in a rushed voice said, "I don't understand any of this. What are you doing here with *that*?"

"Gunnar's a friend," she insisted. "You don't need to read anything more into it."

Slade regarded Gunnar leaning on the cane as the delivery

man made change for the pizza. He gave Mallory a look that said he didn't believe her.

Mallory stiffened, but said nothing. She owed him no explanations.

Gunnar brought the pizza in, put it on the kitchen island, and opened the box. "This looks great."

Mallory hurried over to the counter intent on diffusing the tension in the room. "I love the smell that fills the room when you first open a pizza box." She took three dishes from the cupboard, forks, and napkins. "Are you hungry, Slade? Want to join us?"

"I guess I'll have one piece," he said.

"How did you get here?" she asked.

"My private plane, of course. Then I had a car waiting for me."

"The Boise airport?" she asked.

"Yes."

She put a slice of pizza on Slade's plate and set it on the dining table. He grimaced as he sat. She dished out for Gunnar and herself while he opened bottles of beer for them.

"Beer?" she asked Slade.

"Do you have any bottled water?"

"Yes, I do." She got him a bottle from the fridge, and then she and Gunnar joined Slade at the table.

Slade didn't take his eyes off Gunnar as he twisted the top off the water bottle. Gunnar stared back with equal resolve.

"Extra Parmesan, anyone?" Mallory asked, waving the jar between them, breaking their death stares.

"No, thanks," Gunnar said, taking a sip of his beer and putting the beer down with a thud on the table.

Slade chugged down half his bottle of water, then smacked the plastic water bottle down with such force, Mallory was sure it would break.

"How about some extra pepper?" she suggested holding up a

bottle.

"Definitely," Gunnar said, taking the red pepper flakes from her. He sprinkled some onto his pizza slice.

Slade snorted. "Why did you even bother?" He picked up the bottle and shook at least twice as many flakes onto his own slice.

They ate the pizza in silence.

"I think one piece is enough for me," Mallory said, then looked from one man to the other. "Did you need to leave? Either of you?"

"I could go for another slice." Gunnar reached for more pizza.

"Same here," Slade said. He then poured on the pepper.

This time, Gunnar used more pepper than Slade, and added Parmesan.

Slade did the same.

Only one slice was left. They glared at each other and Slade grabbed it. He put it on his place and picked up the pepper. He turned the bottle upside down to shake out some flakes when the plastic top with pour-holes fell off. The top and all the flakes landed on his pizza. He was putting the now-empty pepper jar down, staring with shock at pepper flakes all over his plate, when his hand must have hit his water bottle because suddenly it not only fell over but somehow managed to fall in his direction. Water splashed from the bottle across the counter and onto his lap.

He jumped up. "What the—"

"I'll get paper towels," Mallory said.

"I didn't touch the water. How did it spill?" He looked down at himself as the water left a large, round stain over the entire crotch area of his trousers.

"Oh, my," Mallory said with a grin. "I hope you don't have to see anyone looking like that."

"Probably not the first time," Gunnar muttered under his

breath.

Black fury flashed in Slade's eyes. "I'll be back here tomorrow, Mallory, around lunch time. We need to talk."

She showed him to the door. "See you then."

He didn't say a word but stormed through it and to his car.

She went back into the great room to find Gunnar leaning back in his chair and looking at her strangely.

He shook his head. "You were engaged to *him?*"

She began to clear the table. She hadn't expected such a tone from Gunnar. "I was."

"He looks old enough to be your father."

"He's prematurely gray, that's all."

"Horse ... pucky." Gunnar scowled. "He must be filthy rich."

She put her hands on her hips. "I don't like your tone."

He raised his chin. "Actually, I don't need to ask. He made it a point to tell you he got here on his *private plane*, and that he's friends with your *new brother-in-law's boss*. And while I was paying for the pizza, I saw a big Audi on your driveway with his driver sitting in it."

Mallory wiped off the table top. "I don't believe we have anything more to talk about tonight."

"So what happened between you two? Why no wedding?"

She shrugged. "I changed my mind about getting married, that's all."

"Why?"

Good question, she thought. And answered honestly as she could. "I'm not sure."

He snorted, eying her. "For a guy like that to come out here, I'd guess he really is in love with you. But then, how could he not be? Did you meet someone else? Someone richer, maybe?"

"That's hateful and you know it's not true!" She put her hands on the top rail of the chair she'd used earlier. "Why this third degree?"

"Just curious." He tried to sound calm. "You're here. This rich dude, your fiancé, comes after you, and you clearly didn't want to be alone with him. He seems to love you, and you did agree to becoming his wife, so I don't get it. What more could you ask for in a husband?"

She stared at the distant wall instead of a man beside her. "Maybe the problem is that I have no answers to that question."

"Do you still love him?" Gunnar asked.

She shut her eyes a moment. Still love Slade? Did she ever? "I don't know."

"I see," he murmured, and then stood. "If you're afraid he might come back and hassle you or anything, I can spend the night here ... on the sofa."

She was torn, wanting him to stay, but knowing it wasn't necessary. "I'm not afraid of him, if that's what you're asking. He's just ... he's a man used to getting his way. He can be extremely persuasive, and I don't want him to turn on the charm and make me feel guilty for trying to say no."

"Guilt?" His eyebrows rose. "I see. Guilt is a powerful thing to hold over a person."

She remembered when she first started dating Slade, how he'd casually let it be known to her how expensive the places were that he brought her to. And later, when he started giving her gifts, he'd make it clear, for example, that the bracelet didn't have any old emerald in it, but it had a high-saturation grade Columbian emerald. Once he learned about her background, he could subtly point out that he, and no one else—especially not her family—had ever been that good to her. It was enough to make her feel guilty if she wasn't overjoyed by him. "Slade is a master at it," she murmured.

"I'm not surprised." He grimaced as he walked to the door. "Well, if anything comes up—anytime of the day or night, don't hesitate to call me."

"Thanks, Gunnar," she said.

"Anytime, kid." He then left without a backward glance.

CHAPTER 16

Mallory could scarcely sleep that night. And it wasn't fear of ghosts that got to her. In fact, Slade's sudden appearance had all but completely driven the episode with Emma Hughes from her mind.

But she couldn't as easily drive away thoughts of Gunnar and how she felt whenever she was with him. And to top it off, he was a great kisser. But that was lust, nothing more. Her mother had warned her how feelings of lust—attractive faces, great bodies, melt-your-heart gazes, *sexiness*—could cloud a woman's mind, make her do things she'd spent a lifetime regretting. Roxanne had carefully schooled her on the type of man she should put her faith in, a man who could take care of her, place her on a pedestal, and provide for her every want.

Roxanne would never have approved of Gunnar.

She kept waking during the night and finally gave up trying to go back to sleep.

At five a.m., she opened up her Dear Nellie emails, wondering if she still had a job at the *Village Gazette*. Her only source of income at the moment seemed to be hanging by a very thin thread.

She went through her inbox. Half way through, she found a letter that interested her.

Dear Nellie,

I have a soul mate. I will call him Brad. He is perfect for me and I am madly in love with him. He says he is with me, as well. The problem is that he is married and has three children. He refuses to leave his family for me, and he says that they must be the priority in his life. Of course he must say that because he is such a good man. We had a brief affair, but he called it off saying he was too consumed with guilt to continue. I dated others and met a nice fellow I will call Joe. Joe and I have dated for a year. He loves me and asked me to marry him. The problem is, I still love Brad. My friends tell me to forget Brad—that a bird in the hand is worth, etc., and since Joe is such a sweet guy, I should marry him. I am torn. Can you help me? [Signed] Conflicted in Connecticut

Oh, wow, Mallory thought. How she would love to tear Conflicted a new one for even thinking of using poor Joe that way. What a self-centered moron! How would Conflicted feel if she found out that a guy married her not because he loved her, but because she happened to be "the best around" at the moment?

But instead of saying what she wanted to, because of Brian's latest edict, Mallory had to be "nice."

Dear Conflicted,

Your friends are right when they advise you to forget about Brad. He's trying to do what's right for his family, and for you to be there mooning over him like a lovesick cow ...

Scratch that! She hit the delete key several times.

...for you to hope he'll return to you, is doing no one any good. He rightly feels a responsibility toward his children. Many studies show that fathers are extremely important to the well-being of children—girls as well as boys. For Brad to recognize that, is a wonderful thing.

"And believe me, I can tell you all about what it's like to have a crappy father," Mallory muttered. Roxanne had given Eric Conway full custody of Mallory when they divorced. She was six at the time. She never forgave the way Eric—she hated to use the title of father with that man—had brought her to Roxanne's house when she was eleven years old and left her there. She never even got a birthday card from him after that. She went back to her response.

And then there's Joe. You asked how you should respond to his proposal. You sound like a good person, Conflicted. That means you do know what you need to do. You know it isn't right to marry Joe when you don't love him. Especially since he's such a nice fellow, he deserves someone who loves him the way he loves you.

So do everyone a favor. Tell Joe the truth and let Brad know it's really over. And then, hold your head high, go out there, and find yourself someone you genuinely love, not someone who's a substitute for another man.

She was about to end the letter, but for some reason she hesitated. Her thoughts turned to the cabin.

The image of Elijah Donnelly wasting away grieving for his dead wife filled her. And the wife ... the hauntingly sad eyes of the woman's face that Mallory saw—or, imagined she saw—in the mirror her first night here came back to her. She remembered them clear as day.

Was that woman Elijah's wife? Was she the nameless mother who died giving birth to a son—a son she never got to hold, never got to nurture as he grew into a fine man, a soldier?

What if they really were trapped here, those three, Elijah, his wife, and his son, Lucas?

From Roxanne's stories, Elijah had built the cabin alone, wanting to fill it with love for his little family, but then tragedy struck. Could it have been his love that trapped the family here? Could it have been his dream to help others find the happiness in this life that his family was denied?

She had no idea if ghosts or hauntings "worked" that way, or if the madness of her life over this past week finally drove her to the brink of insanity, but if the only joy the ghosts had was to bring lovers together, she should help them. No one in this life or the next should look as sad as Elijah's wife did.

She wrote an ending for her column:

How do you do that? Good question! My sister went to an out-of-the-way cabin where she met the man of her dreams and a month later, married him. A number of others have gone there and been similarly fortunate. As my readers know, I haven't exactly been lucky in love myself. I'm thinking of giving the place a try. I call it the Cabin of Love and Magic. [Signed] Nellie Ever-Seeking

Mallory reread her response and smiled. Not only was the response to Clueless as sweet as Brian said it should be, but she had added a tease that she was sure would cause people to write and ask for more information about the Cabin of Love and Magic.

Should she tell them, or not? She hadn't decided yet, but needed to see what kind of results the column got. Still, if there really were ghosts here, she hoped they'd help her come up with an answer.

The next day at noon, Slade picked Mallory up in the Audi, driving it himself. He was wearing country club attire—a white pullover with a collar, tan slacks, and dark brown Italian leather moccasins.

"This is a nice rental car," she said facetiously.

"You look lovely," he said as a quick aside, glancing at her white sundress and teal high-heeled sandals. "My dealership had it waiting for me at the airport. That's the kind of service one gets after years of leases on multiple cars."

"I can imagine."

"Where to?" he asked.

"There are very few choices. If we stay in Crouch, we have a choice of the Rusty Nail, or buying pre-made sandwiches at the grocery store."

"The Rusty Nail it is. I saw it as I drove through the town this morning. My stomach is on East coast time and I'm famished. Is this Rusty Nail any good?"

"Three-star Michelin rating."

"I wouldn't expect less," Slade said with a smirk.

They reached the restaurant in a matter of minutes. Mallory was afraid he was going to question her about running out on what should have been their wedding day, but he didn't. When the conversation veered in a direction that could have led to such a discussion, he directed it elsewhere and spent most of the meal telling her about a huge condo and townhouse development he was building along the ocean near Savannah, Georgia. She tried to pay attention to what he was saying, but after a while she found herself daydreaming and nodding. She doubted he even noticed.

"So tell me about you," Slade said suddenly.

"Me? I'm okay," she said.

"Are you ready to go home? You can fly back with me on my plane. I'd like nothing so much as to show you the whole country from miles high. It's beautiful, but not nearly as much as you."

One thing about Slade, she thought, since he dealt with so many difficult people in business, he could turn on the charm with ease. She knew that was exactly what he was doing, but it did cause her to remember why she'd been attracted to him in the first place.

"I'm not ready, yet."

He stared into her eyes. "It's okay, sweetheart. Take your time and know I'll always be there for you."

She swallowed hard. "I appreciate that."

"Now," he said after he paid for the lunch, "that we've had these fine hamburgers, if the amount of grease hasn't killed us, is there anywhere you'd like to go?"

They headed out to his car. "No. I really should go back to the cabin. I have some work to do."

"Oh?"

She then realized he probably knew she had been fired from Piaget Realty. "I'm working on the cabin. My sisters want to make it a vacation rental. With my experience in real estate, I should be able to help them do that."

"I see," he murmured with a frown and the uncharitable thought struck Mallory that he might have been glad she'd been fired. No job, no income, and soon, no apartment. Nothing like desperation to make one look at a rich man's proposal with fresh eyes.

As he headed back toward the cabin, he asked, "Where would we end up if we stayed on this road?" he asked.

"Forest land. It's huge and has a number of campgrounds."

"Ah yes. I read about all the national forests in Idaho—that it's a land of steep mountains, fast rivers, and dense forests."

"That sounds about right."

"Do you mind if I take a quick look at it?"

"Oh, well—"

"It'll only take a minute."

"Okay, sure."

Slade drove into the forest. Little sunlight found its way through the tall trees. The road hugged the river, and there were interesting views around every bend—and there were lots of bends. Mallory suggested he turn around, but he claimed he was too fascinated by the beauty of the surroundings to do that. Yeah, right. She was starting to realize exactly how much he enjoyed having power over her. Eventually, she stopped saying anything. They kept going north for nearly an hour, even after the paved road ended, which slowed them down considerably.

Slade found a turn-out spot and stopped the car. They got out, and he walked over to the river and peered all around. "It's hard to believe such emptiness still exists in this country," he said after a long while.

"This is nothing," Mallory replied. "I've been told that much of the land in the state is roadless. Gunnar says this road is like Grand Central Station compared to those other areas."

"Then it must be so," Slade said. If sarcasm were blood, he'd need a transfusion. "But here, if someone were to put in townhouses, and a golf course, this could be quite a vacation paradise."

Fortunately, Mallory thought, it was state land. "You certainly have vision," she muttered.

He nodded in agreement.

They soon left. Between the warm car, the big lunch, and since she hadn't slept well, Mallory fell asleep as Slade drove.

"You're home," he said, as he stopped the car.

She opened her eyes. "Oh, I'm so sorry!"

"That's okay." He stroked her arm. "I like it that you're so comfortable with me you can relax and sleep. It makes me feel good."

She sat up straight and pulled her arm away. "Well, that's better than you telling me how rude I am!"

"So, can I see this cabin of yours this afternoon since, now, you don't have any protective old friends sitting around inside?"

"Maybe another time, as I said earlier, I really have a lot to do today. And I didn't expect our jaunt out to the Boise National Forest to be so time consuming."

His face grew pinched. "Well, can I at least see you tomorrow?"

She drew in her breath. "Don't you need to get back to all your businesses? You're always so busy when you're in New York."

He grinned. "You aren't the only one who's able to work from home." He leaned close. She slightly turned her head, causing him to redirect his kiss to her cheek.

She opened the car door and got out.

He straightened. "Have a good rest of the day. Even though you're busy, you still need to eat dinner. Would you mind terribly if I joined you tonight?"

How could she say she'd mind? His question made it awkward to answer. And he certainly hadn't come here to go fishing or hunting like most tourists in the area. "Fine," she said finally. It seemed easier than to try to go into any explanations that he'd probably feel obligated to counter, and on and on.

"I'll pick you up at eight."

She nodded. "All right."

He gave her a dashing grin and drove off.

CHAPTER 17

Gunnar was busy working on an electrical circuit when Nathan called him. "Gunnar, look."

"Look at what?" Gunnar asked. "This is delicate work."

Nathan pointed to the driveway and Gunnar saw Mallory getting out of her Subaru.

"Wonder what she wants?" Gunnar muttered. He hoped his words sounded cold, but he couldn't stop the sudden thumping of his heart at the sight of her—long legs, a knock-out body, and thick black hair. The memory of how it had felt to hold her, only to have her fiancé—or ex-fiancé—show up, was almost more than he could bear. "Maybe her fiancé needs a jump start," he growled as he grabbed a rag to wipe his hands, then took his cane and went out to meet her.

"Car trouble?" he asked.

"No. I took a chance you'd be here on a Sunday, and it turns out I was right," she said.

"Yeah, well, one of my guys is having troubles, and we got backed up. It happens," Gunnar said. "That's why I'm here. What's your excuse?"

He could see her wince at his words, which made him feel bad. But it couldn't be helped. And she looked nervous. "I just wanted to explain about Slade and ... and other things."

He drew himself up, squaring his shoulders, as he wondered just what her game was. "You don't owe me any explanations."

"But I feel as if I do." She tucked a strand of hair behind her ear. "Is there somewhere we can talk?"

Her expression said this wasn't a talk about auto parts. "Let's go to the Rusty Nail. I think this might call for a beer." He turned to Nathan. "Take a break. I'll be back before long."

They drove separately to the Rusty Nail. Gunnar got there first and as he approached the door, Emma Hughes came out.

"Gunnar!" she said with a big smile and a quick hug. "I just got myself a sandwich-to-go, but if you're here for a late lunch, I can join you."

"I'm sorry, but I'm here for a ... a business meeting."

Emma glanced past him and saw Mallory approaching, then faced him with the saddest puppy dog eyes he'd ever seen on a grown woman. "Oh? Oh, I see. Well, don't let me detain you." Her cheeks reddened, and she hurried on her way.

"Did I interrupt something?" Mallory asked as she reached his side.

"Not at all. Let's take a booth." He held the door open for her. As they passed by the bar, he ordered two draft beers.

They sat and faced each other. Mallory kept folding and unfolding her hands until Butch set the beers in front of them. Then she placed her hands flat on the table top.

"I hadn't realized how much your friendship means to me," she began.

Friendship? Yeah, right. His lips tightened. His feelings, exactly.

"We go back many years," she continued, "and when I hear you talk about those days, I see that not only do you remember more about my past than I do, but you even know Carly and Julia better than I do."

He nodded, having no idea where this was going.

"Because of that, I like you. A lot. And that means you deserve to know just how crazy everyone thinks I am. Or, if they're right, how crazy I really am."

What kind of gibberish was this? he wondered. "You're one of the sanest people I've ever met," he said. "Where is all this coming from?"

"You need to know that"—she took a long drink of beer, then fidgeted as nervously as if she were about to confess to a murder—"Slade Atchison isn't the first person I've ever been engaged to."

The way she announced it, he guessed it was a big deal to women. "So you've been engaged before. And, I'm guessing, no marriages, no divorces, right?"

She nodded.

He shrugged. "Well, then, seems to me, that puts you ahead of the game compared to what most folks go through these days."

She shut her eyes a moment. "I need to tell you the whole story."

He both wanted to hear it, and *not* to hear it. But he had the good sense to let her talk.

"The first time I got engaged," she said, "I was eighteen. I was living with my mother in the San Fernando valley near Los Angeles. I was a valley girl. Anyway, Roxanne had just broken up with the man who would've been husband number five, and I think she was feeling bitter about men in general."

"Okay," he said cautiously.

"I dated Arturo for two years in high school. He played baseball and had been picked up by a minor league team. I chose him over college. We were going to marry and end up wherever baseball sent him. Roxanne threw a conniption. But I insisted. She gave me a bridal shower and bought me a wedding dress, and everything. All the time, though, she kept insisting I was making a mistake—that Arturo and I would be broke and without any prospects for a good job if we didn't get more education. Finally, on the night of our bridal dinner, I was so upset and nervous about the future, I told Arturo I couldn't marry him. I said we were too young, and I needed to go to college. I'd hoped our relationship could survive long distance, and after I graduated, he might even be in the majors, and we'd both be more ready for marriage."

"That must have been really hard," Gunnar said.

"It was. It hurt, but at the same time, the idea of going to college, being on my own, was exciting. In any case, our relationship didn't survive. Arturo never made it to the majors, and while I was still in college getting a useless degree in English, he married someone else."

Gunnar analyzed her words. "So, thanks to Roxanne, your relationship fell apart. But in her defense, it does sound as if you two were plenty young. What happened is nothing to be ashamed of. Kids make mistakes."

"True. But then there was Wendell."

"Wendell?" Gunnar repeated.

She nodded. "After Arturo, I vowed to have nothing to do with any man who was involved in sports. Then, to help pay for my college tuition, I got a part-time job in an insurance office. Big mistake. But an even bigger mistake was when I dated a co-worker, Wendell Spitz. He was an insurance claims adjustor. He liked fast foods and movies that involved car chases, but he would sit through chick flicks with me."

"Oh, my." Gunnar couldn't suppress a shudder. "That man was truly in love."

She couldn't help but smile at his expression. "I'm afraid so.

In fact, he was willing to do anything I wanted. Roxanne started saying I really should concentrate more on marriage than college, maybe because I was still living at home. So, since Wendell seemed to adore me, but was shy and unsure of himself, I proposed to him."

Gunnar found himself stunned, perplexed, and more than slightly amused. For the first time, he had to wonder, did she not realize how gorgeous, smart, and desirable she was? "You proposed?"

"I had thought about it for quite a while," she admitted folding her hands on the table. "I knew Wendell would never abandon me the way my father had. And even though Roxanne took me in, she hadn't wanted to. Wendell would be true blue, completely devoted. And as expected, he said yes. I picked out a ring I loved, and he bought it for me, even though it was more than he could afford. Roxanne wasn't thrilled by him, however. She kept saying, 'Are you sure you can't do better than Wendell Spitz? Do you really want to become Mrs. Spitz?'"

Gunnar bit his bottom lip, the last thing he could let himself do was grin, but Roxanne's words were funny. Mal must have read his mind because she glared at him. He did all he could to wipe any hint of amusement from his eyes. "What did Wendell think of Roxanne?"

"You know, I never asked him. I think she scared him. Whatever, I gave Roxanne the money to throw a bridal shower for me—it wouldn't have been cool to throw it for myself, especially since the only people there were from my work. Anyway, at the shower I overheard two women talking about Wendell and saying how dull he was. They couldn't imagine being married to someone like him. And then one of them said, 'Mallory must love power, because she'll have it all. Wendell never did anything on his own, and never will.'

"I swear, I was so embarrassed, not only by what they said

but because everything they said was absolutely true. The next day, I gave Wendell back the ring he'd bought for me."

"Wow," Gunnar said.

"I know." She glanced heavenward. "I quit my job and never went back. The whole thing was beyond embarrassing."

"And then came Slade."

She shook her head.

He swallowed hard. "No?"

"I finally met someone that Roxanne approved of," she said. "And the few girlfriends I had approved, too. I had just gotten a new part-time job at a bank and met one of the customers who was a golf pro."

"Back to sports?" Gunnar asked.

"Yes. But he wasn't just starting out. He was good at what he did and often played in tournaments and even won. He asked me out and Roxanne had visions of him becoming the next Tiger Woods. Or at minimum someone who could bring in quite a bit of money."

Gunnar nodded.

"Anyway, when I graduated from college, he gave me a present of free golf lessons from him."

Gunnar could well imagine where this was going. He ran a hand through his hair. "Of course he did."

"Exactly. One thing led to another, and—this time, I was determined not to rush things—we'd been together over a year when he proposed. I said yes, and Roxanne was beside herself with joy."

Gunnar's teeth were grinding at this point. "Sounds perfect."

"Not quite. I noticed that Colin—that was his name—had a way with women, and that lots of women were always around him wanting to get lessons or play rounds of golf with him. I mean, that was how the two of us got close—especially when he stood behind me and wrapped his arms around me to show me how to swing."

Gunnar's stomach churned at the idea of Mallory with a sleazeball like that. "I can imagine."

"I told Roxanne I simply didn't trust him. And shouldn't I trust that my husband would be faithful? But Roxanne was adamant that everything I was worried about with him was in my head, and he was the perfect man for me. She said I'd finally done something right. I would soon become Colin's wife and my life would become 'perfect.' I went along with everything. This time, things went very far. Our wedding was at an exclusive clubhouse connected to a golf course, and lots and lots of people were there—important people. Since my father was nowhere in the picture, we were going to do the avant-garde thing of having Roxanne walk me down the aisle, plus, the big event during the reception was to be Roxanne singing 'Endless Love.' And in case the party-goers demanded an encore, she practiced 'I Will Always Love You' to show she had as strong a voice as Whitney Houston. And, if you know the words to the song—about a couple leaving each other—she didn't care that it was scarcely appropriate for a wedding."

Gunnar kept his mouth shut. He always knew Roxanne was a piece of work, but he didn't think she'd try to hog the spotlight at her own daughter's wedding. He raised his eyebrows and nodded sagely.

"So, I kept forcing myself to go through with it. It was already weighing on my mind that I'd ducked out on two engagements, and I didn't want to be a three-time loser. Roxanne was happy, Colin was happy, the bridesmaids and groomsmen seemed pleased. Everyone but me. Finally, we were at the clubhouse. I was in my dress, and the music started playing Pachebel's Canon. That's when I panicked. I couldn't do it. Roxanne was furious. She took my arm and pulled me out of the clubhouse to walk to the portico where Colin and the pastor stood waiting. She let go of me for a moment to smooth her dress, head high, shoulders back—and that's when I turned, ran, and kept running."

"Holy smoke!" He shook his head. "You really were a runaway bride." All of a sudden, he found himself smiling. "I must admit, I am impressed."

"It's nothing to joke about! People told me that someday I'd be able to laugh at it. But I still can't. Roxanne wouldn't speak to me after that. Colin wouldn't either. I didn't care about him, but Roxanne not taking anymore of my calls or anything—that hurt. And she never forgave me—the embarrassment of her life, she called it. I never even heard from her when she started having problems with her heart. The next thing I knew, a friend of hers called to say she'd died."

"I'm sorry," he murmured. Despite Roxanne's flaws, and there were many, he saw that Mallory had cared about her mother.

"But all that was years later," Mallory said. "Right after the wedding fiasco, I moved to New York City and found a job as a listing assistant at Piaget Realty. And there I've been until I came here last week. After running away from yet another marriage." She covered her face with both hands.

"Hey, stop that." He took hold of her hands and kept them in his. "It's okay, Mal."

She looked ready to cry. "But it's not. It's ridiculous. I'm ridiculous. I should just shoot myself! Or at least enter a nunnery. I'm not sure which would be a bigger penance."

"You don't mean that." Gunnar gave her hands a light squeeze. "You've had a bout of bad luck, that's all. From what you've said, you were lucky not to marry any of those guys. And hasn't Slade come here to win you back? So you can't be as awful as you think you are."

"He says he still loves me." She sighed. "Maybe I haven't been fair to him, lumping him in with other losers who wanted to marry me. I guess I didn't realize how important I must be to him. Maybe I was too hasty running off like I did. And maybe because of my past, I was just scared of the whole marriage thing. But I wanted you to understand all of it."

He felt sick. That wasn't the reaction he'd hoped for. But what could he do? He should say something, but what? Any attack on the guy would only make her defend him. So he kept quiet. He didn't like it one bit, but he could understand the whole picture. He'd heard a fair amount about Roxanne and her many husbands, and how she would give up custody of her children whenever she got a divorce. People scoffed at and derided her for doing it, but nobody thought about the effect it had on her daughters.

All Roxanne's daughters were intelligent, sensitive girls, and he couldn't help but wonder if Mallory wasn't the most delicate of them all.

"It'll be okay." He let her hands go. She had a decision to make. All he knew was he shouldn't have let himself touch her, shouldn't have let himself feel how silky her skin was and imagine how soft and delicate she must be all over. He could understand too well why those other guys had proposed. And from her story, it was crystal clear she'd been well taught that the man she married needed to be someone rich, in a big city, and preferably powerful.

It was good he'd never thought about getting married. For one thing, he couldn't imagine anyone wanting to marry a small town, disabled, auto mechanic. And for sure, not anyone as smart, beautiful, and fascinating as Mallory Conway.

What in the world had he been thinking to get involved in her life, let alone hoping that something more might develop between them ... despite the way she had looked at him when they'd kissed. "I appreciate you telling me." His voice was soft, hurting. "You do what you must, and just remember, I'm here. I'm your friend and always will be."

She looked at him a long time, as if that wasn't exactly what she'd hoped to hear. But he wondered if she even knew what she wanted to hear from him. She took a long draught of her beer and then stood. "I should go. But thank you for listening." She bent and kissed his cheek, then hurried out the door.

CHAPTER 18

That night, Gunnar and Nathan were seated at the bar at Mama's Folly. A country-western band was playing. They were drinking beer and listening to the music.

"Hello," Emma Hughes walked over to the two men and smiled. She leaned an arm on Gunnar's shoulder. "How are you guys tonight?"

"Okay," Nathan said.

Gunnar mumbled something similar. Ever since Emma split up with her old boyfriend, who was never going to make anything of himself, she'd been popping up wherever he was and looking at him with a glint in her eye that he might have liked, had it come from a woman he was interested in. But Emma Hughes would never be that woman.

"I'm sorry about the way I acted after visiting the old Donnelly cabin," she said to Gunnar. "You must be wondering what kind of nutcase I am, carrying on about ghosts and such."

"I have no idea what went on out there," Gunnar said. "I suggested to Mallory that she get an electrician to look at it."

Emma forced a smile. "You're so helpful to everyone,

Gunnar McDermott, I just don't know what we women would do without you."

Nathan started coughing and turning red, having nearly choked on his gulp of beer. Gunnar jumped to his feet and slapped Nathan's back a couple of times. Nathan was also "single, but looking," as he put it. The two men couldn't help but give each other a knowing glance that was a mixture of both amusement and horror over the way Emma always gushed over Gunnar.

Now, standing, Gunnar spotted Mallory and Slade Atchison walk into Mama's. Slade, with his slicked back, styled gray hair, sports jacket and tie, appeared completely out of place. The two of them took a seat at a table near the wall. Gunnar couldn't help but smirk at the confused look on Slade's face before he followed Mallory's lead and pulled out his own chair and sat.

"I saw the old Donnelly cabin," Emma said to Nathan.

"You did?" Nathan's eyes jumped from her to Gunnar.

As soon as Gunnar sat again, Emma leaned her shoulder against his as she continued talking to Nathan. "I already told Gunnar about it. God, but it's a weird place. I can't imagine any woman in her right mind staying there more than one night, if that. I suspect the latest Donnelly to try to stay there will soon give up just like everyone else in the family did. In fact, she might be on her way back to New York already. I know I could never stay in a place so creepy."

"I'd say she hasn't gone anywhere yet," Gunnar said. "She's sitting by the far wall having dinner with her former fiancé."

"Former fiancé?" Emma said, trying to see where he was looking. "Him? Well, I'll be. It all makes sense now. My, but he is handsome! A bit old for her though. But rich. Women like her always look for rich ones, you know."

"She looks even prettier than usual," Nathan said, eying Mallory. "Especially compared to the way she looked that first morning."

"What morning?" Emma asked, looking from one man to the other.

"I always thought she was cute," Gunnar admitted, ignoring Emma's question. "And I felt sorry for her, the way she had to tag along with her big sisters. They even tried to ditch her a few times. Especially Julia. She was one mean kid."

"They were all kind of odd," Nathan said. "Like their mother, who was something else."

"I don't remember them," Emma said. "My mother wouldn't let me have anything to do with them. She said they were white trash."

Gunnar just shook his head and decided it was safest to say nothing. Emma was just preening—trying to make herself look good, when all she was doing was making herself smaller than ever.

"I never heard anything like that," Nathan said. "All I know is, when the girls' mother would get up and sing at the Fourth of July picnic and stuff, everyone enjoyed it. She had a great voice. I heard she used to sing and dance and act on stage. I didn't think she was trashy. I thought she was great."

Emma ordered herself a beer and sat down with them.

Gunnar faced her. "What did you mean, earlier, when you said 'it all makes sense now?'"

"Hmm. Maybe I shouldn't say."

"Why not?" Gunnar asked.

"You're right. Why not?" She eased closer to the two men and lowered her voice. "Last week, I got a call from a rich New Yorker's assistant that his boss wanted to immediately rent the very best house in Garden Valley in or near Crouch. I said, '*What?*' thinking I certainly wasn't hearing right. But that was what he said. I named a few places, but they were either too far away or not fancy enough. Finally, the assistant offered to pay so much money for the right house for one week's rental, that I made a few phone calls. The Beemis family was out of town for a couple months, so I called them with the offer of $3500 a night for seven nights. Plus a ten-grand deposit. Charlie Beemis took it, saying I had to make sure nothing bad happened to the place. I'm watching it real close, believe me. And that man, with Mallory Conway, is the one who rented it."

Emma went on and on about how rich Slade Atchison must be until Gunnar was ready to leave the bar, but at the same time, he didn't want to go anywhere when Mallory was still there with her ex-fiancé—emphasis on the ex, at least in his mind. He couldn't help but wonder if Slade was still an "ex" in Mallory's mind.

Finally, the two of them finished their meal. He noticed they didn't do much talking, and Mallory scarcely seemed to smile, let alone laugh. A couple of times, Slade even took out his phone and answered it.

Slade raised a finger and caught the waitress's attention. He seemed to be ordering coffee or dessert, or both. Gunnar guessed the two would be there a while longer. Good. The later it got, the better he liked it. Old men like Slade should go to bed early. Alone. Or so he hoped.

He noticed Mallory kept turning around and looking at the band. He guessed she still liked country music. She certainly had heard enough of it during summers up here when they were kids. He even remembered hearing her mother sing some classic Loretta Lynn and Patsy Cline songs.

He also saw that Mallory appeared more interested in the music and dancers than she did her ex-fiancé. Which showed extremely good taste on her part.

She really did seem to want to dance. He couldn't take watching that oaf with her do nothing about it. But Slade Atchison wasn't the type to be caught dead on Mama's dance floor.

Emma was still chattering on and on about something, when

Gunnar said to Nathan, "Remember how Mal liked to dance when she was a kid?"

"No," Nathan replied.

"Sure you do! Why don't you invite her to two-step?" He gave Nathan's shoulder a light shove. "I'll bet she doesn't have a chance to dance that way in New York."

"What?" Emma cried. "Are you suggesting Nathan interrupt her when she's with her fiancé? I don't think so!"

"*Ex*-fiancé," Gunnar said.

"Emma's right. Why should I bother her?" Nathan asked Gunnar.

"Because she's an old friend who deserves to dance if she wants to. You can see her feet tapping from here, and she's way more interested in the music than the geezer she's with."

"He's not a geezer," Emma insisted. "I know I wouldn't throw him out of bed for eating crackers."

Gunnar had to bite his tongue not to say what came to mind with that statement.

The song ended, and he watched Mallory join others enthusiastically clapping for the country-western band and singer. Gunnar had been right that she was paying attention.

"I don't care much for dancing, myself," Emma said with a quick glance at Gunnar's cane as she sidled closer to him.

Another jaunty song began. Gunnar gulped down some beer, then put his glass on the bar. "Come on," he said to Nathan.

Nathan followed as Gunnar headed over to Mallory's table. Mallory glanced up as they approached.

"Gunnar, Nathan, hello," she said, and made a quick name-only introduction of Nathan and Slade. "Are you two having dinner here?"

Gunnar answered. "We just came in for beers and to listen to the music."

She faced Nathan. "I don't know how you two put up with

each other all these years." Then she winked at him. "But I find it nice that you do."

Nathan hooked his thumbs in the front pockets of his jeans. "I admit I was kind of a terror as a kid, but I've mellowed."

"A terror?" She wrinkled her mouth. "You were more than a terror. I remember you throwing a garter snake at me. I swear I thought it was a rattler. I still have nightmares about it!"

Nathan's mouth dropped, horrified. "I didn't mean to scare you that much. It was just a baby." Gunnar elbowed him in the ribs. "Uh, maybe I can make it up to you," Nathan said to Mallory and held out his hand. "Dance?"

She watched the dancers a moment and shook her head. "I don't know how to do that."

"It's a two-step. Quick, quick, slow, slow," Gunnar said. "You used to dance it all the time at picnics and stuff here as a kid. I mean, you didn't have a partner, but you knew the steps. You'd even spin yourself."

"I did?" She chuckled at the image he gave her. "I don't remember."

"I do," both Nathan and Gunnar said at the same time.

Just then, the band began "Chattahoochee," a fun song with a strong beat. Mallory couldn't help but smile.

"This song is fun." Nathan again extended his hand. "It'll come back to you." He faced Slade. "You don't mind, do you, sir? Just one song."

"Go ahead." Slade shooed them away with his fingers. "I'd love to see this."

Mallory took Nathan's hand, and he led her to the dance floor. Slade now leaned back in his chair, arms crossed, and stared hard at them.

Gunnar went back to the bar. Emma was gone. He sat and, like Slade, focused all his attention on the dance floor.

After just a few warm-up steps, Mal and Nathan were soon two-stepping around the room. He saw how Mal laughed at her mistakes and even appeared to take the blame when Nathan stepped on her toes. In fact, that seemed to cause them both to laugh even more than before. Gunnar was dying of envy, and could only wish that he were the one out there with her. But his two-stepping days were over. Mallory deserved a fun guy like Nathan. One who could at least dance with her.

To his surprise, when the song ended, instead of Nathan taking her back to Slade, he remained on the dance floor with her. The next song was a slow one, "I Just Fall in Love Again."

Lucky man. He guessed right. Gunnar wasn't sure how he'd stand it to watch his best friend take Mallory in his arms. But instead of doing that, Nathan led her toward the bar.

They stopped in front of Gunnar. "Here you go," Nathan said. He faced Mallory. "He can dance slow. He just doesn't like to admit it."

Nathan then put Mallory's hand in Gunnar's.

Gunnar's fingers wrapped around her hand, but he remained seated. "Don't listen to him. You don't have to dance with me," he said.

"Maybe I'd like to," she said and stepped backward in the direction of the dance floor, but not letting go of him.

Gunnar searched her eyes looking for a sign of sarcasm or mirth, but there was none. He stood up and handed his cane to Nathan.

Mallory slipped an arm around his back, smiling at him. He caught a hint of her perfume—delicate roses with a hint of spice, much like Mallory. It, more than the loss of his cane, made him unsteady. He slung his arm across her shoulders as they took a few steps onto the dance floor, then she stopped and faced him.

She put her hand on his shoulder; he put one on her waist, and then their other hands joined. She smiled at him and to his surprise, stepped in close to him. Real close.

They moved in time to the music, small, box steps, that

caused him little pain and less unsteadiness. "How are you doing?" she asked.

"Never been better," he murmured.

She smiled into his eyes. "Me neither." Their gazes held a long moment, then she rested her head against the side of his face. The clean scent of her hair filled him and he could feel her soft curves against him. She was all softness and warmth. He couldn't remember ever touching anything like her. This had to be what heaven was all about.

He kept her close. He was fairly steady on his feet without the cane, but it was more painful to walk without it than with it, so he used it whenever he could. He suspected he would have a miserable time trying to sleep tonight after using his hip muscles the way he needed to in order to move around the dance floor, but he'd rather spend the time thinking of how she had smiled up at him, how it felt to hold her, than to sleep anyway.

He could have danced with her forever.

At some point, the music stopped. It had scarcely registered until she turned to his side and put her arm around his back again, and he slid his arm across her shoulders, the sides of their bodies pressed together. In that way, she led him back to Nathan.

"You're right," she said to Nathan, even as she was smiling up at Gunnar. "He's a very fine dancer."

"So I noticed," Nathan said, his eyebrows high as his gaze caught Gunnar's.

Gunnar sat on a barstool. "You should walk the lady back to her date," he said to Nathan. "I think we've monopolized too much of her time."

"I don't need anyone to walk me," Mallory said to him with a wry grin. "I'm not a dog, Gunnar!"

"That, you're definitely not!" Nathan told her.

"What's this about dogs?" They all turned at Slade's voice. "I've paid the bill, my love. It's time for us to go."

Her eyes met Gunnar's, and he sensed the longing in them. It was almost more than he could handle, but she immediately caught herself and turned to Slade. "I guess so."

"Mal?" he whispered. The slightest hint from her, any indication, and he would have stepped in.

But her lips formed a smile, her voice soft and a bit breathless. "Thanks for the dances, you two. This was fun."

"Thank you," Nathan said. But Gunnar couldn't say a word. With his stomach feeling as if a lead weight were in it, he could do nothing but watch as Slade led her from the restaurant.

CHAPTER 19

Mallory called Gunnar early the next morning. "I've got a problem. I was hoping you might help."

"Sure. What is it?" He sounded a little groggy, and she imagined he was still in his bed.

She swallowed, hard, and then said, "I'm not certain, but the more I think about it, someone may have broken into the cabin."

"What? While you were home?" he asked, much more alert now. And then he added, "Were you alone?"

"No. I mean, yes, I was home alone last night. But the break-in, if it happened, may have been while I was at Mama's Folly."

"I'll be right over."

He was there within fifteen minutes. She showed him a broken candy dish in the great room, and then led him upstairs to the room she was using as an office, and pointed out that her papers were strewn over the dresser, the bed, and on the floor. "Last night I saw the broken dish, and I assumed Pumpkin had done that. Not until this morning did I come into this room and find this mess. I think someone was here."

His brow furrowed with worry. "I don't get it. Who would come in here and do this?"

"I have no idea. Plus, the computer isn't the way I left it. I always leave it on, so I just have to put in my PIN, but I had to start it up. For some reason, it had been turned off."

"Your PIN—how secure is it?"

"I don't do anything much on my computer. No banking or anything like that. I—"

"How secure?" he asked again.

"1-2-3-4."

He ran his fingers through his hair. "Someone could have easily gotten into it, then. But if someone was here to rob you, they would have taken the laptop. It looks fairly new. There's not much else in the cabin to take, but that candy dish downstairs is troubling. And these papers look like someone's riffled through them. But still, this is no ordinary break-in. I just don't understand why anyone would have thrown your papers around. Is anything missing?"

"Not that I've noticed."

He glanced at the papers on her desk, and she realized her Dear Nellie notes were there. She often printed out the letters and scribbled her reactions before she wrote the short, concise, final copy for the paper.

"What's all this?" he asked, picking up an email to Nellie.

She grabbed the papers out of his hands and added them to the ones on the bureau, forming them into a stack and then turning them face down. "It's for a friend. She writes those and I edit them before she sends them off to the paper."

He frowned, as if he saw that the notes were written in long hand, not edited computer printouts. But most likely the difference meant nothing to him.

"They aren't important. Worthless, in fact," she continued. "But my worry is that someone managed to get in here. Not only why did they do it, but how?"

He shook his head. "Where's your ex-fiancé? Why did he go off and leave you? Even if you thought Pumpkin had broken the dish, why didn't he double-check things, look around a little?"

"He didn't know. I said goodbye at the door and didn't invite him in."

"Oh." He looked as if he liked that answer. But then he gave a quick nod and stepped away from her.

"You look like you're ready to say something," she said.

He hesitated. "You won't like it."

"Since when has that stopped you?"

"Okay." He sucked in his breath and then sat on the bed. "Here goes. Break-ins don't happen out here. Or, I should say, the only ones I've ever heard of were teenagers looking for booze or money. But here, at this cabin, this is no random happening. Someone was looking for something."

She sat down beside him. "I agree."

His mouth tightened a moment before he added. "Nothing like this ever happened until Slade arrived. I know he's got a man with him—some guy who shops for groceries, is seen driving him around, and seems to be at his beck and call all day. Believe me, everyone in town has noticed. I'm thinking that I don't remember seeing you with your purse in the restaurant. If you left it in the car, Slade's man could easily have come here to see what you've been up to. Breaking into your computer would be a way to do that. A man like Slade would want to know."

"That's crazy."

"Is it?" he asked.

Her mind was roiling, but she hated to believe Slade could be behind this. "This room is such a mess, why would Slade's man leave it this way? It would be as if he wanted to scare me." Her mind went to Slade again ... and the great possibility that he did want to scare her into returning to New York City with him. "Still, it could have been Pumpkin. What if she were after a mouse? She easily could make a mess chasing one."

"And then Pumpkin turned off your computer after catching

it?"

"Oh." So much for that theory.

"How did Slade react to you dancing with a couple of cowboys last night?" Gunnar asked.

"He didn't care for it. But that's nothing new. He tends to think I do silly things. That ranked high among them."

He grimaced. "Why do you put up with being treated that way?"

"He loves me."

"And you love him?" he asked.

God, but she hated getting grilled by anyone. It reminded her of Roxanne harping at her, *'Why don't you love him? He's rich. He'll give you everything you could ever want.'*

"Look," she said finally, "I said I'd marry him, didn't I?"

"That's not an answer," he snapped right back. "Maybe it's because you don't love him."

Tears filled her eyes. "But he puts up with me. With my fears. How many men would come out to this nothingness to be with me, to offer to wait for me, to put up with me dancing with other men?"

He grimaced. "So that's how it's done. I need to find a woman who likes to dance with other men, and that's how I'll know she's the one."

"Exactly. But also, he loves me. And ... and not many people do." Her voice was harsh. She folded her arms. "Besides, who are you to be critical of me? I don't see a wife with you."

"Because I haven't met the right person. At least I'm not leading some poor woman on, making her think I care enough to marry her when I don't."

She cocked an eyebrow. "So who is the poor woman you're looking for?"

Her question seemed to take him aback. "Well," his voice lowered, and his words came slow and—she had to admit— rather sexy. Especially sitting on a bed with him. But she wasn't about to move away like some nervous schoolgirl. "First, she'll be a country girl. That's for sure. The girl next door type. Someone who'll be happy with what we've got. And even if the rest of the world doesn't think it's much, it wouldn't matter to her because we'll have each other. And, if we're lucky, we'll have kids, too. Lots of them."

"Kids?" Thinking of Gunnar and kids surprised her. He would be a fun father for a boy, and any daughter would absolutely adore him.

"You know, those two-legged critters that often show up when two people get married. The stork brings them."

Darn, but why did he always say something that made her smile when she was trying to be angry with him? "Oh. Those things."

"Haven't you and Slade talked about kids?"

Sore subject, fellow. But she answered truthfully. "He's already got three. I don't think he really wants more."

He frowned. "You're okay with that?"

"I'm sure if I insisted, he'd go along."

"Would you?"

Slade had mentioned kids yesterday, but she had the feeling he was just saying that—that he might say anything to win her back, and later reality would set in. She played with her too-short fingernails. "He's a busy man. He's forever traveling. I think a child should have a father nearby. Not one who rushes off to business meetings around the world."

"And what about you? No kids, and a husband who travels without her. Sounds like a lonely life to me."

"It's a different kind of lifestyle from the one you know," she said.

"It sure is." He couldn't hide his sarcasm. He put a pillow up against the headboard and rested his back against it, shifting in a way that made her realize his hip must have been hurting.

She turned, one knee on the mattress, to better face him. "I have a number of women friends who live that way."

"Are they happy?"

"They're certainly busy. They're forever on the go."

"Why?"

"Why do you keep asking so many questions?" she demanded.

He leaned toward her. "Maybe because I'm trying to figure out what makes you tick. What is it that you want?"

"Happiness."

He backed away, resting against the pillow once more. "No. I think what you want is money. And that's all I see Slade giving you. I don't get it, Mal."

"At least money doesn't disappoint you!" she shouted.

"Really? I see it as the most disappointing thing out there. People spend their whole lives trying to gather more and more of it, and in the end, when their lives are over, they look around to see what they have. And you know what?"

"What?"

"They realize they have nothing. Numbers on a ledger. That's it."

How dare he? "And what is it you want, Gunnar, since you're so smart and above all the rest of us money-hungry peasants?"

"Me?" He spat the word at her, now angry, too. "I'd love to walk around like I used to and not feel any pain. That's all it'd take to make me happy."

His words made her heart hurt, and she was sorry she had pushed him. But she wouldn't give in to pity. "Surely you want more than that. You can get that by taking enough pills. Don't you want a family and some of those kids you were praising just minutes ago?"

"First off, pills aren't the answer. You saw the guys working for me—even Nathan. A lot of them turned to pills to mask what they saw and did while in Iraq or Afghanistan. Not all injuries are as obvious as mine. And you know what, now they're facing new kinds of demons trying to get the pills out of their systems. Some can't. Ever.

"And as for the rest of your 'solutions' for me, what woman would want to put up with me?" He gave a bitter laugh and turned his head. "It's kind of ironic, me learning from you all about Lucas Donnelly, the hermit of the cabin. We're nearly a hundred years apart, yet I'm in the same kind of mess as he was. It makes me wonder why he isn't my relative instead of yours. He and I surely have lots in common."

"No." She got up and moved to sit at his side, facing him. She placed her hands on his forearms. More than anything, she wanted to hold him. "From all I've heard, Lucas came back here because he was broken. You aren't broken Gunnar McDermott. Not at all."

"I'm not? Could have fooled me." He abruptly got up off the bed and stood.

She wanted to pull him back to her, to hold him until he listened to her. But instead, she just looked at him, hating that he felt that way about himself, and worse of all, hating that he'd rejected her. She stood as well. "If we ever decide to sell the cabin, I'll let you know. You can rot in here all alone just like Lucas, and maybe die way too young, just like he did!"

"And then I can haunt the place, too." Gunnar said.

She put her hands on her hips. "You try it and I'll find a way to rid this cabin of all its ghosts! Starting with you!"

He cocked an eyebrow. "So you do think there are some here?"

"No, I don't! And ghosts mean nothing to me."

He shook his head, grabbed his cane, and headed out of the bedroom and down the stairs. "I'm leaving before I *do* want to kill myself just to end this stupid conversation!"

She leaned over the bannister, yelling down at him like some shrew of a housewife. "Good. Because you keep talking this way, and I just might assist you in getting your wish!"

He couldn't help but grin as he glanced up at her, then turned and walked out the door.

At least, she thought with a heavy sigh, he stopped feeling sorry for himself.

After Gunnar left, Mallory paced back-and-forth around the cabin for some ten minutes, steamed and thinking about their conversation. She pulled herself together, ran around outdoors until she found a spot with two bars on her phone, and then downloaded her emails and sat on the bench on the back porch and read them.

She read Brian's first. *"Lots of great responses to today's write-up. People love, love, love the Cabin of Love and Magic. Need more ASAP. This will get the public's mind off your own 'marital situation.' Send me another column mentioning the Cabin ASAP and I'll get it printed ASAP."*

Mallory rolled her eyes. Brian's favorite expression, used three times in a short message, showed his complete lack of patience.

She'd figure out something tomorrow. Surely, he could wait another day. *ASAP, my eye!*

She received a message from Julia asking how everything was going, another from Carly apologizing profusely for giving Slade the cabin's address, and one from Abby, the closest thing to a best friend she had while in Manhattan, who wanted to know what was going on with her.

Most surprising was a terse text from Slade saying he was off to Los Angeles for business, but he would be back the next day.

She didn't expect to hear from Gunnar again that day, not after the way they'd parted company that morning.

From inside the house the lively strains of Roxanne singing "This Can't be Love" began again.

"What in the world?" Mallory jumped to her feet and rushed inside.

She shut off the CD player, and this time took the cassette out of it. She hated hearing the song. Did that mean she was in love? Or wasn't?

She had no idea. She could stand no more, got into her car and drove to a used bookstore in Horseshoe Bend. There, she bought several romances. It would be nice to read about sensible relationships for a change!

When Mallory returned from Horseshoe Bend, she opened up her Dear Nellie folder. Sure enough, as Brian had indicated, her email was flooded with questions about the Cabin of Love and Magic.

One email stood out above the rest:

Dear Ever-Seeking Nellie,

When you called yourself "ever-seeking," I had to write to you. I've also been looking for true love for a long, long time. When is it time to give up? No one I meet seems special. They are all kind of the same. More interested in sports than in me. Looking at other women when we're out on dates. Talking about ex-girlfriends or ex-wives when we're out on dates. Or even worse, talking about their health problems. I'm no longer a spring chicken, Nellie, and at my age—not quite winter, but definitely late fall—lots of men are sickly. Still, I'd love to meet someone who's there for me. Do you think the Cabin of Love and Magic that you mentioned might offer me some hope? [Signed] Ever-Hopeful Autumn

Mallory responded immediately.

Dear Ever-Hopeful Autumn,

Believe me, younger men have the same boring topics of conversation, not to mention swiveling heads when a "looker" goes by. They might not talk about health issues, but substitute business and bosses who make them every bit as miserable as sciatica or bursitis or, God help us, hemorrhoids. You're doing what you need to. Go out, meet people, and if the one you're with isn't interesting, head back home pronto. There are many fish in the sea, and one of them will be right for you. And me. We're both ever-hopeful about that.

So what are the signs that a man is right for you? I'm looking for someone who not only understands me—whatever that means—but puts up with my quirks and my fears as well as my joys. Someone I can always count on to be there for me, who won't simply criticize when I screw up—which I tend to do with great regularity—but is also accepting that I'm not perfect. Some shared background is nice, though not essential. But if you have it, it helps build more bridges for you both. I want someone who really listens when I talk to him, and if I need advice, gives it honestly even if it's not what I want to hear. And most of all, he needs to be a man who, when I look into his eyes, I love what I see. I'm not talking physical beauty, but warmth and compassion and a reflection of the love I feel in my heart for him. And, frankly, if we can laugh together, that's icing on the cake.

As far as the Cabin of Love and Magic goes, I'll have to try it before I tell anyone where it is. I don't want to lead people astray (apparently some readers feel I've already done that, and for that, I'm truly sorry). For all I know, the cabin is more a state of mind than anything. But it does have a physical location. I'll have to think about how much more I should say about it. Maybe it's best if I keep it a secret for now. [Signed] Nellie the Cautious

She sent the back-and-forth off to Brian asking if that was the sort of response/write-up about the cabin he'd been hoping for.

She soon got back a one-word reply: *"Yes!!!"*

CHAPTER 20

The next morning, Mallory heard a knock on the door. It was too early for Slade, and she didn't think Gunnar would be dropping by after their conversation the prior morning. She went downstairs to see who it was and was stunned to find two women. They looked to be in their late forties or early fifties. And could have been twins. Both had short dyed blond hair, were a bit plump, and one wore a teal top with a midi length floral teal skirt, and the other a pink top and a midi-length floral black skirt.

"Is this the Cabin of Love and Magic?" the teal-wearer asked. Mallory noticed her eyes were blue, and the other woman's eyes were brown.

"The what?" Mallory looked from one to the other, hoping she hadn't heard what she'd feared.

"Cabin of Love and Magic," the pink wearer said. She then held up a printout of a newspaper.

Mallory grabbed it from her hands. It was from the online *Greenwich Village Gazette*, an article on page 1, *Dear Nellie's Cabin of Love and Magic Exposed!*

"No, no, no!" Mallory cried.

The article claimed fans of "Misery Loves Company" managed to track down the cabin. It explained the cabin had been built in the late nineteenth century and had since become a place where people could go to find their true love. The article talked about the legend of the ghosts, using few facts, and lots of lurid innuendo.

"This is crazy," Mallory said.

"We drove over from Walla Walla," Ms. Teal said. "My sister in Hoboken is a big fan of 'Misery Loves Company' and often emails the column to us. We couldn't believe it when we learned Nellie's cabin was in nearby Idaho—only some five or so hours away! So we left home at four this morning. We figured if we drove straight over, we could get a room here before anyone else."

"We'll share," Ms. Pink said. "As long as we're here, we don't care."

"I'm sorry, but this is a hoax," Mallory told them.

"What? It can't be," Ms. Teal announced. "It says it's true. And that Nellie herself is going to come here. Maybe we can meet her, depending on when she arrives."

"No, Nellie hasn't contacted me. In fact, no one has," Mallory said, thankful that the cabin's landline phone number wasn't given in the article. "You should leave."

"But we have nowhere to go!" wailed Ms. Pink. "Please, if you have no one here, you must have space. Can we stay just for one night, at least?"

Mallory shook her head. "I'm not set up for guests."

"We're not guests," Ms. Teal said. "Think of us as friends. On an adventure." She looked at her companion and gave a long, woeful sigh. "Even if it hasn't turned out as we'd hoped."

"I guess we suspected it was too good to be true," Ms. Pink said, equally morosely.

Her friend nodded, and both turned sad eyes on Mallory.

"Anyway," Ms. Teal continued. "I'm Babs Stennick, and this

is Imogene Rorehm. We don't care for any fineries. In fact, we can help, if you'd like. We'll make our beds, whatever you need."

"You don't even have to feed us," Imogene said, a desperate wail sounding in her voice.

"It's just that we left our houses so very early to get here." Babs did look on the verge of collapse. "And now we're tired—"

"And hungry," Imogene added.

"And disappointed." Babs gave a sigh as weighty as she was. "But if we could just lie down for a while…"

"In the cabin," Imogene interjected.

"We'd be so grateful—"

"And we wouldn't tell anyone about it."

"So you wouldn't have to worry about others doing the same thing."

"Stop. Please." The way the two women jabbered at her, Mallory even lost track of who was saying what. Not that it mattered. They seemed to be nice women, both plain of face, but brimming with misplaced enthusiasm, their eyes hopeful. After all the misery she'd been around recently, she couldn't turn them out. "We charge one-hundred thirty dollars a night. I have two bedrooms available. If you wish, you can share a room to save money, but the beds are queens, and I don't have any room with twin beds. I won't be cooking breakfast for you, but I have eggs, bacon, sausage, pancake and waffle mix, lots of fruit, yogurt, and all kinds of cereal available. Just look around. I'm sure you'll find something you want to eat. So, it's up to you if you want to stay here."

"We do," the women chimed. They glanced at each other, then announced. "We'll take the two rooms."

They each opened up their handbags and pulled out one hundred thirty dollars apiece and handed it to her.

"Cash?" Mallory said.

"We figured anyplace that had ghosts might not have credit

card processors, and who uses checks anymore?" Imogene, clearly the practical one, said.

"True enough," Mallory conceded. "But don't you want to see your rooms before you pay for them?"

They glanced at each other and shook their heads. "No need," Imogene said.

"Okay. My laptop is in one of the spare rooms. I'll move it and give you towels and fresh sheets for the beds. We will need to share the upstairs bathroom. It's the only one with a tub and shower. There's a half-bath downstairs. We also have a garage if you want to put your car in it. Come on inside."

Mallory was a bit stunned by all this, but the women seemed nice enough—and the thought of not being here alone after the strangeness of the prior night, actually was a good thing. She showed them the great room and pointed out the kitchen and pantry for their food.

"Oh, my! This must be the builder of the cabin," Babs squealed as she stood in front of Elijah Donnelly's portrait and gawked. "And he haunts the cabin to this day!"

"Yes, that's him!" Imogene stood next to her. "Look at those eyes! They're so penetrating! And what a beautiful color! It just gives me goosebumps. He's so handsome!"

"He is, isn't he?" Babs said. "And died so young. It's so tragic. I could just cry!"

"Shall I show you to your rooms?" Mallory asked, thinking this was all getting a little out of hand—although she hadn't seen Elijah looking so pleased by anyone in a long time.

"Yes! Wonderful!" Both said at exactly the same time.

As they left the great room, Imogene gazed over her shoulder. This time her sigh wasn't in the least bit morose. "Elijah can come haunt me any time!"

Babs' squeal of laughter was ear-splitting. As Mallory led them up the stairs, she feared this was going to be a long twenty-four hours.

Mallory was glad Julia had brought a week's supply of food when she visited. How she knew extra people might end up in the cabin was anybody's guess, but here they were. The women oohed and aahed over their bedrooms along with everything else in the cabin. They cooked themselves bacon, eggs, and toast, and even cleaned up the kitchen after eating. Then they went to their bedrooms to take naps since they were both exhausted from their long drive.

As they ate, they'd been filled with questions about the cabin. Mallory wished she'd paid better attention to its history.

As soon as the women went off to their bedrooms, Mallory drove closer to town where she'd have good cell phone service and phoned Brian at the *Greenwich Village Gazette*.

"What do you mean by publishing a story about my cabin?" she cried. "Not to mention that the stories about the ghosts helping people find true love are wildly ridiculous fantasies. Of course they aren't true! But also, how am I supposed to maintain any degree of anonymity when people are showing up here?"

"Wait a minute! I'll admit, it wasn't written with your usual wit or caustic remarks, and there were plenty of opportunities for both, but you never indicated it was a draft. You said it was ready to go."

"What are you talking about? I did no such thing!"

"You sent me the article, and I published it. End of story! Why are you so surprised? I told you this morning how much people loved the write up."

"I thought you were talking about my column," she cried.

"Uh, no."

She didn't like the way that sounded. "All that aside, I would never have sent you such an article. No one is supposed to know about the cabin."

"I'm now forwarding the email you attached the article to. Tell me if it isn't your email."

It took just a few seconds before she saw a notification of a new email. She opened it, and it did look as if it came from her email address. The email itself was beyond terse:

Brian,
    I've decided to tell the world about my cabin. I hope you like the attached article.
    Mallory

"I've never written you such a short note in my life," she said. "Didn't that seem suspicious?"

"Not really. I knew you were busy, and I assumed your fiancé tracked you down."

"My fiancé? He doesn't know I'm Dear Nellie."

"Of course he does. He's friends with Tom Campilongo, who suggested I hire you for the job, remember?"

"Oh, no." She had told Tom to keep it a secret, but of course Slade would have gotten the information out of him. Her breath caught. At the same time as she lost her job at Piaget, there was a sudden social media attack on her Dear Nellie column—demanding she be fired.

And Slade knew she wrote the column. Could he …? She hoped not!

"But tell me," Brian continued, "why was your fiancé having to call all over the place trying to find you? I thought it was because you simply weren't answering his calls, but now I can't help but wonder … you aren't in Idaho, are you? At that cabin?"

"What if I am?"

"Take photos!" he sounded more excited about the possibility of pictures than she'd heard him in ages. "You can't imagine how many people want to know about all of it. That article had a photo of the outside, but I want some of the inside.

And especially anything that looks ghostly! Maybe we should send some of those ghost hunters from those TV shows to see if they can detect any presence. That would really get the readers pumped!"

"No! I'm not turning my cabin—my retreat—into a sideshow."

"Why not? It'll make money. Can you imagine how many people will be clamoring to get a room there?"

"I can," she said, without bothering to explain about her two lodgers. She realized what a mistake she'd made even mentioning the cabin. Julia had been right about that. "I want you to put a retraction in the paper. Tell them the whole thing is a mistake—a hoax—and Nellie won't take part in it and neither should her readers."

"You've got to be kidding," Brian said.

"I'm not. I want that story pulled."

"Not gonna happen, Mallory."

"I insist! I didn't write it."

"There's no byline, so no one thinks you did."

"I'll sue."

"Get in line." He hung up.

She was beyond furious and phoned Julia.

"You won't believe what's happened," she cried as soon as Julia answered.

"If it has to do with the cabin, I'll believe anything. What's going on?"

Mallory gave her the whole story, beginning with the fact that she had been writing an advice to the lovelorn column for seven months. That, more than anything, seemed to capture Julia's imagination. "What am I going to do?" Mallory asked when her long tale of woe ended. "What if more women like the two that showed up today start arriving?"

"It'll be like a theme park. Well, I'll tell you one thing. You'll need to at least double the nightly rate."

"Jules! That isn't funny."

Julia was silent a long moment. "My question is, who wrote the article? Where did anyone find all that out?"

"I don't know. No one knows about it except the three of us."

"Are you sure of that?"

"Well, there's also Gunnar. And I suppose he told Nathan, who he still hangs around with. But they don't know anything about Brian and my column."

"So you're still seeing Gunnar?" Julia's voice sparkled with good humor.

"So?"

"Very interesting. That's all."

"He's not my type." Mallory was emphatic. "I'm a total city girl. You know that. Also, Slade is here."

"Slade is at the cabin?" Julia sounded shocked.

"No. But he's renting a beautiful mountaintop retreat overlooking the Valley. I haven't gone there yet, but he pointed the house out to me when we went to dinner."

"Your stuffy New York guy is in Crouch, Idaho?" Julia spoke slowly, laughter clearly in her voice, as if she couldn't believe what she was hearing. "That would be something worth seeing, I do say."

"He thinks he can win me back."

"Hmm. Does he know about the ghosts?" Julia asked.

"I've never said a word to him," Mallory said.

"Okay. Well, you need to figure out who would have told such a story about you. Who would benefit from making you miserable at the cabin? That would be a way to start. And I'd keep an eye on the people around there. Including Gunnar and Nathan. You never know what goes on in men's heads."

"I'm sure this has nothing to do with Gunnar or Nathan," Mallory said. "But you're right about one thing, who would benefit from making me miserable here?"

"Keep me posted."

CHAPTER 21

"Yoo-hoo! Here we are again," Babs called to Mallory as she and Imogene wandered into the great room from their naps some three hours later.

Mallory was busy writing an article for Brian about the cabin, and how it might have been seen as a place of love and magic for the family that once lived there, but not for anyone else. If she could get him to publish it soon, maybe no one else would track her down. So far, the cabin's landline hadn't rung.

"I'm surprised you're both already up."

"We don't want to miss a minute of being here." Imogene said, gazing lovingly at Elijah Donnelly's portrait. "It's so exciting. Is there a museum in town, or anything else that might give us information about the Donnelly family?"

"I'm afraid not. There was nothing special about the family, other than they built this cabin."

"Nothing special?" Babs questioned. "Not many family members become ghosts."

Mallory needed to be nice to her lodgers. "We don't know for sure that Elijah and his family are doing anything but slumbering in the ground. That newspaper article was all rumor."

Babs fluffed her hair. "Maybe. Maybe not. And I'm feeling lucky."

"Me, too," Imogene said with a giggle.

The two women high-fived, and then Babs turned to Mallory, her expression suddenly serious. "That newspaper article was a wake-up call. We can't just sit around and wait for Prince Charming to knock on our door. We have to go out. Push ourselves. Work at meeting someone we want to spend time with. Maybe we won't meet the right men here, but we can sure try."

Babs nodded. She was about to speak when a knock at the door stopped her.

Mallory opened it to find Gunnar there. "I left work early today and was thinking of heading up to McCall." He seemed to study her a moment before adding, "I was wondering if you'd like to join me. Payette Lake is beautiful, and huge. Plus lots of shops. Most are kind of touristy, but it also has good restaurants."

Where was this coming from? He said nothing about their prior spat. Nothing about Slade. Only an invitation. Was this his way of apologizing? What had they fought about, anyway? She couldn't stop her smile. "Shops, restaurants, and a lake. What's not to like? Won't you come in?"

Babs and Imogene hooked arms and gawked as Gunnar entered the great room. "Maybe I was wrong about knocks on the door," Imogene murmured, a little too loud. Babs chuckled and nodded.

"Let me introduce my lodgers," Mallory said quickly, and then made introductions.

"Is this your young man, Mallory?" Babs asked.

"We're old friends," she replied with a smile.

Gunnar cocked his head toward Mallory, "I didn't realize you were taking in lodgers."

"I didn't either," she said with an eye roll. "But it's just for tonight. And bed only. These poor ladies had to make their own breakfasts today."

"We're here because of the ghosts," Imogene said, giving him a wink. "And we've got to give them time to work their magic."

"Their magic?" Gunnar asked.

"We can go now, Gunnar," Mallory interrupted, taking his arm.

"The magic of the cabin," Babs whispered.

"If you're talking about the old legend of the ghosts," Gunnar said. "It's just a story. It's not real."

"Are you sure of that?" Imogene asked, waggling her eyebrows.

Mallory tugged on Gunnar's arm. "Ready?"

"You know, Babs and I haven't had lunch yet," Imogene said. "And we love seeing new places."

"You should start with Crouch," Mallory said. "It's just down the road a bit. You'll love it. See you later!"

"Wait!" Imogene said giving Gunnar a coy smile. "If you two are just friends, and the ghosts send nice men to this house ... and he's here and we're here ..."

"What?" Gunnar stopped, dumbfounded as his gaze jumped from Imogene to Mallory.

"I'm sure the ghosts didn't send you Gunnar," Mallory said, all but dragging Gunnar toward the door.

"So you *do* think there's something to the story," Babs said.

Mallory had had enough. She stopped, and all but gave them an order. "I think the two of you need to head down to Crouch and get yourselves an ice cream cone at Miss Sandie's and then walk around and take in the local color. There's a cute little antique shop. I won't vouch for the antiques, but it has some adorable souvenirs in it."

"Ice cream?" Imogene raised her eyebrows hopefully as she looked at her friend.

"Sounds even better than a man," Babs said with a chuckle,

then glanced at Gunnar. "Sorry, dearie. You lose."

As a perplexed Gunnar gave Mallory a "what just happened?" look, she could only shake her head and, finally, got him to leave the cabin.

Gunnar drove through McCall to a small beach along Payette Lake. He and Mallory got out of the truck, walked along the concrete boardwalk for a ways, and then left it to go closer to the lake. A number of people were there, including families with young children wading in the water.

"You're right," Mallory said, looking out over the blue waters of the huge lake to the mountains surrounding it, "this area is beautiful."

After walking around a bit, the hot sun drove them to find a restaurant with a covered, colorful outdoor patio. There, they ordered burgers, fries, and beer.

"So," Gunnar said after a while, "are you ever going to explain to me why you have two women at the cabin hot to trot about finding true love?"

"It's beyond awful!" She put both hands to her forehead. "Oh, my! Somehow, word got out about the cabin's ghosts, and those women drove here all the way from Washington state. Fortunately, the small paper that published the story is only found in the New York area, but they have a friend who emailed it to them. It's not easy to track down the cabin's phone number, so at least I'm spared phone calls."

He grinned. "Tell me your cabin hasn't been written up as some sort of supernatural match-dot-com."

"It's not funny, Gunnar!" She frowned as he couldn't help but laugh. "If I ever find out who put out all this information, they'll be extremely sorry."

Just then, the waitress brought out their food. When they

were alone again, Gunnar chewed a French fry, then said, "Maybe it's just someone who believes in ghosts and wants to share your cabin with the world. The whole world. And I'm afraid some hackers will have found your landline number by the time we get back."

He said those words in such a serious tone, she peered hard at him to see if he was joking. He wasn't, but the gleam in his eyes told her he was still amused. "This. Is. Not. Funny."

"Seriously then," he said, "who could have done it? Is this something personal against you, or does it have to do with the cabin and ghosts?"

She was hungry enough to bite into the juicy cheeseburger—with a slice of bacon and a breaded onion ring included—before finally answering. "I wish I knew."

Gunnar also picked up his burger and began to eat. "You said the article told the cabin's history. Your sisters know the story, most people in the town do, but sending it to a small paper in New York City connects it to you. So you're clearly the target of the piece. Are you named in the article?"

"I'm not."

His eyes narrowed. "Then why use that newspaper to get such a story published? And why would a New York paper take a story about a cabin in Idaho? None of it makes sense. What are you not telling me?"

She shut her eyes a moment. This was harder than she imagined it would be. She put the burger down, reached for a fry, but then stopped and faced him. "It makes sense if you know that the cabin was mentioned in an advice to the lovelorn column called 'Misery Loves Company'." She wished she could stop there, but she couldn't. She blurted out the rest. "And if you also know that I'm the one who writes that column. People write letters to Dear Nellie, and … and I'm Nellie."

Gunnar was speechless. "You are pulling my one good leg."

She slowly shook her head. "I'm not, and I wouldn't. Not

about this, anyway."

They both went back to their lunches. After a while, Gunnar said, "So, whoever did this also has to know that you're Nellie."

"And no one does except my editor, my real estate boss, Slade, Julia, and now you. And I only told Julia this morning."

Gunnar's mouth slanted in disgust. "I know where I'd put my money."

"I know, but …" She shut her eyes a moment. "Oh, no!"

He looked at her with worry. "What?"

"I just remembered that my newspaper editor thought the article was from me because it was sent from my email address. Remember the other day when I told you it looked like someone broke into the cabin and had gotten into my computer?"

"Of course. I was worried about you. And I still am, frankly."

"The computer has my Dear Nellie files. And my emails."

"So you're thinking that whoever broke in could have gotten into your computer not to steal anything, but to use your email?" Gunnar asked.

"Yes, which means that whoever did it might want to come back and send out more emails from Dear Nellie." A chill zipped down her spine and she shifted in her seat. "That's scary."

His lips tightened. "Very. Or, they might have used a program that could download and then mimic your files."

"What do you mean?"

The burger gone, he pushed aside the rest of his fries and reached for his beer, taking a sip before explaining. "A sophisticated program could copy your files and programs to a movable device, and then someone could take their time going through them. Plus, they could send out emails, such as the one with the article, under your email address anytime they wanted."

"That's crazy," she wailed, also no longer wanting more of her meal. She could have predicted his next words.

"We both know one person who would have access to people with the equipment and know-how to do all that," Gunnar said.

Her prediction would have been correct. Just then, Gunnar's cell phone began to buzz. He tried to ignore it. "Besides, Slade has a reason for wanting you to leave the cabin."

"I don't want to believe he would do that to me. I can't believe it, in fact."

The phone kept buzzing and Gunnar was growing increasingly irritated. "Since you find him so great, why didn't you marry him?"

"Maybe I will!"

"So you keep saying!" The cell phone didn't stop and, furious, he finally glanced at the caller. "It's Nathan. I'd better take it."

Mallory couldn't hear what Nathan said, but the look on Gunnar's face told her it was bad. "You're sure? ... No, don't call the sheriff ... okay ... okay. I'm in McCall so it'll take a while. Stay with him, I'll get there as fast as I can."

He hung up, lost in thought and not facing her.

"We've got to return?" she asked.

"One of my guys," was Gunnar's only explanation, as he paid the restaurant bill and they hurried to his truck.

Once they were on the road, Mallory asked, "I heard you say 'don't call the sheriff.' Did he do something illegal?"

"No. At least, not yet. He's been having a really bad time lately with his wife and all." Gunner drew in his breath, then said, "He wants to end the problem. He just needs someone to talk him down. Nathan's hoping I can."

"End the problem?" she repeated. The term was frightening. "You don't mean ..."

"I don't know."

The winding road back to Crouch seemed more twisting than ever as Gunnar did his best to drive quickly down the high mountains around McCall to the medium high ones in the Garden Valley area. She stopped talking and held her breath as they sped along the two-lane highway.

CHAPTER 22

A sheriff's car blocked a street with a cluster of old homes a few miles past Crouch off the Banks-Lowman Road.

"Stay in the car," Gunnar told Mallory as he pulled to the side of the road, got out, and spoke to the deputy who was sitting in the car.

Nathan was standing in the middle of the narrow street. A woman holding a baby with curly blond ringlets stood beside him. Another sheriff's car was parked in front of a driveway, the deputy out of the car and leaning against it. All were staring at a small wooden house in need of paint. It had a front porch, and a stand-alone, single-car garage off to the side.

Nathan and the woman hurried over to meet Gunnar. Mallory got out of the car and moved close enough to hear what was being said.

"The deputy was already here when I showed up," Nathan said. "He came over to serve an eviction notice, and that's what set Kyle off."

Gunnar faced the woman. "You're Kyle's wife?"

She nodded. "LouAnn. He's bad. We've been having money

troubles and fighting and when the deputy showed up with his tough-guy swagger and barking orders, Kyle was right back in that Al Qaida prison. There was no reasoning with him. As soon as I saw his face, I feared he was going for his guns. I told the deputy to get out, and I grabbed the baby and ran, then phoned the Auto Repair, just like Kyle told me I needed to do if he was ever in trouble like this."

"You did good," Gunnar said as he surveyed the situation. "Is the deputy listening to you?"

"So far. I think. I hope."

"He called in back-up," Nathan said. "As you can see, they've blocked the road, but they're staying out of sight, which is good. I convinced them to give you a chance."

Gunnar looked back at the car blocking the road and took a few steps toward it, then returned to Nathan and nodded. "Okay. I see the backup. Just make sure Kyle doesn't see them."

"I will. But don't you mess up, brother. If he's too out of control, don't take any chances," Nathan said. "I'm counting on you to make it back here in one piece."

"I haven't been in one piece for a long time," Gunnar said.

Nathan put his hand on his shoulder. "You see the situation here. It can get ugly. You don't have to do this if you aren't comfortable with it."

Gunnar took in the house, the deputy, Nathan, the wife, then his gaze met Mallory's. She moved a little closer, there was so much she wanted to say to him. Mainly, "Don't do it," but she couldn't do that.

She watched as he faced Nathan again and nodded. "I need to try."

"If things go south, get out of the way," Nathan said. "The deputies will go in, and you know these yahoos will probably be so scared, they'll shoot anything that flinches."

Gunnar called to Mallory. "Mal, will you take care of LouAnn and her baby?"

"Me?" She had no idea what he meant.

"Take them down the street." He pointed in the direction meant. "Maybe behind a car. You three don't need to be around here."

Mallory could feel herself going pale at his words. He was afraid shots might be fired. She could hardly breathe but somehow she heard herself saying, "Okay, sure. Come on, LouAnn. My name's Mallory. Let's get your little one far from all this."

LouAnn shook her head and angrily stepped toward Gunnar. "What about Kyle? He said he won't let himself be taken, that he'd rather be dead. They said you'd help him."

He looked her straight in the eye. "I will. I'll take good care of him, LouAnn. You listen to Mal."

Her anger vanished, replaced by confusion and worry. Mallory took LouAnn's arm. "Let's do as he says," Mallory whispered, and all but steered the woman and her child down the street.

As they stood there watching, Gunnar took off his jacket and handed it and his cane to Nathan. Then, with his arms spread wide, he slowly approached the house.

"Oh, God," LouAnn said, the child on her hip and a hand over her mouth.

"What's he doing?" Mallory asked.

"I'm thinking he hopes Kyle will let him in the house so they can talk. He's got to get Kyle to listen and then make him realize he's safe here. Although … we are being evicted."

Gunner stopped about ten feet from the front door. Mallory guessed he and Kyle were talking, but she couldn't hear any words.

Mallory and LouAnn stared at the house and at Gunnar, both scared of what the next moments might bring. Nothing happened for about five minutes, then they saw a slight movement, and the front door opened just a crack.

Gunnar slowly walked up the two steps to the front porch and then went inside.

"I'm so sorry all this is happening to you and Kyle," Mallory said, needing to talk, needing to do anything, rather than to think of the danger inside that house.

"Not much help for it," LouAnn said. "The baby was real sick for a while and I got laid off. Things were tight, and then some bills came due, and now, once again, there wasn't enough money for the rent. Kyle was under pressure to begin with, and when he saw a big man at the door saying we had to leave our home, he snapped. In Iraq, he spent three days being tortured before his guys rescued him. He has the scars to prove it—and the worst ones aren't physical. It's like he's another person when he gets this way, and he's in another place."

"How awful for him," Mallory murmured.

"My Kyle is one of the toughest men I know, but when it hits, he screams at night when he's sleeping."

Mallory didn't want to imagine such terror. "Do you think Gunnar can get through to him?"

"I don't know. It's like he doesn't see what's in front of him. He only sees *them*. That's why I took the baby and ran out." Her tears began to flow. "When he's that way, I can't trust my own husband."

Mallory put her arms around the woman and let her cry.

After a while she said, "May I hold your baby? What's her name?"

"Sure." She handed the child over. "Her name is Holly."

"That's pretty. As she is."

"Yes, she is," LouAnn said, calming down a bit.

Mallory rocked the baby as she asked, "Tell me, has Gunnar ever come here and talk to Kyle before?"

LouAnn shook her head. "He's never had to. This is the first time I've met him."

"I see," Mallory whispered. That wasn't good news. "You

mentioned Kyle might not see what's in front of him. But he'll recognize Gunnar, won't he?"

"I don't know," LouAnn whispered.

The full realization of the danger Gunnar voluntarily walked into made Mallory's legs go weak.

LouAnn's eyes were empty as she reached for her baby and hugged her tight.

Mallory's breathing had all but stopped. She wanted to ask Nathan how much Gunnar knew about Kyle. Between hallucinations, guns, and paranoia, how was Gunnar supposed to handle all that? He wasn't that well himself.

Minutes slowly ticked by ... thirty ... forty-five. The deputy kept checking his wristwatch.

Nathan walked over to the women. "You two okay?"

"What's Gunnar doing?" Mallory asked, and she took his arm and walked him away from LouAnn. "He could be killed! Does he know how bad Kyle is?"

"I'm sure he does," Nathan said, his voice hushed. But the worry on his face made her more scared than ever.

"Tell me he'll be all right," she pleaded.

He took her hand and gave a squeeze. "I can't. We can only hope. And pray, if that's something you do."

"I can't remember ever needing to before, but I pray God is with Gunnar and watching over him now." She squeezed her hands together, her eyes never leaving the house.

Somewhere in the distance she heard the baby cry, heard a plane fly overhead, a large truck rumbling along the nearby Banks-Lowman Road. But nothing diverted her attention from the bungalow and worry about what was happening inside.

An hour and five minutes went by before the front door opened.

"It's okay." It was Gunnar's voice. "We're coming out now."

Nathan and the deputy faced each other, smiled, and

nodded. He got on his radio, probably to tell the others the situation had ended.

LouAnn and her baby started walking back to join the others, but Mallory stopped them. They needed to wait, to not make any movement that might upset a delicate balance.

And then Gunnar and Kyle appeared in the doorway, side by side, and then stepped onto the porch. Kyle raised his hands as Gunnar slowly walked with him toward the deputy.

All Mallory's attention was on Gunnar. She could see the white pallor along his mouth with each painful step he took, could see how hard he was trying not to grimace or show how badly he was hurting. But she could also see the relief in his eyes that this had ended well, that he had been able to help his brother. Never before in her life had she witnessed what real courage looked like.

CHAPTER 23

Nathan drove Mallory back to the cabin as Gunnar went with Kyle to the sheriff's office. He would do his best to have Kyle admitted to the Veteran's Hospital in Boise rather than jailed. He needed some good psychiatric counseling.

Mallory kept thinking about Gunnar. It was odd, but when she wrote her answer to Ever-Hopeful Autumn on what she was looking for in a man she could love, she had described Gunnar—not Slade, or Arturo, or Wendell, or Colin, or anyone else she'd ever thought she might have been in love with. Only Gunnar.

"We're going to pass a hat at the auto shop," Nathan said, interrupting her thoughts. "Hopefully, we can take care of Kyle's rent payment. Kyle's a quiet guy who never talks about himself or his troubles, so none of us had any idea what he's been going through."

"Good idea," Mallory said. When they reached the cabin, she asked Nathan to wait a moment even though he wanted to get going quickly in case Gunnar needed his help.

She was soon back at Nathan's pickup and reached in the

window to hand him two hundred sixty dollars, cash. "There should be more tomorrow, but for now, take this for LouAnn and Kyle."

"It's a lot of money," Nathan said. "Are you sure—"

"Absolutely."

She stood watching Nathan drive away, then looked at the land around her. The cabin. The mountains looming behind it, and in the opposite direction, the footpath down to the river—sometimes low and placid; other times roaring and raging fast and deadly. But it was all so very alive, as were the people who lived here. Good people.

How could she leave them?

She walked back into the cabin to find Babs and Imogene sitting by the fireplace, cups of tea and plates of cookies in front of them. The contrast between the harmony of the cabin and what she had just witnessed wasn't lost on Mallory. There were, she realized, much more terrifying things in this world than ghosts.

"Did you two have a nice time in town?" she asked, trying to sound cheerful.

"She did." Imogene pointed at her friend.

Babs smiled, her full cheeks growing rosier by the second. "Oh, well, it probably means nothing." She took a bite of a ginger snap.

Oh, dear, Mallory wondered, now what? "What means nothing?"

"Well," Babs sipped her tea, a clear sign she had something to say. "We went to the antique store first, but it was a bit of a dud, so we got ourselves some ice cream like you suggested, and then we walked around town. We noticed a store with a sign that said it's a hardware store, but the things in the front and in the window were more interesting than the stuff in the antique shop. They seemed like old-fashioned tools and household things that might have been used a hundred years ago. So we went inside and looked around."

"We saw an interesting man behind the counter," Imogene said. "And Babs marched up to him, bold as brass, and started asking questions."

"I did," Babs squealed, which was an alarming habit coming from a woman her age. "His name is Fred Wilkins and he not only answered all my questions, but began to tease me a bit. I couldn't get over it."

"She was like a schoolgirl," Imogene said, with a firm nod. "And then, Fred said our ice cream looked mighty delicious, and did we mind if he got one and joined us? So of course, Babs here said it was just fine with her."

"And why wouldn't it be?" Babs asked archly.

Just then, the landline rang. Only Julia and Carly knew that number, so Mallory hurried to it.

"Hello. I'm trying to reach the Cabin of Love and Magic. I'm hoping there's a room available."

Mallory was aghast. They had tracked her down just as Gunnar said they would. "I'm sorry, you've reached the wrong number." She hung up and smiled stiffly at Babs and Imogene. "Sorry for the interruption. What happened next?"

"Oh—that call reminds me," Imogene said. "We received three calls before you got back. We told them there was no room now, but they should call back and talk to you."

"Three calls?" Mallory's heart sank. That was no good. The cabin's phone number was definitely out there.

"Anyway," Imogene said, picking up her story, "Fred Wilkins went over to Miss Sandie's where there were a gazillion flavors of ice cream to try, and you know which flavor he picked out?"

"Vanilla," Babs answered and giggled like the schoolgirl Imogene had accused her of being. "Which gave us something to tease him about! These men, they're never adventurous when it comes to ice cream flavors."

"Anyway, he shut his shop and put a 'Be Back Soon' sign in the window. We sat in the shade across the street from it so he could see if a customer came by. None did, which he said was pretty standard in the middle of the day around here, so we sat and talked for the longest time."

Babs continued, "Turns out he's a widower, and has been for nearly ten years. And he's got a great sense of humor. We both really enjoyed talking to him."

"Some of us more than others," Imogene said, cocking her head in Babs's direction.

"Very funny. But he's a nice man."

The landline rang again. Mallory answered, and this time she was much faster telling the caller she had called the wrong number. She hung up, and almost immediately the phone rang again. This time, the caller explained she feared she had mis-dialed and had tried again. Mallory reworded her statement. "There is no Cabin of Love *or* Magic. There never has been. Never will be. And if you call again, you will be haunted."

She then unplugged the phone. Gunnar had warned her this would happen. He'd been right.

And she couldn't help but think of his idea that Slade was the one behind the break-in at the cabin, and the article "exposing" the cabin. She'd argued against Gunnar's suggestion, but deep down, her gut told her he'd been right. And she knew why. For Slade to go on the attack that way was his "vanilla ice cream"—his comfortable fallback position. It was what he did in business all the time. It was how he managed to nearly always get his way.

She shook her head and returned to the great room. "Sorry, again. Please go on," she said.

"Not much more to say," Babs said, put-out by the interruptions. "Especially since we agreed to meet Fred for dinner tonight at a place called Mama's Folly. After he went back to work, we drove down Crouch's main street until we found the restaurant."

"How nice!" Mallory said trying to make up to Babs with enthusiasm. "So, you two have a date tonight," Mallory said.

"One of us has a date. The other is just tagging along," Imogene explained.

"But Mama's is great," Mallory added, as thoughts came back to her of her evening there—dancing with Gunnar while Slade watched, probably growing angrier by the minute. "Go tonight, Imogene. You never know who else might show up."

Imogene pursed her lips and then nodded. "Not a bad idea."

After Babs and Imogene left the cabin, Mallory sat alone in the great room. *Do what's right.*

She looked around. Who said that?

She saw no one. Maybe she'd just thought it. And if so, she knew why. She knew what was right, but she'd been ignoring it. Perhaps she put it off because she hated confrontation. In fact, she hated anything but "to go along to get along." She always had. But the time had come to stop that, the time had come to do what was right.

She got into her car.

Slade had pointed out to her the house he was renting at the top of a bluff overlooking the entire valley. She had no idea how Slade had managed to rent such a beautiful home in the area, but he was one of those people who knew everyone. He probably put out feelers and found someone who, for the right price, gladly turned over their home for a few days.

She aimed her car in the direction of the mansion and eventually found the road up to it until she was stopped by an iron gate. She buzzed, and the gate opened.

The house, up close, took her breath away. Massive and

constructed of wood, logs, and stone, the front was nearly all glass to take in the view.

He had found it to impress her. And he had. But it didn't matter.

His assistant stood at the front door as she approached. "Hello, Faruk. I'm here to see Mr. Slade," Mallory said. "I'm guessing he's now back from his trip to Los Angeles."

The assistant nodded and opened the door wide. "He is. I'll let him know you are here. I'm sure he'll join you in a moment."

It was longer than a moment. He left her waiting fifteen "moments," in fact. But instead of calming down, she was even more determined to speak her piece when he walked into the living room.

"Mallory, my dearest. What a wonderful surprise!"

"Did your man find what he was looking for?" she asked.

"What do you mean?" He frowned. "You seem upset."

"In my cabin. The other night, while we were dining at Mama's Folly. It appeared he did a search. What was it for? Was it proof of some infidelity? Is that what you hoped to find? Some excuse to give your friends as to why we aren't married? You can feel free to tell them you were the one who walked out on me, you know. I really couldn't care less."

"I have no idea what you're talking about, my sweet."

"Don't lie to me, Slade. It's bad enough you cost me my job with Piaget, and I'm sure any day now I'll be getting a letter from your friend the professor saying that my sublease is being terminated early. But this latest stunt is the worst one yet."

"I haven't done anything to you!"

"You've destroyed my one place of sanctuary. The one place I could try to get my sanity back."

He strolled away from her, as if needing to give her space, then spun her way adding, "You're being ridiculously melodramatic, Mallory."

"I know you wrote, or more likely paid someone to write,

the story about the cabin printed in the *Village Gazette*. Don't bother to deny it. There's no one else that would have done it. And your assistant hacked into my email so Brian Abernathy would think I'd written the article. But what I don't know is what you were searching for. A broken dish and messed up papers were sloppy, wouldn't you say?"

At the bar area he poured himself a straight shot of Macallan and didn't offer her any. He drank it down in one gulp, a waste of good Scotch, she thought.

"If my man hacked your email, you would never know it," he said archly. "And there's no way he would've snuck into your home and broken anything or messed up your papers. In fact he wouldn't have needed to even enter your house. He'd do it all online."

"Except that the cabin is in an Internet and cellular dead zone. So that wouldn't have worked for him."

He sneered. "How can you set foot in a place so ancient, let alone live in it?" Disgust dripped from his lips. "Anyway, what if I did help word got out about the cabin? It would have been exposed, eventually. So what?"

"So what? This is my life you're destroying."

"What about my life?" he roared. "I cared about you! I was ready to give you everything, all the riches and adventure you could ever want. And you rejected it."

"So this is about your pride," she said, her shoulders sagging and her voice soft. She shook her head. "I thought you were a bigger man than that."

"I'm plenty big. If I wasn't, I would have squashed you for your behavior." But then his demeanor changed as if he flipped a switch and suddenly sounded concerned, a man in love. "I'm worried about you. How can you live with no job, no income? So much of this, I see now, is my fault. Let me help you."

"It always comes down to money with you, doesn't it? Come to think of it, that was all we ever talked about." She walked over to the picture windows that looked out over the valley and clearly delineated the south fork of the Payette River running through it, forming it. How was it that she once had been so fascinated by Slade's stories of his business ventures and all the money involved?

She never heard anyone in Garden Valley talk about money beyond what was necessary—such as Kyle and LouAnn not having enough at the moment.

"You can still make this all go away, you know," Slade said as he strolled to her side.

She faced him again. "What are you saying?"

"I'm not a vindictive man."

"But, you are," she whispered. "I've seen you in action in New York. I thought you were clever, a big operator, now, I think you were simply being nasty."

He glared at her, then smirked. "It's nothing to get upset about. That's the way of the world."

"Your world, for sure." She strode to the front door. "By the way, whoever told you about the ghosts had most of the story wrong," she added. "You really need to do a better job vetting your sources if you do anything like that in the future."

He followed her. "Perhaps it was a mistake for me to come here. I had hoped we'd be able to overcome whatever caused you to leave the judge's chamber last week. But it appears we can't."

She nodded, and to her surprise, sadness over the miserable situation filled her, particularly her foolish role in it. "You know, when I first saw you here in Garden Valley, saw that you'd come all this way to try to win me back, a part of me hoped I could change my mind. I'd hoped I'd been wrong to leave you. But my heart didn't agree. And I finally had to face the fact that this marriage wasn't right for me—or for you. You can be a good man—"

"Don't." He held up his hand. "Don't give me the old 'it's

hurting me more than you,' or 'I'm doing this for your sake' lines. I've gotten through two marriages and myriad affairs without having any woman say that to me. I'd prefer not to change. To me, those words are only said to someone who's a loser. And I'm not the loser in this relationship, Mallory. You are."

She raised her eyebrows, but then nodded. Maybe, in Slade's—and Roxanne's—world what she was doing now made her a definite loser. But if so, she didn't care. "And sometimes, losers can win."

Slade opened the front door. "I hope you realize, if you walk out again, there's no coming back. I won't have you. I'll find some other young, beautiful woman to show off to the world. You were special to me, so I wanted to give you a second chance."

"Goodbye, Slade." She headed for her car.

"I'm sorry that it turned out this way," he said.

She didn't react to his words. It would have been a lie to say she was also sorry. In fact, she wasn't sorry at all.

CHAPTER 24

The next morning Imogene and Babs announced they wanted to stay one more night. They were cooking their own breakfasts of omelets filled with cheese, bacon, and mushrooms, plus drop biscuits—and made enough that Mallory could join them. Everything was delicious, especially when Mallory smeared the warm biscuits with the homemade lemon curd the ladies had bought in town.

"And here I thought I'm supposed to be cooking for my guests," Mallory said. "You're lucky I'm not. Hard-boiled eggs and cold cereal are the extent of my breakfast skills."

"That's okay," Babs said. "You youngsters seem to buy everything ready made. But this is real food."

"Actually, my sister, Carly, had a catering business," Mallory told them. "She's a great cook."

"How nice. Where's it located?"

"She gave it up when she got married. She'll be opening a nursery in Boise soon. The sale won't be completed until next month, so this month she and her new husband are taking an extended honeymoon to visit his parents and to see London, Paris, and Rome. She'd never been to Europe before this."

Imogene joined in the conversation. "Isn't that lovely! That's the sister who found her husband right here, isn't it?"

"Yes, but it really had nothing to do with the ghosts," Mallory said with a smile.

"You don't know that for sure," Babs said.

Mallory had to agree.

The two not only cooked breakfast, but cleaned up the kitchen afterward. And seemed happy to do it, as they chatted nonstop about the area and things to do and places to see.

Mallory scarcely paid attention to them. She wondered why Gunnar hadn't come by. She'd expected him last night to tell her all that had happened with Kyle, and she would tell him she had sent Slade packing. When he didn't show up, she believed he might still be busy. But the morning was a different story.

She walked over to the phone and plugged it back in. It wasn't there for five minutes when someone phoned about reserving a space at the Cabin of Love and Magic. Mallory told them that the story was fake and not to call back. Then she unplugged the phone and went back to stewing about Gunnar.

"It's time for us to be off," Imogene said, breaking through Mallory's reverie. "We're going to drive to Boise and see what the area is like. We've never been there."

"Don't worry about us," Babs added. "I have no idea when we'll be back. And by the way, you might want to change your cat's food. She won't eat a bite of it. She's such a sweetie, I'd hate to see her starve herself. Cats can be very fussy."

"So I've heard," Mallory said. "I'll give that a try. Be careful out there."

"We know, but"—Imogene pointed to Elijah's portrait—"he's looking after us. We know it. And he's going to find a companion for me, aren't you Mr. Donnelly?" She gave him such a fierce look, that Mallory couldn't help but think if he weren't dead, that would have struck him down for sure.

"Have fun, ladies," Mallory said.

Much as she was irritated at how they arrived at the cabin, she had to admit, having them there made it a whole lot less scary.

Mallory spent the rest of the day going through emails from Dear Nellie's readers. Brian had informed her that anything negative, particularly using words like "hoax" or "fantasy," about the Cabin of Love and Magic would not be printed. As a result, she simply answered the questions with Nellie's newly warm and caring tone, difficult though that was.

Once her Dear Nellie column was finished, she sat on the sofa, feet up on it, engrossed in one of the romances she'd bought. Pumpkin was curled up asleep on the other end of the sofa. But then, about ten o'clock, the cabin's front door burst open and Babs and Imogene came fluttering into the great room.

"Oh, such a night!" Babs exclaimed. "You should have been there!"

Mallory had hoped Gunnar would stop by, so she had stayed home and had a grim dinner of canned soup and a salad.

"After returning from Boise we stopped at Mama's Folly for dinner. A visiting country-western band was there and tons of people turned up. The place really jumps. We love it here!"

"I'm glad you had fun," Mallory said with a smile. "And was Fred Wilkins there, too?"

"He was, but he doesn't dance." Babs frowned. "It made me decide he's just too old for me. I mean, if that young man—your friend—could go out there and dance when he has a bum leg, I should think Fred could, too, wouldn't you?"

"Gunnar was there?" Mallory asked, surprised to hear that.

"Sure was. And very popular with the ladies, I must say. He's one good-looking fellow." Imogene chimed in. "It's good you two are just friends, or you'd have your hands full keeping that one in tow, I tell you."

Mallory felt as if she had a lead weight pressing on her chest. She had been telling herself he hadn't stopped by the cabin because he was too busy taking care of Kyle and his family. "I see," she murmured.

"Anyway, we think we should be heading home tomorrow," Imogene said. "We've loved our time here, and we would like to come back. But maybe we'll plan better next time about what we want to do, which clothes to bring, and so on."

"That's right. And I have a doctor's appointment in two days," Babs said. "Those are getting harder and harder to get. You have to wait forever for them, so I don't want to have to cancel."

"Sure," Mallory said. "I understand."

"And even though neither of us met the man of our dreams," Imogene added, "we have hope. The cabin gave us that."

"In that case," Mallory said, "I'm sure the ghosts here are quite happy."

Pumpkin gave a sweet little meow at that, which caused the two women to laugh. Mallory's spine felt a cold chill. It only confirmed what she had long suspected.

The women said they were going to be leaving at dawn, probably before she even got up, and so they paid her for the additional night, in cash, and then headed up to bed.

CHAPTER 25

The next day, the cabin seemed unnaturally quiet without the two chatty women from Walla Walla. Mallory's only company was Pumpkin, who was actually a pleasant, affectionate companion, even though she still wouldn't eat the food Mallory put out for her.

Do ghosts eat? She had no idea. But just admitting she had such a thought sent a cold chill along her back. Still, if Pumpkin actually was ... *what was she thinking* ... ghosts might not be nearly as frightening as she'd feared.

She managed to download her email and when she looked at it, she found the message she'd been expecting from the professor whose apartment she was subletting. Her sublease was being terminated early. He would have her clothes and personal belongings packed up and shipped to the place of her choice as a means of showing her how sorry he was to put her out so abruptly.

Nothing like starting over. But she'd done it before, and she could—and would—do it again.

She also heard from her boss, Brian, who was happy with the more emotional turn the Dear Nellie column had taken.

Although she hadn't continued to mention the Cabin of Love and Magic, it had attracted a lot of readers' attention, which brought a number of new people to the *Gazette* to find out what all the fuss was about.

For the time being, at least, Nellie had survived to write another day.

By three o'clock, Mallory had finished the next Dear Nellie column.

And she had no idea what to do with herself.

Her lodgers were gone; Pumpkin was out of the house doing whatever ghostly little cats did; Slade was gone.

Even Gunnar was gone.

And Mallory was alone.

By four o'clock, she couldn't take it any longer.

First she drove to the grocery to buy more brands and flavors of cat food—maybe Pumpkin was simply an extremely fussy but otherwise normal cat—plus to restock some of her own grocery shelves, and then she drove to the McDermott Auto Repair.

She parked and, carefully this time, approached the car bays where the men worked. Nathan saw her and hurried out to meet her.

"Hi," he said. "Is everything okay?"

She nervously drew in her breath. "I'm looking for Gunnar. I haven't seen him for a while."

Nathan looked sheepish. He glanced back at the office, then faced her once more. "He's, uh, gone down to the VA hospital in Boise to see how Kyle is doing. That money you gave was a big part in helping pay off a chunk of the rent so the family won't be evicted quite yet. Hopefully, Kyle will be able to get back to work soon and we'll see that his wife and little girl are taken care of in the meantime."

"Good," she said, then reached into her handbag, pulled out an envelope, and gave it to Nathan. "Here's more cash for them.

Another two hundred sixty dollars. Tell Gunnar I was here, won't you? And let him know I ... I'd like to see him."

His eyes turned sad and shifted slightly away, as if he couldn't look directly at her. "Sure. And thanks so much. You should know, the money you alone have contributed is close to a whole month's rent for Kyle."

She was stunned. She suspected the tiny bungalow's rental would be inexpensive here compared to Manhattan, but not to that degree.

"I'm glad to hear that," she said. "But ... is anything wrong, Nathan?"

His eyebrows rose innocently. "Wrong? No, no nothing at all."

"Gunnar is all right, then?"

"Yeah. Yeah, sure. I'll tell him about your visit."

"Thanks," she said, and returned to her car.

Mallory drove from the auto repair to Emma Hughes' office.

Emma lifted her eyes from the paperwork on her desk when the bell chimed to let her know someone had walked in. "Mallory Conway," she said, her mouth down-turned. "What brings you here?"

"Curiosity," Mallory replied. "By any chance, is your office receiving calls about the cabin?"

"Oh, you mean the 'Cabin of Love and Magic'? I must say, that's a great marketing tool. I never suspected you would go that route, but it seems to be working."

"Are you giving out the cabin's landline number?"

Emma leaned back in her chair, her eyes cold. "Why not? In fact, I was going to talk to you about that. If the volume of calls keeps up, I will be asking for some compensation. Right now, I'm glad to help out, and give callers your number. Of course,

I'm also informing them that if the cabin itself is booked up, I can find them other suitable accommodations. So far, though, none of the people have called back, which means I've been acting as your receptionist for free. That isn't anything I enjoy or that I can afford to keep doing."

"How did you get the cabin's landline number?"

"I have all kinds of access to phone numbers, listed and not, reverse directories, and so on." Her arch expression turned smug. "But I first looked up your sister's name since she was the one here last winter getting the cabin fixed up. I figured that if she put in a landline, it was probably in her name. And sure enough, when I phoned it, one of your lodgers answered."

Mallory sat down across from Emma. "I'm sorry about all this, I really am. There is no Cabin of Love and Magic. That was a sham story sent in to a newspaper by my ex-fiancé who has more money and contacts than he knows what to do with. I think he was hoping that word of the ghosts in the cabin would drive me out of it and perhaps back to him."

"Really?" Emma's eyebrows rose, then she folded her hands on her desktop. "That's interesting. I had no idea who he was when his assistant called wanting to get a beautiful house in the area for a week's rental, and money was no object. I suspected some big celebrity or even royalty was coming to spend a week here. If I'd known he'd been your fiancé, I would have asked you before I said anything to him about the ghosts."

"So he asked you to tell him about them?" The pieces, Mallory thought, were all falling together.

"A couple of days after he arrived, he stopped by the office and said he'd been hearing rumors in town about a cabin that had ghosts. He wanted to know all about it. I told him the only one who really knew much about it was you. He pretended he didn't know you and didn't want to bother you, so I told him all that I could about the sad Donnelly story, and how the ghosts try to help other people find the kind of love they had shared."

"What was his reaction?"

"He laughed."

Mallory shook her head. "Of course he did."

"Most men probably would," Emma said.

"Maybe."

Emma eyed her. "Just out of curiosity, now that you and Mr. Atchison are no longer a couple, does that mean that you and Gunnar...?"

Mallory stiffened. Gunnar hadn't tried to reach her for over forty-eight hours, and he'd gone to Mama's Folly last evening. She couldn't help but suspect that he changed his mind about getting involved with her. And why not? She was a mess. Now, looking at Emma, she recalled the hopeful way Emma always gazed at him. "We're not," she said. "We're just friends."

"Oh." Emma couldn't help but smile. "Well, if I hear anything more from your fiancé, I'll be sure to let you know."

CHAPTER 26

Mallory spent another evening alone at the cabin, waiting and hoping Gunnar would show up. Always in the past, whenever she indicated she wanted to see him, he turned up at the cabin almost before she'd hung up the phone.

This time, she'd gone to see him at his auto shop, and later, she phoned there to make sure he got the message.

But she never heard back.

The next morning, she worked on more responses for her Dear Nellie column, and then decided to write proposals for syndicating the column, rather than to wait for small-town newspapers across the country to somehow discover her. She was, after all, popular in one of the country's largest and toughest markets. One of the songs her mother sometimes sang about New York had a line that said something like, if you can make it there, you can make it anywhere. She guessed Nellie was making it there, even though Mallory had completely struck out.

But to tell the truth, Mallory didn't care.

For some reason, she thought about her mother's songs and

found the group of CDs in a box in the family room. She put them on, and listening to Roxanne's beautiful voice, she was able to remember the good times with her mother. Roxanne had made mistakes, but Mallory knew she had as well.

Few people could sing a love song with the emotion of Roxanne. Listening to them, Mallory became more and more upset about Gunnar. Her gaze went to Elijah Donnelly's portrait and held. She stayed as if frozen, as a sense of great sadness filled her, the sadness of love lost.

"Why?" she whispered, stepping closer to the portrait. It was as if he wanted to tell her something. But what?

As Roxanne sang "They Can't Take That Away from Me," Mallory grew teary-eyed and suddenly she knew she couldn't just sit here and do nothing about Gunnar.

Mama's Folly always had live music on Friday nights. My God, she thought, only two weeks had passed since Slade's proposal. It seemed like a lifetime ago and maybe, in a sense, it was.

Since Gunnar had been at Mama's having such a good time two nights earlier, he just might return again that night.

She took her time getting ready. First, she washed and styled her hair by adding a few curls to the waves, and then put on lots of eye make-up. Tonight, she was going for a saucy look. She felt saucy. She wanted to *be* saucy. Especially with Gunnar. She chose a short, sexy, very New York nightclub designer dress, in black, of course. And then added black high, high-heeled shoes.

She waited until nearly ten before entering Mama's. If Gunnar were there, he'd probably be there late.

Sauntering into the nightspot, she smiled at the cowboys who were looking her over with much appreciation, but she didn't bother to stop when more than one gave her a clear invitation to join him. At the far end of the bar she saw Gunnar, a bottle of beer in his hand. Emma was next to him.

He turned his head and his eyes met hers. She smiled, but he didn't. She walked toward him as he raised the beer to his lips, took a quick drink, put it down, then took Emma's arm and led her onto the dance floor.

Mallory stopped cold, and stood there, gaping. She watched a moment as the two slow danced to the old country classic, "Crazy."

No kidding! She spun on her high, high heels and left.

Mallory went home, took off her fine clothes, washed away the makeup and climbed into bed. But then all her thoughts turned to Gunnar. He'd told her he had no feelings for Emma, but if that was the case, why did he dance with her as soon as he saw Mallory?

Had Emma finally worn him down?

Why, after all they'd said, the closeness they'd shared, had he suddenly turned against her?

She didn't get it, and maybe she never would. Maybe this was why she only went for older, more reliable men like Slade. He wouldn't have broken her heart.

A broken heart? Really? She had never had her heart broken before.

She rolled over in bed, punching the pillow a few times to make it more comfortable so she could sleep. It didn't work.

Instead, she thought about her "love life." The only time she'd felt a lot of sadness was when she'd ended her engagement to Arturo right after high school. But she was so young, and so influenced by her mother, her emotions were more scattered than focused.

The truth was that no one had ever made her feel the way she did when she was with Gunnar—not the thrill, the fun, or the desire.

But for some reason, he didn't share those feelings. He once told her why bother with one tree when he could have the whole forest? Obviously, the forest was what he wanted.

She should have known. Leopards don't change their spots, and Gunnar had been devil-may-care when he was young. Pretty clearly, he was still that way.

In time, she would forget about him, about this entire nightmare of moving from New York City to the cabin. My God, what had she been thinking? All she had to do now was to figure out where she wanted to go next.

Maybe she'd return to Los Angeles, where she'd lived as a young child with both her father and mother. She'd been happy there.

Somehow, finally, she fell into a restless sleep.

The next morning as she sat on the sofa with her laptop, she was pleased to discover that she had received some nice responses to her queries about expanding the Dear Nellie circulation.

Ironically, now that she'd decided to leave, the jeans and boots she'd ordered online showed up at her door. She was tempted to return them, but instead went upstairs and tried them on. She rather liked the country girl look she now sported. When she and Gunnar had walked down to the river, she realized that linen slacks and strappy sandals weren't the best attire for trooping around the Payette River, or pretty much anywhere in Garden Valley outside of town.

She hiked down to the river now, and sat there a while, looking at the water, the birds, and a couple of elk grazing on the field on the other side of the river. This area was known for the many elk it had. She liked watching them.

As much as she didn't want to think of the time she'd been here with Gunnar, her thoughts kept going there. It was funny how much more interesting the river had seemed with him than with Slade. She'd never forget Slade perusing the natural beauty of the place and then talking about spoiling it.

She kept hoping, irrationally, that Gunnar would show up here, at the river. But, of course he didn't, and she finally returned to the cabin.

She walked into the great room and froze.

Surely, she was seeing things.

The woman in a calico dress was in the kitchen and she had baking supplies all around her, flour, butter, milk, cherries. She was paying no attention to Mallory or anything else, not even to Pumpkin who was sitting up on one of the barstools watching her.

Mallory took a step closer, but the woman, who was quite pale and ... thin, not as in skinny but as in almost transparent ... kept working.

Mallory's blood ran cold, but she couldn't move, couldn't do anything but stand there and watch as the woman scooped a bowlful of cherries into a pie crust and then put another layer of pie crust on top of it. She then put the pie in the oven, turned, walked through the wall, and vanished.

Mallory gasped and then stumbled backward until she bumped into the sofa facing the fireplace. Her whole body was shaking with the realization of what she saw. Or, if she hadn't really seen it, she was losing her mind.

Gripping the sofa, she turned and glanced up at Elijah Donnelly's portrait. Usually, his eyes seemed to look right at her. No matter where she was in the room, his eyes found and followed her. But not now. Instead, he had a soft, loving look on his face, and his gaze was directed toward the kitchen, toward the woman who had been there.

His wife.

Tears filled Mallory's eyes and she no longer felt frightened by what she had witnessed, only a deep sorrow for all that the two didn't get to share in their lives.

She hurried to the kitchen and opened the oven door.

It was empty. There was no cherry pie.

She sat on the barstool, her mind racing with how strange it was that the woman had appeared to her that way. What did it mean? It wasn't as if Mallory had ever baked a pie in her life, so it clearly couldn't have been about the pie. In fact, the only pie she'd eaten since she'd been here …

Gunnar had brought her a pie. One that his mother had made. A cherry pie.

Was the woman trying to tell her something?

CHAPTER 27

Mallory drove to McDermott's Auto Repair to see Gunnar. Once again, a sad-eyed Nathan told her he wasn't there. "Well, then, can you tell me how to find his parents' farm? He might be there."

Nathan looked puzzled. "He might, but why do you want to know? Aren't you going back to New York in a day or two?"

"No."

"You sure? 'Cause that's what I heard."

Mallory was stunned. "You heard wrong."

He gawked at her a moment as if trying to decide if he believed her not, and then he smiled as he gave her directions.

The farm wasn't far from town. As soon as Mallory turned onto the driveway, she saw Gunnar's truck near the barn.

She parked in front of the house, marched up to the front door before her nerves got the better of her, and knocked. An older woman with short, curly brown hair and Gunnar's big blue eyes opened it. "Hello," Mallory said, "I'm—"

"Mallory," she said. "It's good to see you again. I'd recognize you anywhere."

"Thank you, Mrs. McDermott. I'm—"

"Call me Faye. How are you doing?"

Mallory wanted to see Gunnar, but she also didn't want to be rude. "I'm fine. And I want to thank you for the cherry pie you sent over. It was really delicious. I'm sorry I didn't come by earlier to thank you for it."

"You're most welcome. And you certainly didn't have to drive all the way out here just for that. Would you like to come in and have some iced tea?"

Mallory bit her bottom lip. "Actually, I'm looking for Gunnar. I'd like to talk to him."

Faye's lips pursed. "Oh, well..."

She sensed Faye's hesitancy to let her see Gunnar and had no idea why. "I see his truck," she quickly added. "I was hoping he's around somewhere."

Faye's eyes scrutinized her, and she looked troubled. Mallory couldn't help but wonder what Gunnar might have said to her. "Well..." Faye began.

"I know he's busy, but I just need a minute of his time. Really," Mallory urged.

"Could you come in? Please." Faye's words were stern and, feeling like a child in trouble but wondering why, Mallory did as told.

She stepped inside the country home filled with quilts, candles, and needlework scattered about comfortable-looking furniture. The home smelled of freshly baked bread and was as warm and cozy as something in a magazine.

They sat in the parlor, and Faye got right to the point. "I suspect you think it's none of my business, but I can't help but wonder why you want to see Gunnar now."

She's right, Mallory thought. It was none of her business. "We had a misunderstanding, and I hope to straighten it out."

Faye's lips tightened. "The whole town was talking about the rich New Yorker and his driver staying in the area. Gunnar told me that was your fiancé come here to take you back home with him."

"It was, but—"

"I think, maybe it's best that you say whatever you want to Gunnar in a letter."

Mallory didn't understand. "A letter?"

"Or text or whatever you young people use these days." Faye grimaced. "Gunnar's been through a lot. And I just don't want to see him upset."

"But I won't—"

Faye stood. "I think you should leave. I'm sorry."

Mallory remained seated as she met Faye's gaze, her eyes much like her son's. "First, my former fiancé has gone back to New York without me. It's over between us. But also, I'm not sure what I'll say to Gunnar. I know what I want to say, but what happens between us also depends on him, of course. That's why I need to talk to him."

Faye squared her shoulders, her head high. "That's not the way I've heard it, but also it's not as straightforward as you say. My son has been through a lot, and he's still fighting against his demons. He's better, lots better than in the past." She sucked in her breath before adding, "I can tell that he cares about you; more, I suspect, than is wise for him. But I don't know how much you know."

"He's told me facts about what happened to him, but not a lot more," Mallory said.

"He wouldn't," Faye remarked, her lips tight. "Did you know he joined the Army to learn to fly helicopters? He wanted to become part of search and rescue operations in Idaho. Maybe even do life flight work."

"Yes," Mallory said. "That sounds like Gunnar."

"He loves getting involved and trying to help people. But after three tours in Afghanistan he was given a forced medical discharge. His dream ended. That probably hurt worse than the physical pain. I just don't want to see him hurt again."

Mallory understood, and given her history, she didn't blame Gunnar's mom one bit for wanting to protect him. "Believe me, the last thing I'm here to do is to hurt him. I care about him. A lot. I want him to know that. And I need to tell him face-to-face."

Faye took a long, hard look at Mallory. Finally, she nodded. "I suspect he's inside the barn tinkering with the tractor. It needed a new part that finally came in."

Mallory stood. "Thank you."

Mallory entered the barn. Gunnar was bending over a tractor's engine, attacking it with some sort of tool. He didn't look happy.

She walked about halfway in, then stopped. "Hello."

He bolted upright, staring at her incredulously. Then his eyes hardened. "Come to say goodbye?"

She frowned. "No. Why does everyone think I'm leaving?"

"We figured as much since your marriage is back on. Unless, of course, you decide to run away again."

He picked up a wrench.

She was stunned. "What? My marriage isn't back on. Why would you think that?"

He went back to studying the motor as if it were the most interesting thing in the world. "Emma let the cat out of the bag. She told us your no-longer-'ex'-fiancé had already gone back to New York to get things ready, and you'd soon be following him."

She stepped forward. "No, Gunnar. That's not true. Why would Emma say such a thing?"

Gunnar glanced at her, but just as quickly turned back to the tractor. "But he *is* gone."

"Yes, because I made it clear to him that he was wasting his time here," her voice was pleading. "Believe me, it's over between us. I know, now, that I never had real feelings for the man. His power and his money enticed me, fascinated me, I'm sorry to say. But someone wise once told me that money was never enough."

He put down the wrench and faced her. "You telling the truth?"

"Yes! The question really is, why did Emma lie to you and everyone else?" She then gave him a look that she tried to make steely eyed, but feared only appeared sad. "Could it have something to do with her dancing with you at Mama's Folly last night? You two were looking pretty chummy."

He gave her that slow half-grin she found equally infuriating and wonderful. "Why, Mallory Conway, you do sound a might jealous."

She marched right up to him. "I wouldn't waste my time! But I'm not here to talk about all your other women."

His eyebrows rose. "*All?*"

"I never had a chance to tell you," she began, but then hesitated as memories of that frightening afternoon came back to her, "I wanted to tell you I thought you ... that helping Kyle the way you did ... was the bravest thing I've ever seen. I truly never watched anything like it, and hope I never need to again. But I was so proud of you, and proud to call you my friend."

He shook his head. "I didn't do anything one of the guys wouldn't do for me. Kyle's one of us and got in a bad way. The money you gave, by the way, that'll be a big help to him and his family."

"I like his wife. She's got a tough job there, but she loves her man. It was good to see. And Nathan—he looked really worried about you. He's a good friend."

Gunnar nodded. "He was a medic. Deployed four times. It's

one of the toughest jobs out there. He saved lives, but when he tries to sleep at night, it's the faces of the ones he couldn't save that keep him awake. When you're a medic in a unit like he was, those guys are your friends, your brothers. So when you can't save someone, it hurts really bad."

"I had no idea," she said.

"It's not anything we like to talk about with civilians."

"If you ever want to, I'm here," she said.

He went over to an outdoor faucet and turned on the water to wash his hands, then used a paper towel to dry them before tossing it aside. His expression turned hard. "For the moment. When are you heading back to New York?"

She had followed him outside. It took her a moment to reach an answer. "I don't think I will. I don't think I fit in there anymore. And the strangest part is, I don't think I want to."

"You're kidding," he scoffed. "Where else would you go?"

"I have no idea. I'm such a screw-up. I don't know that I'd want to live in any place that would have me."

"Mal," he said, and then walked over to some stools stacked against the barn, pulled two down and put them against the wall on the shady side of the barn. He got them each a bottle of water from a small ice chest in the barn and offered her one. They then sat, side by side. "I wish you could see yourself the way others see you." His voice was soft, even velvety. "You're smart, witty, and fun to be with. Why do you think those men proposed? It's not because they pitied you. You're great—just the way you are."

"You really see me that way?" she asked. "Not as some flaky bimbo who can't figure out if she even wants to get married or not?"

He opened his water and took a long swallow. "Well, maybe a little flaky. But not totally. And you can get over that easy enough."

She also drank some water. This task, of trying to get back

into Gunnar's good graces, was hard work. "How?"

He leaned back against the barn wall and stared out at the farm's alfalfa field. "Do what you want and not what you think someone else wants."

"Trust myself, you mean?"

"It works."

"So ..." Still seated on the stool, she turned to face him. She wasn't sure she should go this way, but she couldn't help herself. "Do you, possibly, care about me?"

He glanced at her, one eyebrow lifted, then faced the field again. "Well ... as a friend," he said.

Her shoulders sagged. "I see. But what about when you kissed me?"

He scrunched his face. "Did I? Oh, yeah. Now I remember!"

"Thanks, loads," she cried, wanting to shake him. "It happened twice! And I found both times quite nice."

"Well, good!" He faced her now and grinned. "I've had lots of practice, you know."

"So I've heard." She fumed. "Especially with Emma."

"*Emma? Again?* Why in the world are you so hung up on Emma?"

"Because I've seen the way she looks at you! And you were holding her pretty close last night. Is there something between you?"

He nearly jumped up from the stool. "No!"

"Ever?"

He settled, and leaned back against the barn wall again. His voice was quiet as he added. "God, no! And maybe I was holding her close to try to help me forget the woman I wished I was holding—the woman Emma told me was leaving to go back to her fiancé, Methuselah."

"Really?" she liked that, despite the crack about Slade's age. She sipped a little water, then quietly asked, "So if Emma isn't your type, who is?

He put the water bottle down on the ground and faced her. "At the moment, she's a former New Yorker who doesn't seem to have her head screwed on straight, but she's pretty and smart, and always has me in a dither about the crazy things she finds to talk about. There, happy now?"

She grinned. "Yes, I am. Because you aren't my type at all."

"Thank God!" he said. "I see what happens with your type, and I'm very glad to learn I'm not one of them."

"The sad part is," she said, "although you aren't my type, I like you better than anyone who is my type. Why is that?"

"Good taste?" he said with his half-grin.

"Definitely not!"

"Could it be because you don't play games around me?" he suggested, placing his hands on his knees. "Could it be because you're yourself? Just Mal, the sweet kid who got a raw deal when it came to both her parents, but still has a heart as big as the moon and a great lust for life. You don't fool me, Mal, so don't try to fool yourself."

Her mouth went dry over what his reaction might be, but she made herself continue. "I've thought about staying in Garden Valley. I love it here—the beauty, the quiet, the people. I can write my Dear Nellie columns from here, and the money I make will go a lot farther than it does in New York."

Big blue eyes searched her face as if trying to see if she was joking, or was only saying what he wanted to hear and not really meaning it. His head tilted slightly. "Don't you think you'd be bored in such a small place?"

"Actually, I've found being here more interesting than New York. I'm not talking about restaurants and shops and all that city stuff. I'm talking about more personal reasons."

He caught her eyes, and this time he was the one struggling to find the right words. Finally, he murmured, "What about me, Mal?"

She smiled. "Don't you let it cause your already ego-swollen head to get any bigger, but yes, you especially. If I stayed, would you spend time with me?"

He scrunched his mouth as if he were pondering his answer, but the glint in his eyes gave away that he was teasing. "I'd say it wouldn't be terrible."

"And maybe," she asked, "could you see yourself as my boyfriend so that women like Emma Hughes would know it's hands off?"

He again forced a serious frown. "Boyfriend? Hmm. Well, we did go from being little kids together to being adults. It seems we jumped right over the teen years, so hey, boyfriend and girlfriend? That could work. But I don't have a class ring for you to wear."

Her heart swelled. "I'll survive."

"Good. But we've got to get one thing straight," he said, looking at her intensely, then placed his hands on her forearms. "Given your track record, there's no way I'd ever propose. Got that? I mean, for one thing, if you ran away from the altar, there's no way I could run after you."

Her heart pounded. "I guess that means, if things were to progress the way we're talking about, since I could never be a runaway bride, I'd have to stick with you, no matter what."

"Absolutely." He pulled her from the stool to sit on his one good knee and wrapped his arms around her. "I say we start this togetherness right here, right now, and see where it gets us."

She put her arms around his neck. "I like the way you think."

"Good."

Gunnar kissed her. As she drew him even closer, she smiled as the scent of sun and hay and tilled earth and even tractor grease that was her man filled her heart. Maybe all those years that she thought she was running away, she was really running toward something. And now, in her arms, she found exactly what, and who, that was.

PLUS ...

Dear Reader,

I hope you've enjoyed book two in The Cabin of Mystery trilogy. Book 3, SENTIMENTAL JOURNEY, presents Julia's story, and it will answer a lot of the questions about the ghosts and even Roxanne Donnelly.

For your enjoyment, here's the opening scene:

Chapter 1

Julia Perrin lifted the cat carrier from her Jeep. "We're here, Otis, and I'll spring you from jail soon as I'm sure it's safe. Don't worry, little guy, things will look up soon. Or so I hope."

She unlocked the door to the family cabin in Garden Valley, Idaho. She owned it jointly with her two half-sisters, Carly Fullerton-Townson and Mallory Conway. Or, at least, she'd been told they were her half-sisters. Julia couldn't help but wonder if the hospital hadn't switched her at birth because while her mother and sisters were tall, buxom, and beautiful, she was short, with a slight build, and—she believed—quite plain. Her ash blond hair was twisted into a single braid that reached halfway to her waist, while large cobalt blue eyes were framed by surprisingly dark brows and lashes given how pale her hair was. She rarely wore make-up and preferred baggy, comfortable clothes. At age thirty-five, she was the oldest of the three sisters. She had never married, never came close to marrying and, frankly, had never met anyone she wanted to marry.

Julia entered the cabin's foyer, glanced at the stairs that led up to three bedrooms and a full bathroom, and continued past them to the great room.

She unzipped the cat carrier. "Come out, Otis. You'd better get used to being here."

Otis was a gray and white tuxedo cat—a very friendly, affectionate little guy. But for some reason, instead of springing from his cat carrier the way he usually did, he poked his head out, and then shrank back inside and hissed.

"What's with you, cat?" Julia said. She lifted him from the case and petted him, telling him all would be fine. She filled a bowl with water for him and put Otis and the bowl on the floor in the kitchen area, but the cat scooted behind a chair, his eyes wide and round.

Julia shook her head. Most likely, the long car ride from her apartment in Bend, Oregon, had upset him. He usually was curious, not scared.

She looked around the room and had to admit the cabin looked no worse for wear, despite her sister Mallory having run it as a bed and breakfast for the past few months.

Some months earlier, Mallory, who answered letters addressed to "Dear Nellie" in her advice to the lovelorn column called "Misery Loves Company," wrote of a cabin that might house some ghosts who enjoyed the decidedly unghostly habit of helping visitors to it find true love.

Mallory even gave the cabin a name, calling it "The Cabin of Love and Magic."

When a newspaper article "exposed" the location of Mallory's "Cabin of Love and Magic," an avalanche of interest followed. People wanted to book a room. Lots of people. Single people.

Julia imagined many of them believed life would be much easier if some disembodied spirit could find love for them. It was certainly easier than the usual way, a way paved with heartache and wasted time when one's supposed love god or goddess turned from angelic into a sleazy, unfaithful demon.

Or sometimes, as in Julia's case, when true love never emerged at all.

Not that she was looking.

Julia remembered how she had hated the idea when Mallory announced she wanted to turn the cabin into a bed and breakfast. But so far, the gambit was actually making money. Not a lot, but it was better than nothing. And no one had, as yet, threatened to sue when they didn't find the love they sought.

Of course, with only two guest rooms, it wasn't as if Mallory had had to deal with a lot of people. And she knew how to make each guest feel important and welcome. But Mallory suddenly had other things on her agenda—most of all, a handsome veteran named Gunnar McDermott as well as the growing popularity and demands on her advice column—and she could no longer fit running a bed and breakfast into her increasingly busy life.

That created a dilemma for the three sisters. Mallory wondered if they shouldn't close the B&B and either sell the cabin or find someone else to manage it as a simple vacation rental.

But since Julia had recently lost her job due to downsizing, she volunteered to run the bed and breakfast herself.

Even over the telephone, Julia could sense her sisters' reluctance to agree to her idea. They'd both, at times, bore the brunt of her acerbic personality. It wasn't, she liked to say, that she was cranky or bossy or unwilling to compromise, but she was overly honest—and some people couldn't handle that. Still, she understood why her sisters felt she and "the hospitality industry" weren't a match made in heaven.

Julia pointed out to them that without a job her savings were dwindling. She had to do something, so why not take over running the B&B? At least it offered a roof over her head—a free roof, in fact, since she was *a part owner* of the cabin. Knowing what she was like when she dug in her heels, her sisters didn't even try to argue.

So Julia gave up her apartment, and here she was.

She turned to the portrait of Elijah Donnelly over the fireplace. He was the cabin's builder and one of the three "matchmaking" ghosts said to lurk there.

He looked like a young 1890s farmer dressed in his Sunday best. His blond hair was parted slightly off-center and slicked down straight. He wore a gray jacket with a white carnation in the lapel, a vest, tie, and a white shirt whose collar must have been starched to a torturous degree the way it stood upright on his neck. His eyes were an unusual shade of blue. Others often called them lavender, which made Julia question their color aptitude.

"Well, Elijah," she said aloud, hands on hips, "you're finding this all quite amusing, aren't you? Or you would be if there were such things as ghosts, which we all know there are not. But a fool and his money are soon parted, and let's hope plenty of fools coming out here to stay at"—she shuddered—"the Cabin of Love and Magic."

She really hated that name.

She proceeded to unload her Jeep. She'd sold her furniture and had given away everything she couldn't sell, so she hadn't had much to pack. The only important items were her laptop and printer. She had been a graphic designer for a small tech company, and after losing her job, she had thought it would be easy to find one similar. But at the moment, the need for graphic designers had diminished due to changes in the economy. For now, she could only get small work-at-home gigs that brought in equally small pay. But they were better than no pay at all.

She carried her boxes upstairs. She knew Mallory had used the smallest bedroom and rented the other two. She would do the same.

As she unpacked, she heard a soft whistling sound. She stepped into the hallway to find the shrill noise even louder.

Hurrying down the stairs, the "toots" became a high, loud screech, and once in the great room, it sounded just like…

She stopped and gaped. A tea kettle sat on the stove, steam shooting from its spout and its whistle growing higher and more ear-splitting with each passing second.

She ran to it and shut off the burner.

On the kitchen island sat a teacup and saucer. A tea bag of Earl Grey, her favorite, lay beside it, plus a spoon and a sugar bowl.

"What in the world?" Her eyes searched the room. Otis once again cowered in the cat carrier.

With a hard swallow, she swiveled around to gawk at the tea service. She hadn't set all that up … had she? Was someone else in the cabin?

She checked the French doors that led from the great room to the back porch. Locked. She went to the small hall off the foyer that led to the laundry room, a half-bath, and the door to the garage. That door was also locked.

But she had left the front door unlocked. She shuddered at the thought that someone might have entered while she was upstairs. Could he, or she, be inside now?

She stepped out onto the front stoop. The cabin had been built on a dirt road that edged the Middle Fork of the Payette River. The area had been isolated when the cabin was first built and remained so. Her Jeep sat on the driveway, but no other car was in view, and no other homes were near the cabin.

Julia couldn't imagine anyone sneaking inside to make her a cup of tea. Could one of her sisters be playing games to scare her about the so-called, albeit nonexistent, ghosts?

"Carly? Mallory? This isn't funny!" she called, marching around, and even going onto the back porch and looking over the fenced land behind the house.

All was silent ... and seemed quieter than ever. Julia's breathing quickened, but she steeled herself. She'd never been a namby-pamby, scaredy-cat type, and she wasn't about to start now.

The only explanation was that she had set up the tea service herself and somehow forgot she'd done it.

Otis had come out of his carrier, inched a little closer to her, and now sat in the middle of the room, giving her a quizzical look. She picked him up and hugged him.

Unbidden, her gaze lifted again to the portrait of Elijah Donnelly. He seemed to be staring straight at her and his expression, instead of his usual stoic smile, seemed to be a smirk.

Julia's knees felt wobbly. She put down Otis and turned away, not wanting to look anymore at Elijah, and dropped onto a barstool by the kitchen island. Her imagination was clearly working overtime.

The long drive from Oregon hadn't only made her cat nervous and skittish. It had done the same to her.

Continue with SENTIMENTAL JOURNEY wherever fine books and ebooks are sold.

ABOUT THE AUTHOR

Joanne Pence was born and raised in northern California. She has been an award-winning, *USA Today* best-selling author of mysteries for many years, but she has also written historical fiction, contemporary romance, romantic suspense, a fantasy, and supernatural suspense. All of her books are now available as ebooks and in print, and most are also offered in special large print editions. Joanne hopes you'll enjoy her books, which present a variety of times, places, and reading experiences, from mysterious to thrilling, emotional to lightly humorous, as well as powerful tales of times long past.

Visit her at www.joannepence.com and be sure to sign up for Joanne's mailing list to hear about new books.

Contemporary, Fantasy, and Historical Romance

Seems Like Old Times

When Lee Atchison, nationally known television news anchor, returns to the small town where she was born to sell her now-vacant childhood home, little does she expect to find that her first love has moved back to town. Nor does she expect that her feelings for him are still so strong.

Tony Santos had been a major league baseball player, but now finds his days of glory gone. He's gone back home to raise his young son as a single dad.

Both Tony and Lee have changed a lot. Yet, being with him, she finds that in her heart, it seems like old times...

The Ghost of Squire House

For decades, the home built by reclusive artist, Paul Squire, has stood empty on a windswept cliff overlooking the ocean. Those who attempted to live in the home soon fled in terror. Jennifer Barrett knows nothing of the history of the house she inherited. All she knows is she's glad for the chance to make a new life for herself.

It's Paul Squire's duty to rid his home of intruders, but something about this latest newcomer's vulnerable status ... and resemblance of someone from his past ... dulls his resolve. Jennifer would like to find a real flesh-and-blood man to liven her days and nights—someone to share her life with—but living in the artist's house, studying his paintings, she is surprised at how close she feels to him.

A compelling, prickly ghost with a tortured, guilt-ridden past, and a lonely heroine determined to start fresh, find themselves in a battle of wills and emotion in this ghostly fantasy of love, time, and chance.

Dangerous Journey

C.J. Perkins is trying to find her brother who went missing while on a Peace Corps assignment in Asia. All she knows is that the disappearance has something to do with a "White Dragon." Darius Kane, adventurer and bounty hunter, seems to be her only hope, and she practically shanghais him into helping her.

With a touch of the romantic adventure film Romancing the Stone, C.J. and Darius follow a trail that takes them through the narrow streets of Hong Kong, the backrooms of San Francisco's Chinatown, and the wild jungles of Borneo as they pursue both her brother and the White Dragon. The closer C.J. gets to them, the more danger she finds herself in—and it's not just danger of losing her life, but also of losing her heart.

Dance with a Gunfighter

Gabriella Devere wants vengeance. She grows up quickly when she witnesses the murder of her family by a gang of outlaws, and vows to make them pay for their crime. When the law won't help her, she takes matters into her own hands.

Jess McLowry left his war-torn Southern home to head West, where he hired out his gun. When he learns what happened to Gabriella's family, and what she plans, he knows a young woman like her will have no chance against the outlaws, and vows to save her the way he couldn't save his own family.

But the price of vengeance is high and Gabriella's willingness to sacrifice everything ultimately leads to the book's deadly and startling conclusion.

Willa Cather Literary Award finalist for Best Historical Novel.

The Dragon's Lady

Turn-of-the-century San Francisco comes to life in this romance of star-crossed lovers whose love is forbidden by both society and the laws of the time.

Ruth Greer, wealthy daughter of a shipping magnate, finds a young boy who has run away from his home in Chinatown—an area of gambling parlors, opium dens, and sing-song girls, as well as families trying to eke out a living. It is also home to the infamous and deadly "hatchet men" of Chinese lore.

There, Ruth meets Li Han-lin, a handsome, enigmatic leader of one such tong, and discovers he is neither as frightening cruel, or wanton as reputation would have her believe. As Ruth's fascination with the lawless area grows, she finds herself pulled deeper into its intrigue and dangers, particularly those surrounding Han-lin. But the two are from completely different worlds, and when both worlds are shattered by the Great Earthquake and Fire of 1906 that destroyed most of San Francisco, they face their ultimate test.

The Cabin of Mystery Romances

Three half-sisters inherit a remote cabin, but there's just one problem with it. It's haunted.

IF I LOVED YOU
THIS CAN'T BE LOVE
SENTIMENTAL JOURNEY

The Rebecca Mayfield Mysteries

Rebecca is a by-the-book detective, who walks the straight and narrow in her work, and in her life. Richie, on the other hand, is not at all by-the-book. But opposites can and do attract, and there are few mystery two-somes quite as opposite as Rebecca and Richie.

ONE O'CLOCK HUSTLE – North American Book Award winner in Mystery
TWO O'CLOCK HEIST
THREE O'CLOCK SÉANCE
FOUR O'CLOCK SIZZLE
FIVE O'CLOCK TWIST
SIX O'CLOCK SILENCE
Plus a Christmas Novella: The Thirteenth Santa

The Angie & Friends Food & Spirits Mysteries

Angie Amalfi and Homicide Inspector Paavo Smith are soon to be married in this latest mystery series. Crime and calories plus a new "twist" in Angie's life in the form of a ghostly family inhabiting the house she and Paavo buy, create a mystery series with a "spirited" sense of fun and adventure.

COOKING SPIRITS
ADD A PINCH OF MURDER
COOK'S BIG DAY

Plus a Christmas mystery-fantasy: COOK'S CURIOUS CHRISTMAS

And a cookbook: COOK'S DESSERT COOKBOOK

The early "Angie Amalfi mystery series" began when Angie first met San Francisco Homicide Inspector Paavo Smith. Here are those mysteries in the order written:
SOMETHING'S COOKING
TOO MANY COOKS
COOKING UP TROUBLE
COOKING MOST DEADLY
COOK'S NIGHT OUT
COOKS OVERBOARD
A COOK IN TIME
TO CATCH A COOK
BELL, COOK, AND CANDLE
IF COOKS COULD KILL
TWO COOKS A-KILLING
COURTING DISASTER
RED HOT MURDER
THE DA VINCI COOK

Supernatural Suspense

Ancient Echoes

Top Idaho Fiction Book Award Winner

Over two hundred years ago, a covert expedition shadowing Lewis and Clark disappeared in the wilderness of Central Idaho. Now, seven anthropology students and their professor vanish in the same area. The key to finding them lies in an ancient secret, one that men throughout history have sought to unveil.

Michael Rempart is a brilliant archeologist with a colorful and controversial career, but he is plagued by a sense of the supernatural and a spiritual intuitiveness. Joining Michael are a CIA consultant on paranormal phenomena, a washed-up local sheriff, and a former scholar of Egyptology. All must overcome their personal demons as they attempt to save the students and learn the expedition's terrible secret....

Ancient Shadows

One by one, a horror film director, a judge, and a newspaper publisher meet brutal deaths. A link exists between them, and the deaths have only begun ....

Archeologist Michael Rempart finds himself pitted against ancient demons and modern conspirators when a dying priest gives him a powerful artifact—a pearl said to have granted Genghis Khan the power, eight centuries ago, to lead his Mongol warriors across the steppes to the gates of Vienna.

The artifact has set off centuries of war and destruction as it conjures demons to play upon men's strongest ambitions and cruelest desires. Michael realizes the so-called pearl is a philosopher's stone, the prime agent of alchemy. As much as he would like to ignore the artifact, when he sees horrific deaths and experiences, first-hand, diabolical possession and affliction, he has no choice but to act, to follow a path along the Old Silk Road to a land that time forgot, and to somehow find a place that may no longer exist in the world as he knows it.

Ancient Illusions

A long-lost diary, a rare book of ghost stories, and unrelenting nightmares combine to send archeologist Michael Rempart on a forbidden journey into the occult and his own past.

When Michael returns to his family home after more than a decade-long absence, he is rocked by the emotion and intensity of the memories it awakens. His father is reclusive, secretive, and obsessed with alchemy and its secrets—secrets that Michael possesses. He believes the way to end this sudden onslaught of nightmares is to confront his disturbing past.

But he soon learns he isn't the only one under attack. Others in his life are also being tormented by demonic nightmares that turn into a deadly reality. Forces from this world and other realms promise madness and death unless they obtain the powerful, ancient secrets in Michael's possession. Their violence creates an urgency Michael cannot ignore. The key to defeating them seems to lie in a land of dreams inhabited by ghosts ... and demons.

From the windswept shores of Cape Cod to a mystical land where samurai and daimyo once walked, Michael must find a way to stop not only the demons, but his own father. Yet, doing so, he fears may unleash an ancient evil upon the world that he will be powerless to contain.